COPYRIGHT NOTICE

© Copyright 2010 Larry Charles Holt: Almost Home

All rights reserved

DISCLAIMER

This is a work of fiction. Any similarity to places, circumstances, scenarios, and persons living or dead (unless explicitly noted) is merely coincidental. As a work of fiction statements and descriptions do not imply fact or warranty performance of any individual item or items described herein.

WARNING

Language and descriptive imagery may be offensive to some readers.
Reader discretion is advised.

ALMOST HOME

Dedicated to

Zeke, Zoie, and Little

For being the inspiration, they will never know they are

Special thanks to

Brian, Dr. Laura L., SK, and Stephanie

Your help bringing the story alive made all the difference

Almost Home

CONTENTS

APPENDICE

FOREWARD

Lights go out and do not come back on. No one at the time had a clue how life changing that annoyance would be. As days pass and events unfold, some people will bend under the strain. Some will break. In their own way, each person will wrestle with choices they make. That's the way life is, especially life in the dark. All anyone knew at the time was the lights were out. The next logical question was, "Now what?"

Charles William Stanton (Cdub, to his friends) lives in the country and works in an office complex in the suburbs, an hour drive from home. On his journey through the darkness to get his life back, he finds more than he could imagine or hope for.

"I'll do what it takes; I'll shoulder any burden, protect, and defend family and friends.

I love my God, my family and my country;   I'm a man living my days in America."

CHAPTER ONE
PAPÉ CAP

Friday morning, October 18

Gently squeezing four pounds of trigger pull until the hammer fell seemed to take forever. Inevitably, I shot him dead where he stood with a single 5.56 caliber armor-piercing bullet fired from a prone position sixty yards behind him. Traveling twice the speed of sound, the bullet tore between his shoulder blades, below his neckline. Its impact violently jerked his head back, pinning his face skyward. In an instant, he loosed a spray of misty blood, as if he had a mouthful of strawberry milk when surprised by a laugh he could not contain.

The would-be killer wearing the dirty, frayed Papé logo embroidered baseball cap deserved what I gave him. I would have killed his friends too if they hadn't run off. "Prick, you could have left. Now look at you, ugly dead and me having to clean up your sorry ass."

~ Three Days Prior ~

CHAPTER TWO
LOST AND FOUND

Early morning, Tuesday, October 15

Without opening my eyes, I smile for the first time today. I was dreaming a good dream and its sweet memory lingers, not yet having fully disappeared. Rolling over and finding a comfortable position again, I exhale with deep satisfaction, reveling in warm sheets and the soft pillow of my bed made perfect through the night. As long as I keep my eyes closed, lying perfectly still under my bed covers, life will remain innocent and uncomplicated. Right now in the stillness of this new morning, the world outside is far away, out of sight, held at bay. There are no ugly deadlines, sharp edged responsibilities, endless morass of worry, or regret. When I drift and dream in the quiet of the morning, I am perfect. I am weightless. I am wanted, loved, new, young, and safe. I am everything I need to be, and all I desire will come true. Inhaling fully, exhaling slowly, I surrender. My spirit floats inches above my bed for a few luscious, serene minutes more.

Too soon, much, much too soon, insolent ringing from the alarm clock behind the closed bathroom door rudely intrudes, uninvited, into my perfect world. It casually deflects any feeble attempt of mine at ignoring its incessant interruption. Throwing back my bed covers, I relinquish any further effort of mine to ignore it. Groggy, I make my way to the alarm clock, fumbling with it a bit too long for my liking before finally silencing the necessary but hated thing. As much as I would love to go back to bed, I nevertheless set about my morning routine. As the shower runs to get the water hot before I step in, I shuffle down the hall, check on my sleeping dogs and open the front door of the house so they can go out to take care of their business without a need of personal attention from me. Stumbling back to the bathroom, I flick the wall switch, squinting sleepy eyes against the bright light. Regardless whether I possess the necessary mental or emotional stamina for the inevitable challenges, I am powerless to do anything else but submit to the day.

Stepping into the shower, I close my eyes. Turning my face into the hot stream, relishing the water pouring over me, I pray again, somehow, this time, the volume of worry racing through my mind will mercifully wash away. I know I will not be so blessed. My strength of will, my zest for the future seem imprisoned - tortured by inescapable anxieties of maintaining a paycheck to pay my bills, heat my home, pay my taxes, put food on the table, and perhaps save a little for a retirement that seems increasingly out of reach.

Vivid and painful memories of combat, failed relationships, my third divorce not many years ago, the devastating financial hit at the end, and countless shriveled entrepreneurial dreams pummel my self-esteem as if together they are an endless combination punch delivered by a prizefighter I am unable to defend myself against. Middle-aged hope for better days ahead is bloodied, reeling, dazed, and on the ropes. Much of the time, the most progress I feel I am making is slogging toward an indefinite and undefined end. Feeling the way I do leaves nothing much to offer a prospective significant other. Therefore, I do not even consider love to be within the realm of possibility for me any longer in this lifetime. I simply have nothing left to give.

Life was not always this bleak. I was not always so slump shouldered. When I was younger, I possessed an ability to make dreams come true, through nothing more than force of will if need be. Life before its most ugly moments meant trusting my commanders and foxhole buddies when the chips were down, and later believing it was the gospel truth when she said I was her one true love. When my third marriage failed and she left, I packed up what little I had left, put Zeke and me in the truck and headed out to the country to start over. I had always found solace in nature and decided I might as well go through bad times in a place that could nurture me even if I could not nurture myself. I have never regretted choosing me over staying in bondage of her peculiar version of love.

Nonetheless, fundamentals of the man I self-manage now seem incomplete, as if too many puzzle pieces are missing from the box, leaving me feeling perplexed and woefully inadequate for the task of renewing the life ahead of me. Regardless, if nothing more than from sheer stubbornness, I move forward every day, privately nurturing my belief in the will of God, a frail belief in luck, and the element of surprise I bring to the equation.

Against seemingly insurmountable odds, the hot shower, soft dry towels afterward, a good shave, and pressed shirt and pants all work their magic, helping prop up my flagging spirit set forward to face another day at work in the city. Standing in the kitchen, I involuntarily yawn, staring at my nearly worn out toaster with its heating elements glowing orange, transforming my bread to toast one more time. After breakfast dishes are in place in the dishwasher and the timer is set to activate a normal wash cycle during my absence, I herd the dogs from the comfort of their beds, out into their heated penthouse-garage full of blankets, food, clean water, and a rawhide chew bone for each. Without fail, my two-year old puppy, Little, is the first into the garage. With a smile and bright eyes, without ever being commanded to do so, he dutifully sits facing me in the doorway ready for his morning treat, as if saying to the other two dogs, "See, I'm a good boy." A good boy he is too. The next one out the door without coaxing is Zoie, wagging her tail as she goes. She too expects a treat, but she does not sit for it, and I do not ask her to do so. Zeke, the old soul, is a different story altogether, always the last one out of bed each morning, grumbling as he goes, and the last one into the garage.

Every morning his is a slow progression of halting, trudging steps in stages from the bedroom to the garage, punctuated with numerous pauses to stretch, yawn, and look back with longing toward the warm comfortable king size mattress in their bedroom he is being forced to vacate yet again, against his will. Eventually, Zeke is in the garage, and always stands with his back to me, one last gesture of protest. Sometimes he will take the treat I offer him but most times not. They all make me laugh regardless of what they do or anything else I may have on my mind at the time. They have access to a covered side pen to do their business and get fresh air; therefore leaving them in such luxurious accommodations is not difficult for me. They have one another for company and I return home more times than not at a reasonable hour. Before I leave for work, I pat each of their big heads, rub their ears, turn and lock the door behind me before making my way to the car. With security lights on and the alarm set, I ensure my cell phone is active for calls I will make while on my drive to work. With a press of the electric gate switch, I head down my gravel drive and over the metal bridge spanning the creek, while the gate swings open and then shuts behind me, as if bidding me a pleasant day in the city.

As the day progresses, I somehow pull myself together and do the best job I know how, "cap facing forward", one foot in front of the other, minding my own business. I do each of those things in hopes I am incrementally rebuilding a future for myself, while daily securing a home for my dogs and me.

I cannot begin to describe how deeply grateful I am for everything Zeke, Zoie, and Little add to my life each day just for being who they are. Those three are the ones I come home to at night and wake up to each morning. Their loyalty to me and their need of mine know no bounds. Seems to me, I owe them my best effort.

Zeke, also called "Biggie", is the male and the oldest of the three dogs. Tacked to my wall at work, I have several favorite pictures of him as a puppy that always make me smile. He was the only spotted grey, black, and white one in a litter of solid black brothers and sisters. When I brought him home, he was just eight weeks old. As I drove, I cradled him in the crook of my arm, his huge paws dangling off to one side, very large and quite pink. While he slept the entire way, my smile never faded. I don't know how much he weighed when I took him home, but he is a healthy, 175 pounds now. Zeke has never been any trouble and has always displayed a loving, gentle spirit toward people and other animals.

When Zeke was a little over a year old, I moved to the country. That meant leaving him alone for ten to twelve hours a day. After awhile I felt bad for him and decided it would be good if he had a companion. That's when I went to visit Zoie. When she and I first met, she was 14 weeks old, the last of her littermates - small, skinny, spunky, and altogether adorable. My heart tells me Zoie picked me the very first time we met. As I stood in the kitchen discussing my plans with her owners, at one point I looked down and saw a small Great Dane puppy.

With ears perked up and an intrigued look in her bright eyes, she sat ramrod straight not making a sound at my feet in the middle of the group. When our eyes met, she ran to the next room, jumped up on their sofa, laid down, and curled up with her eyes locked on me, watching my every move. She stole my heart at that moment and I knew it. After a few minutes more talking with the owners, I excused myself and sat beside her on the sofa, petting her small head and rubbing the tummy she offered. Before her, I didn't think I had capacity to love another dog, firmly believing Zeke had taken all I had to give. How thankfully wrong I was.

Several years passed with Zeke and Zoie having thoroughly bonded as brother and sister. Life was good. One day I realized because of his age, Biggie could not play with Zoie as they used to and would at times get hurt from the rough play they loved. Although they are only a year and a half apart in age, Zeke has always been somewhat prone to injury. To protect him and provide a playmate for Zoie, all three of us piled into the pickup truck and drove to a breeder in the area. We picked out a black and white Harlequin Great Dane and brought him home to be part of our family. I named him Little and he fit in right away, settling in like he had always been part of the tight group with Zoie taking immediately to her role of teaching Little the rules of the place and especially how to play. It made my heart happy knowing my decision was a good one.

It is magical watching those two run and chase each other in the wide-open spaces on the six acres of our home. Even Big Zeke occasionally feels spunky enough to get in on the act but generally stands next to me watching as I do the antics of the other two.

Often throughout my workday, I think of those three goofballs. They make me smile because of who they are. When I return home from work each day and open my garage door, my spirit lifts as I watch them race out, Zeke always the first one: tails wagging wiggly bodies, all three jumping around together acting like goofballs on the front lawn, welcoming me back home in their fervent, unabashed enthusiasm. It never ceases to amaze me how cares and worries of my day evaporate in the warmth of their greeting. Their joy upon seeing me is as if I had been lost and now found.

CHAPTER THREE
CASCADE EFFECT

Early afternoon, Tuesday, October 15

On both sides of a remote country road, wooded hills filled with bright orange, yellow, and rust colored leaves on tall, tightly packed trees adamantly refuse to be anything less than dramatic and vivid, even though skies are grey and misting rain. The serenity is broken by an echo of a lone tree limb as it cracks and snaps free from the top of its 60-foot Douglas Fir growing within an acceptable distance from power transmission lines below. The limb in and of itself is altogether unremarkable, ordinary, of no significant size or length. What is special is how it did not fall to the forest floor, a few inches right or left of transmission lines; but by chance, fell in such a way as to come to rest, balanced across power lines already overheated and sagging from an increased load demand. Because the tree limb fell where it did, it arced the power load, causing a circuit breaker to trip at a critical moment of high electrical demand, putting a strain on other high-voltage power lines connected to the electrical grid - ultimately forcing one hundred or more power plants to shutdown one after another. Within two hours, eleven states and millions of people are without power. A fallen tree limb impacts everything connected to or dependent on the electrical grid including television, internet, cellular phones, transportation infrastructure, fuel supply, water supply, and law enforcement response.

As events unfold a series of grid operator and IT system errors add to the chaos, further fracturing a power generation infrastructure unable to avoid a resultant cascade effect.

Grid control power station A5 is like hundreds of other power stations scattered throughout the United States; a windowless, cinder block box crammed with electronics equipment and load capacity readouts critical to grid operators whose job it is to keep circuit breakers from tripping. It is a tight space, with operators and electronic gear heating up the room, a bit too stifling for most people to call it anything close to comfortable. Nevertheless, rotating shifts of grid control operators at station A5 call it home 24/7, 365 days a year. Overloaded transmission lines trip circuit breakers. A critical function of a grid operator is to ensure that does not happen. There are many intricate moving parts to the machine of the largest power grid in the world and every part of it, both systems and people, must perform at all times in perfect synchronicity in order for the electrical grid to function efficiently.

[1.] 2:14 PM: Local grid operators at station A5 stop receiving power interruption alarms although receiving alarms are a usual and customary part of the job. An Energy Management System (EMS) generated alarm is the foundation a grid operator relies on to identify events on the grid that need their attention. Time passes and no one notices the lack of alarms. More time passes until an operator becomes suspicious and begins to investigate.

2:41 PM: Unprocessed alarms have backlogged the computer system and cause the computer server hosting the alarm software to shutdown. IT staff monitoring the servers switch alarm processing to a backup system.

2:54 PM: The backup alarm system fails and goes undetected for another fifteen minutes.

3:05 PM: The first power transmission line trips and is not detected.

3:08 PM: IT staff restarts the initial alarm server but are unable to bring the server on line. They fail to notify anyone, including grid operators within their chain of command.

3:19 PM: A grid operator from a sister station calls station A5 and alerts station A5 they think a line is down in their area. A5 grid operators are unconvinced by the report because of a lack of alarms.

3:32 PM: A second power transmission line goes down.

A third line trips at 3:41 and calls to station A5 begin in earnest. Personnel slowly recognize there may be a problem with the alarm system but corrective action is not initiated. No one engages the chain of command to report suspicions or request further instructions.

3:39 to 3:59 PM: Seven lower voltage lines sag due to excess load and trip when they touch branches of trees, consequently resulting in a breaker failure causing five more low voltage lines to trip.

Between 4:06 and 4:09 PM, five more lines fail due to high loads straining the system brought on by other line failures. Grid collapse is now in free fall. There is nothing to do but let it fall.

By 4:13 PM, the cascade failure is complete throughout all eleven states, enveloping millions of people in gathering darkness.

Almost immediately, widespread looting, violence, and death erupt from the darkness. Horror will reign unabated for weeks without end.

CHAPTER FOUR
CROSSROAD DANCE

Tuesday afternoon, October 15

Lights go out and do not come back on. No one at the time had a clue how life changing that annoyance would be. As days pass and events unfold, some people will bend under the strain. Some will break. That is the way life is, especially life in the dark. All anyone knew at the time was the lights were out. The next logical question was, "Now what?"

When the crisis started, it was a typical fall day in mid-October. We had a nice but short summer and with shorter days of daylight came the inevitable rain with sporadic clearing soon followed by more days in a row of inclement weather. I was at my desk in my cubicle on the third floor of our multi-unit office complex, when overhead lights and my computer monitor flickered for an instant, went dark, flickered shortly with a hazy yellow light, and then went completely black.

At first, I sit at my desk staring at a darkened computer screen, waiting expectantly for the power to restore any moment. As seconds become minutes, I go from disbelief to frustration. All the spreadsheet work I had completed but not saved is lost. "Not now!" In frustration, I aggressively stab both index fingers on the keyboard - as if by magic I will somehow resurrect this dead machine in front of me. I had meetings to attend, notes to take, schedules to confirm, and plans to make. We all did. "This can't be happening," I mutter to myself. Minutes tick by with the outage registering as an overwhelming silence, unnatural and unnerving. With electricity gone, all the myriad office devices that create white noise, the subtle electrically induced background buzz that goes unnoticed much of the time, is now gone. I check my wristwatch, 4:09 PM, Tuesday, October 15. The late afternoon grey light will be fading quickly.

"Usually, when this happens it's because a thunderstorm is rolling through. But that's not happening," someone says from a cubicle space along the outside wall.

I think to myself the weather outside has been uneventful all week, same old grey skies and drizzling rain with sporadic rain showers for this time of year.

"Same weather we'd had for the past three days straight," someone else says - and then adds, "That's what you get living in God's country."

That thought had also crossed my mind, and I chuckle softly to myself. Ten minutes pass and I seriously begin taking stock of the situation. I hear people from other cubicle areas in the building wandering floor to floor, checking out the situation, asking others if anyone knows what's going on. A couple of people, including our new team manager, Bryan, are standing at one of the exterior windows, seeing what they can see. Hearing my coworkers gathering at Bryan's cubicle, I meander over to the group now engaged in anxious and curious speculation about the cause, but more urgently, debating what to do next.

"Could it be a terror attack?" asks Erica.

"Could be," I reply in a matter of fact tone, although, for some reason this doesn't feel terrorist related.

"Would we know if it were?" Nick says, "Would it make a difference anyway, for us I mean right now?"

No one in the group answers.

Bryan says, "I don't think it's a terror attack. Whatever the cause is, I'm thinking it won't make a difference in the short term for us."

He gives no explanation about why he thinks what he thinks; Bryan simply proclaims it and that's it. "We do know," I say to the group, "our local government emergency response unit told us about three years ago we would be on our own to deal with an emergency evacuation if an area-wide disaster happened."

"Why?" asks Jo Ann.

"They said they would be too busy dealing with other priorities and unable to deal with the workforce in this business park. I don't believe they meant it personally - as if they didn't like us. Just that they are already stretched thin and would be looking to respond to other higher priorities during an area wide emergency."

Jo Ann asks, "What other priorities? Did they say?"

I pause to think, "I don't recall. All I know is we were told by our Crisis Management Team we would have to take care of ourselves in the event of an area wide emergency." All eyes are now on Bryan. He shrugs and says he wasn't here at the time so he doesn't know. After more group discussion, Bryan tells his team to stay put - he will be back with guidance from the leadership team.

"Don't go anywhere until I get back," he remarks in a stern tone of voice, pausing to make eye contact with each one of his direct reports. Bryan leaves the area, turns the corner, and exits out of sight.

Ten minutes pass. I look at my watch. Time is closing in on 4:30 in the afternoon. The electricity is out, and cellular phones don't work. From what I can tell, which isn't much from here, the area surrounding us is also without power. I turn and look out the window. "See there," I point the group to low hills a short distance away that have clusters of houses tucked into them. "Everything is out."

While other teammates press their faces to the window glass and peer out, I start considering what I am going to do. For reasons I do not clearly understand, this blackout has the feel of a major electrical event. Listening to my instincts, I quickly resolve to pack my things and evacuate the building. Facing an hour drive home I am leaving without waiting for instructions. If I leave now, even under normal conditions, it will be getting dark as I pull into the driveway. That is, if we were under normal conditions, which this is not.

"I'd rather be driving in daylight as much as possible, so I'm leaving," I say to our small group. If in the meantime power is restored, I'll connect to the internet from my home office and finish my work from there. If all goes well, I can still get the management report to Bryan before the deadline tomorrow afternoon.

After quickly gathering my laptop and office supplies, packing everything in the roller bag I use to transport my work gear, I flick the switch on my desk lamp a couple of times in one last but vain attempt to give me a reason to stay in place at work. I am half-relieved the light doesn't come back on. Wheeling my gear behind me, I slowly navigate the tight walkway in our small department. Several of my teammates are sitting at their desks. Others seem to be gathering their belongings to leave. I let everyone know I am heading out. They wish me good luck and I wave goodbye. Thinking of my three goofball Great Danes makes me smile. I do not worry for them in their penthouse-garage setup. Taking one-step at a time down the stairs to the second floor offices, I am hopeful of finding my friend Ann. "Rats."

Her office area is completely abandoned, and dreadfully quiet. I scribble a note and tape it to her dark computer screen in case she is still in the office complex: "4:45 PM. Safe travels to you. Give Christian my best. I am leaving work for Point B."

Ann and my other close friends Airisa Severn, Max and Mia West all know, Point B is my home, where my dogs are. In the past, they have all heard me on more than one occasion embark in an impassioned discussion of individual contingency plans in case of an area wide emergency, whether from a terror attack or something natural, such as an earthquake, or an accidental crisis. "A crisis is a crisis regardless of its origin," I have repeated ad nauseum, "And we should be prepared." For all the right reasons, I decided a long time ago, that if something happened I would not abandon my dogs, resolving that if they were to die, they would not die alone. My dogs are my family. "Zeke, Zoie, and Little will not suffer the same fate hundreds of abandoned family pets did in the aftermath of the Katrina disaster." Images on TV of frightened animals, treading water with not much strength left, haunt me still. My dogs depend on me, and in a sense, I depend on them. They cannot survive in the wild, and they cannot fend for themselves or simply make do. "We are a family and I am not going to abandon them."

Considering what might happen if an area wide disaster struck and the fact I work an hour drive from home, I might be unable to drive my car for any real distance – possibly faced with trying to find my way through debris-strewn streets.

Bridges might be collapsed, forcing me to ford at least five creeks along my route of travel. I would need to be prepared for that. Contemplating a worst-case scenario of having to abandon my car, I created a plan that included traveling the entire way home on foot. My research showed that under ideal conditions it should only take 16 hours to walk the entire 43 miles from Point A to Point B. That is, if I walked continuously without a break. Thinking I could do that would be unrealistic. Obviously, I would need to rest, eat, and walk slow enough not to injure myself. Military experience taught me that due to stress and unforeseen circumstances, everything takes longer to accomplish during a crisis. Inclement weather, injury or health problems, or civil unrest compound the problem of making progress, not to mention the effort it takes sustaining a will to survive even under mild conditions of uncertainty. All things considered, I outfitted my car with clothing and four days of provisions. When I get home, I have other supplies that will do for a little while to sustain me until help arrives or conditions improve. Ann will understand what I mean by the note I taped to her computer screen. She, my friends, and my family all know what route I will be traveling by car or on foot to home - to Zeke, Zoie and Little. After I arrive Point B, I will have plenty of time to make other necessary decisions.

Exiting the building, I look up at the growing clouds. It is probably my imagination, but daylight seems to be fading faster than usual for this time of year. I am confident I will get home safe - believing it if for no other reason than I always have. "It'll take a little while longer, that's all."

The volume of fellow employee's streaming from the cluster of buildings is growing, similar to our infrequent fire evacuation drills. This time, we merge and make our way to numerous parking rows and to our waiting cars. Many of us do so at a quick pace, hurrying to waiting cars and the sanctuary the familiarity of that space will afford. Within minutes, I am at my car trunk putting my tote bag in its spot next to the backpack of provisions and the AR15 rifle in the hard-shell case lying at the bottom. Before closing the trunk lid, I pause. A chill claws its way from the pit of my stomach up the back of my neck, standing my hair on end. Motionless, staring at the contents in the trunk, I know the chilly feeling is not from the wet drizzle, but from the uncertainty of what comes next. I inhale deeply and say softly aloud toward the interior of the trunk, "God, give my dogs peace of mind I am coming home. Somehow let them know I am on my way. Give reassurance to my family and friends as well that I am working my plan. Please keep me safe on my journey. As always, I am in your hands and trust I will be pleasing to you."

Shaking myself free from the creeping chill, I close the trunk hood with its convincing metallic thud, unlock the driver side door and slip into the upholstered driver seat. Turning the key, the engine comes to life with a reassuring rev. Taking a deep breath, feeling the relief of being in the car, I glance at the gas gauge, only to become immediately worried about having only a quarter-tank of gas. Gut instinct tells me "I'm not going to make it," and I say as much aloud. On my way to work this morning, I put in less than my usual $20.00 worth of gasoline at Gales Market, seven miles from home.

My budget being what it is, I put in less this time because money was extra tight, counting on being able to watch my pennies until my pay was automatically deposited into my bank account this coming Friday. I shudder with the thought of what is facing me, as I sit in the driver seat waiting for the engine to warm up in a car nearly out of gas. When I turn on the radio in hopes of hearing news of what's happening, I hear only static on every channel I try. "This is bad. I've never seen anything like it." At that moment, I did not know how right I was.

Shifting gears into reverse, I carefully back out of my usual parking space and begin my journey home, looking at the gas gauge for the third time. Parking rows across the complex are emptying, easily taking me just several minutes to thread my car to the main intersection where inoperable traffic lights make getting through the four-way intersection extremely slow. In every direction, as far as I can see, traffic signals, street lamps, storefronts, and front porch lights of houses that dot the road are all dark. When I check my watch, time has jumped. It is 5:35 PM, and I am not a mile away from work with no relief in sight from the crawling pace of traffic. From this spot, I have forty-two miles to travel before I pull into my driveway. The lack of gasoline in the tank has me nearly panicked. Settling back in my seat I simply have no other choice but to calm myself and adjust to a new reality. However, I cannot stop asking the rhetorical question of the day, "Where did all these people come from?" I take a couple of deep breaths. "It'll probably take an hour or two more to get home. That's doable," mumbling to myself.

It's a lame attempt at conjuring up self-confidence, "as long as I can find a gas station open along the way," qualifying myself, actually feeling myself start to relax. Traffic congestion continues for another hour and forty minutes before I am able to get beyond all the intersections with traffic lights not working and into the unincorporated area where traffic flow is usually better. As expected, I make good progress for nearly three miles until, at the intersection where I need to make a right to get to the main highway, I am stopped by a seeming endless line of cars and trucks of every size and description crawling north on the pass road in the direction I need to travel. I am twentieth in line before it is my turn to thread into the crawling stream of traffic. With nowhere to go and nothing left to do but wait, I periodically power the radio but always with the same result, ultimately stabbing the off button with my middle finger that much harder each time, increasingly irritated by a lack of information when I need it most. "The emergency management system should have kicked in by now," I think to myself. "Where in hell do our tax dollars go anyway?" I say aloud – another rhetorical question that will remain unanswered. Not knowing what is going on, combined with not being in control of my circumstances, makes me feel nearly suffocated in my small car. All the while, I try not to stare at the needle on the gas gauge inching its way to empty with each idling minute.

As I will eventually do, cars ahead of me in my lane want to make a right turn at the intersection up ahead to thread into the nearly stalled line on the pass road. It is clear to me, pass road drivers are not allowing cars from my lane to turn right. I have not moved more than an inch in twenty minutes, and when I have, it is only because cars in my lane are shortening the distance between car bumpers. Through streaks of my well-worn windshield wipers, I witness what looks up ahead to be a near collision between a Hyundai station wagon and a pickup truck at the crossroad. The Hyundai is the lead vehicle in my lane. The driver was counting on being allowed to thread in line, but instead nearly had his front quarter panel crushed by a Ford 4X4 pickup truck driven by a rude and aggressive driver. I wonder aloud, "Where's Mr. 4x4 going in such a slow rush anyway?" My simple mutterings are cut short by the beige Kia behind me. The Kia driver has evidently had enough of all this. He guns his engine, turns sharply left from behind me and speeds past all the cars in our lane, pausing a moment adjacent to the Hyundai in first position. Kia and Hyundai drivers exchange glances. Unexpectedly, the Kia driver revs his engine loudly two or three times, sees what he believes is enough open space for his car between the backend of the Ford 4x4 pickup that would not let anyone cut in and the front bumper of a late model Navy blue Mercury Sable. The Kia lurches forward, aggressively injecting half its length in the line of crawling cars, causing the Mercury Sable to slam on its brakes. This results in a ripple effect down the line of screeching brakes and rocking cars accompanied by car horns from their annoyed and aggravated drivers.

As the Ford 4x4 pulls forward a little more, the Kia driver straightens his car and for all to see, stabs a skinny middle finger straight in the air from a pale arm stretched out the driver side window. That is a universal challenge few will ignore. Almost immediately, two pickup trucks down the line of traffic break out of their lane. One goes right and one goes left, traveling up each side of the road along the line of stalled cars until they sandwich the Kia between them. Both pickup trucks, as if on cue, veer repeatedly right and left, crashing their large frames into the soft metal of the Kia's side panels. Awful sounds of metal grinding metal, glass breaking, and loud cursing from several unidentified persons complete the scene. Not long after the assault began, the Kia is thoroughly stalled with a flat tire or ruptured fuel line or both, causing the thing to sputter and the engine to seize. It and its driver are going nowhere fast. The pickup truck on the right side of the mangled Kia disengages and speeds away along the roadside, spitting dirt and gravel behind its tires as it leaves the scene. Gripping my steering wheel, and leaning forward toward the foggy windshield glass, I sit stunned having witnessed a shocking display of road-rage.

The driver of the Kia exits his vehicle through the opening where his passenger window used to be and stands on the outside of his car looking at his damaged and stalled vehicle. Even through dimming light of the grey early evening, I see the unmistakable chrome handgun he has in his right hand. "Oh God no" I hear myself mumble.

The gunman's attention focuses entirely on the pickup truck at his driver door. When the pickup driver also sees the gun, he tries frantically to get his truck engine started again and unstuck from the battered and unmoving Kia. Both vehicles have become locked together during the process of the battering. As Kia driver stands in the roadway at the back right corner of his car, he levels the chrome semiautomatic handgun at the back window of the pickup truck, and pulls the trigger. Six blasts in rapid succession angrily explode orange flames from the muzzle. Glass breaks and bullets spray the cab. Large holes appear in the truck metal while the driver of the pickup ducks and miraculously bolts through his driver door, running, stumbling for his life into the muddy field beyond, away from the line of traffic and the madman with the gun trying to kill him. The female driver in the Mercury Sable watching all this unfold presses her accelerator pedal, perhaps in an attempt to pin the man with the gun. More likely, her foot instinctively hit the accelerator from shock at seeing the man attempt to kill someone right there in front of her. Her car lurches forward barely missing the Kia driver. He jumps out of the way as her car strikes his car with such force the front grill of the Mercury Sable becomes pinned to the rear end of the Kia. Sitting in my car, I am shaking my head in disbelief, impotent, with my eyes wide and my mouth hanging open. The thought of intervening never once crosses my mind. I do not know why.

The mad man swings his aim swiftly left, leveling his outstretched arm at the female driver who I am sure is staring down the barrel of a very large gun.

Surely, her last thoughts were for her baby buckled safely in the car seat on the rear passenger bench. The gunman's bullets don't miss an easy target not more than six feet away. She is murdered where she sits. With terror in her eyes and white knuckled hands clenched around her steering wheel, he empties all remaining 40-caliber ammunition through her windshield, into the body of the female driver. Blasts from the gunman's semiautomatic handgun mingle with agonizing screams of the toddler witnessing the horrific moment of his mother's execution. Except for its tiny face and arms peppered with bits of blood, bone and windshield glass, the baby is physically unharmed, spasmodically shaking and screaming at the top of its lungs. Everyone in the immediate area witnessing the carnage sit in stunned silence for what seems a long time. The Kia driver, with the chrome handgun limp and smoking at his side, passively surveys the destruction, all the while ignoring the heart wrenching screams of the toddler buckled in the car seat. Then all hell breaks loose. Cars and trucks of all kind peel out of what had been a maddeningly slow, but orderly line of cars. Scores of vehicles try at once to desperately flee the scene. Some attempt to crawl through wet ditches that line both sides of the road, ultimately mired in the mud, only adding to the chaos of blockading cars at the intersection. Darting my car left out of my lane of cars and into a wide gravel spot near the intersection of both roads, I brake to a hard stop, skipping the tires a bit in the loose gravel. Trying with all my might to make sense of what just happened, trying to breathe and not faint, I almost break the ignition key trying to get out of the car as quickly as I can, to a crouched position behind the trunk. I don't want to be like that trapped woman, buckled safely in my car if someone starts shooting at me.

Time compresses into itself as I stand at the rear of my car trunk. My senses tingle with the feel of a sky on the verge of tearing open in a violent torrent of rain on all the sinners. It will pour down upon us and cleanse the earth in this spot as a measure of God's furious grief for what had befallen one of his Children.

In the growing drizzle, I stand in stunned silence outside my car and watch the madness unfold. Three individuals, two men and a young girl exit their vehicle some distance down the line of stopped cars and begin making their way quickly toward the Kia Gunman. Aimed weapons of various sorts and strident walk, resolutely close the distance been themselves and the unwitting Kia gunman standing at the passenger side of his vehicle, examining the mangled quarter panel. What Kia Gunman heard that caused him to turn and face his Judgment no one will know. Without warning, as if on command, sounds like a firing squad of various calibers from weapons in the hands of angry and determined drivers brutally hit at once, massive and deadly into the gunman's skin, muscle and breakable bones. For a moment, bullets piercing the gunman's clothing and flesh cause him to dance an awkward puppet dance a hail of bullets can only truly create. His death was not beautiful or sickening. It was vigilante justice I witnessed over the top of my car hood as I crouched in the mist and watched in shock and fear. Stunned and unmoving, nothing comes to mind to answer - how did all this happen?

As suddenly as hell broke loose, the crossroad falls silent. Clouds of grey-white gun smoke slowly drift up and away. The body of the Kia driver streaks wide swaths of blood as he slowly slides down the mangled side of his car into a sitting position on the wet pavement. With his head to his chest, he bleeds through countless holes in his body; blood soaking his shirt and pants until clothing can no longer contain the volume. Dark streams spill onto the black asphalt roadway, down into the gravel, where his blood mingles with the dirt, weeds and cigarette butts at the roadside, as someone reaches in the Mercury Sable, unbuckles the female driver's baby, and carries him away to a vehicle down the line. It's agony slices my heart in deep gashes. Surely, no one within earshot of his cries remains unaffected for the rest of their lives by its screams; knowing for a certainty, her baby has changed as person for the rest of its life. Other drivers and passengers with smoking guns check the woman, obvious to everyone within eyesight, she is dead behind her steering wheel, steam-trails rising from a quickly cooling body. Another person kicks the dead gunman's weapon to one side - out of reach of hands incapable of reaching, as if actually kicking the gun away was necessary. I guess that's what we're supposed to do in situations like this.

After a long while, I suddenly realize I am cold and wet standing outside my car. There is nothing for me to do but get moving down the road toward home. I do not know what to make of what I've seen. I am emotionally numb but get back in my car and weave back in line. Cars and trucks at all angles, stuck in ditches along the roadside, make the crossroad nearly impassable.

With no awareness of time passing, I find myself in first in position to turn right toward home. Sitting motionless in my car, the picture of carnage out my left window is of bullet holes and blood everywhere. The slow roll of tires is hypnotic as they pass outside my car window, tracking Kia gunman's blood in their tire treads onto the pass road, dark and wet. Not soon enough, I notice a friendly signal from a smiling driver, allowing me to turn right. Seems courtesy and progress has been restored. I think, "Maybe he's been waiting on you to notice you can go."

At last I am on the pass road headed north, down to the river road and then to home in the gathering night miles away from here. It has taken many frustrating hours getting to this spot and I do not think I can go much further. My car fuel light has just come on. With gasoline precariously low, I resign myself to what had been an inevitable realization - I will never make it home without more gas and there is no station anywhere close. Even if I had a full tank, I would have to get out of my car and get some air to try to clear my mind. I can't stop now but need to find a good spot to pull over. Sweating the entire way, it takes me another hour to go an additional three miles. My pulse quickens even more when I realize the needle on the gas gauge has fully dipped below the red line. Miraculously I am now nearly to the top of the hill, almost to a small grocery store that does not sell gasoline – a safe place to stop. I cannot go further. To try would be useless, ultimately being stranded in the middle of the narrow two-lane road, not a good place to be when going downhill through the curves.

Starting at the top of the hill where the store is, and ending at the river highway at the bottom, there are steep wooded hillsides on one side of the pass road and on the other, a precariously steep tree and brush covered embankment with a creek far below. Not long ago a car driven by a young woman inexplicably veered off the pass road at one of the many curves, careened headlong down the hillside, and ultimately overturned into the creek. Safely buckled in her seat, she drowned, upside down in the swirling, muddy, dark water before anyone could get to her.

With great relief, I am finally able to point my car toward the gravel lot. This is where I will secure my vehicle and eventually start walking home. Several other cars have pulled in before me and I am fortunate enough to find a spot along one wall at the back of the lot. I pull my car to a stop with my engine idling and set the stick shift in its neutral position. Removing my left foot from the clutch, my leg involuntarily trembles in place. My right leg is cramping and going numb regardless of my efforts to stretch and regain circulation. My hands and shoulders shake uncontrollably as the horror scene of Kia gunman killing an innocent person, "God damn - A woman, and with a baby in the car too!" replays itself in an endless loop in misty rain on my windshield. I am in the car with her, kneeling on the front passenger seat, my face inches from hers, frozen, as she cringes and squints against bullets exploding through her windshield that rip into her chest, jaw and soft perfumed neck. A bullet severs the 2 millimeter Figaro gold chain with its crucifix attached, once playfully dangling above her cleavage, now fallen, hopelessly lost between ample breasts that quiver with each deadly impact.

An overpowering fragrance of Plumeria blossom wafts through the air of my high definition imagination as her head turns slowly toward me. With sad, unblinking, dead eyes, she utterly condemns me for not having prevented her murder. Kia gunman's sinister stare behind his muzzle flash jolts me upright, standing the hair on the back of my neck, my eyes wide but not seeing. Gasping for air, trying hard to breathe, I blink several times, attempting to focus on the pass road beyond my rainy windshield. After for what seems an inexhaustible lifetime, I am finally able to discern headlights of a metal, segmented snake, shiny wet, descending into dark curves. Leaning my head back, I do not close my eyes for fear of seeing the woman's death, my face again-and-again inches away, unable to stop the inevitable. Time passes. How much, I don't care. At some point however, I regain my sense of control enough to realize I need to turn my car off. Only after I turn the headlights off do I notice the engine has stopped with the key still in the ignition. The car is out of gas and the realization of how close I'd come to being stranded on the road rolls like a wave through me, standing again the hair on the back of my neck. Praying thanks repeatedly, I take the car key and put it in my shirt pocket. The only sound within the car is my pulsing heartbeats throbbing in my ears. Outside my car window, the slow roll of car tires crunch gravel as they maneuver into position next to me. Rubbing my eyes, I pause and take several more deep breaths before gathering my wallet. In an attempt to regain control of myself, I turn my attention to the store and prepare to exit my car saying, "The owner will make a boat load of money if he's open."

Taking the compact .357 revolver from my glove box I tuck it into a back pocket of my blue jeans, exit the car and slip into my jacket as I walk to the front of the store. I'm lucky I made it this far and much closer to home. Thankfully, I won't have to walk those miles and the thought makes my jacket feel a little bit warmer as I adjust it around neck. As expected the front door of the store is locked, the interior nearly pitch-black. Standing at the glass and metal framed door, I press my face to the glass trying to see inside, realizing there was no reason for doing what I just did. Obviously, the place is closed, but I rattle the door anyway, pressing my face to the glass again, with my hands on either side. "Too bad dude. You've got a captive audience and you're missing out." Three other people come up, do the same thing I had done. My three strangers and I pause for a moment, silently gathering our thoughts. The man next to me pipes up saying he's going to try the back door and if need be, he's going to break in. Pointing absently in the general direction of the mass of cars parked this way and that, the man says he needs supplies; otherwise he won't be able to make it home ten miles away. He says he has to have something to eat and something to feed his diabetic wife sitting in their car on the other side of the store. "All this caught us by surprise while at her doctor appointment in town. Who would have thought?" speaking to no one in particular. I'm not listening any longer. I think no one else is either. We all follow the man to the back of the building. He rattles the padlock hanging securely on the hasp and jiggles the doorknob finding it locked as well. I think to myself with some unease, "With all the doors locked, likely no one is inside waiting with a loaded shotgun for looters like us to arrive."

I am not completely dismissing the notion of an armed encounter from being within the realm of possibility. Clearly seeing again what happened down the road, I believe nothing is usual and customary any longer. The image of the dead Kia driver sitting and bleeding in the road screams loud and clear I cannot afford to take anything for granted. "Gotta go slow. Think things through," I remind myself. If the shootout down the road tells me anything, and it is saying a great deal, we are all in survival mode whether we realize it or not. Moreover, the quicker I accept that fact, the better off I'll be. "Don't do anything stupid," I mutter under my breath. My goal is to get home to the dogs and do it safely, "period". Being together is everything. At that moment, someone comes forward with a sledgehammer and crowbar. I step away from the back door and take up a position behind the gathering group of people now standing in a half circle, ready to break in and take what they want. The hasp and doorframe put up a small fight. They are no match against an aggressive crowbar wielded by country boys hardened by logging trees for a living. The lock comes loose and the door is summarily kicked aside, yielding the dark interior of the store to the crowd of strangers now making their way inside. I pause for a moment before stepping in, just to make sure no one is indeed hiding with a loaded shotgun. Once inside the store, I do my part without conviction to relieve it of a few items. "This is what it takes to keep going, right?" I hear someone in the darkness prying at the cash register while I gather "dinner." Shouldering my way past the crush of people flooding in from the gravel parking lot, I make my way to my car with four days of food and provisions for traveling on foot.

Although more cars from the pass road attempt to wedge their way in, the parking lot is already chaotically full. Facing the hoard of humanity crawling over the place like ants, with my back against the wall at the rear of my car, the revolver in the back pocket of my Levi's pressing into my right butt cheek, as well as the backpack in the car trunk, I reassure myself I am not like them. I have a plan that goes beyond going with the flow or hoping for the best. In my oasis between cars, with my back against the wall I survey the scene, and for a second time the question of the day comes to mind, adamantly refusing to be dismissed or ignored, "Now what?" I know what. I wish though I had a reasonable alternative other than walking home, but clearly, I don't. There is no way I am camping in my car for an indefinite period. Who knows how long I would be here if I do not get moving now and I'm not going to ask someone for a ride just to sit in traffic. "I'm walking," I say aloud. Affirming it makes me feel better if not slightly more confident. I'm taking control of my circumstance. I'm taking control of my life.

Sitting on the edge of the trunk with an open bottle of water and chewing an energy bar I stole from the store, I feel my body responding to what I am feeding it. For some reason or other I skipped lunch and eating now, even just this little bit, is a delight. One by one, each happy face of my dogs comes to mind, bringing a welcome smile to my face while I am chewing my energy bar. "Goofballs," I mumble aloud with food in my mouth and then chuckle knowing I did that. In a few hours, the dogs will probably start whining a bit, wondering why I am not opening the garage door to let them out to run the front yard.

The dogs will be ok I reassure myself. They don't know what I know, so they won't be worried. Zeke, Zoie, and Little have it better where they are than at the kennels. "Compared to Big Meadow, they're in a penthouse," and the thought of them safe at home makes me feel a great deal better. Being overly anxious is simply an example of how I want to be home with everything back to our normal, if not boring, routine.

I finish eating, and with thoughts turned to the list of immediate must-do items before leaving my car, I notice daylight has completely faded into a pitch-black sky. Lights coming from flashlights many people carry as they walk this way and that in the parking lot combined with headlights of cars on the road will be enough to help me as I gear up. Recognizing the moment for what it is, I stay seated for a minute more on the edge of the trunk in the misty drizzle and talk to myself, "Trust in yourself, Cdub. You have what it takes." Talking to myself aloud in this way now makes me laugh, bringing back memories of how, during some of the toughest times of my last divorce, I periodically called my home telephone. I would leave a message, "I love you Man! You're awesome! You are so cool; I wish I could be like you." Most often, by the time I got home I would have forgotten about having done that. When I listened to my goofy message, I laughed and laughed, and that was the point of it. Leaving messages like that felt awkward and simple minded at first; however, over time it had the desired effect of teaching me how to be my own best friend when a friend was all I really needed.

With renewed energy and a better frame of mind, I set about doing first things first and the first thing to do is strip the car of any details of my name and address. Legitimate authorities will have a way of finding out who owns the car, and they can tow it for all I care. I simply do not want to make it easy for someone to figure out I am not home by finding my abandoned car. Searching throughout the car interior, under the seats, glove box and side pockets, I stuff all identifying papers I find into the backpack I moments before removed from the car and have leaning against the wall of the hilltop store. Using a small screwdriver from my glove box, I take the hard drive and battery out of the computer and place those in the backpack - what remains of the laptop I put in the trunk. Lastly, I pop the car hood, wrangle free the car battery, put it in the car trunk, and then lock the gearshift column with my car key. Whatever I don't take with me, I know I won't miss. In less time than I thought it would, I am able to focus on gearing up for the journey toward home miles and miles away.

CHAPTER FIVE
MY FELLOW AMERICANS

Tuesday, October 15

If the current crisis had not been born from a cascade-induced blackout, another emergency in some other form would have struck with equal or greater effect. For years Federal, State and Local governments' published one catastrophe study after another. Each scenario, imminent and devastating, led news headlines for the day, circulated around the internet for a while, but quickly faded from public attention. After the lights go out and do not come back on, most people try as best they can to get home as quickly as possible, either walking or returning to their cars for the trek home. Fortunate ones get home safely before dark.

Other people must fend for themselves where they are until their situation improves. Some are doomed to spend inexhaustible time trying in vain to escape darkened elevators that have stalled in various vertical positions within concrete building shafts with no one to heed their muffled cries for help. Throughout the metro area, people are stranded within electrically powered mass transit train cars no longer moving. Imprisoned, anxious occupants, breathless and sweating, fan themselves, trying to stay calm amidst growing alarm. Others in the car try every means possible to open doors shut tight for their safety while traveling. In other parts of the city, anarchists, apocalypse seekers, and opportunists coalesce into hordes of roving armies. Comingling their madness, they seize the blackout for their own purpose - whether to vent pent up rage, aid and abet judgment day, or simply act out their criminal intent for no other reason than in that moment they can. Incomprehensively, in the midst of the bedlam, massive dance parties spontaneously appear in the streets - as if lights going out and with a city burning down around them is good cause for a rave.

Minutes before the lights go out; department store windows proudly display a promise of an ideal consumer experience perfectly attuned to the affluent and those aspiring to be. Shoppers, street artists, cops, teachers, lawyers, kids, anarchists, and soon to be arsonists, anonymously moving along the sidewalk outside, might have caught a glimpse through the cold window glass of Mr. and Mrs. Middleclass inside, feeding at a trough of life the disaffected will never know.

When the lights go out and do not come back on, denizens with little regard for anything contained there, mercilessly rape the trendy, self-important department store. Piles of luxury brand mattresses are easily set ablaze with a .98-cent lighter. Finely crafted home furnishings, on-sale for thousands of dollars, are stomped to kindling and thrown into flames of the growing funeral pyre. The human condition pounces on the blackout as catalyst to unleash dogs of hate - hate refusing to be coddled, satiated, or mollified until it achieves its full release. Channeling a collective fury, the street dance raves on in refracted glow of the city on fire while raging through the streets, the anarchist and apocalypse seeker together embrace the blackout as their long awaited judgment day: a day they have panted for, as a groom pants for his virgin bride. Darkness is their signal to bring the city down in a conflagration of their making they will soon come to know has marked them as well for its own consumption.

When the city starts burning, usual and customary population control techniques fail miserably. Law enforcement personnel quickly feel the impact. Unabated rampage overwhelms inadequately staffed and poorly equipped law enforcement and National Guard resources, stripping them of their potency to protect and serve the greater populace of otherwise law-abiding taxpaying citizens caught in the crossfire of the melee and mayhem. Limited resources mean Government priorities during the crisis are taking precedence over usual and customary operations. The result is, in the end, citizens must make do the best they can with what they have.

Emergency response plans now require protecting high-value, critical infrastructure such as fuel storage tanks, National Guard Armories with their stores of weapons and explosives, international airport terminals, and major banks.

As civil unrest takes hold, State and local police begin herding city leaders and their families into basement shelters under City Hall, while the rich and rich looking run for cover. Governors of each affected state flee to mansions in greener pastures to sit out the unfolding disaster. Their safety is critical for spiritual and moral support to all citizens during the dark days of struggle ahead: a visible image of strength and continuity of government. In each safe location they have flown to, each manicured Governor steps down from a state police helicopter onto expansive immaculately kept lush green lawn, to a position of authority at the dais. The ubiquitous gaggle of press stand at a respectful distance, boom microphones thrust outward, recording every word, while TV cameras capture each gesture and nuance. Scripted, each Governor solemnly swears; "My fellow American's, I am in direct communication with law enforcement officials on the ground in the affected areas. As soon as I am able, I will return to our great state to lead from the helm the recovery that will surely come. As your Governor and fellow American, I promise this crisis will pass. I put my faith in the resilient, indomitable spirit of you, the American people.

During hours and days ahead, we must remain calm. Do what is right for our fellow man, for our community, and for our great state in this, our hour of greatest need. God bless us all. God bless America. Thank you. No questions please."

At the conclusion of the speech, camera floodlights illuminate the back of each Governor and their entourage hurriedly walking to a sparkling mansion a short distance away. Strength in the words transmitted to eager listeners is reassuring to citizens watching the live broadcast from areas of the nation not affected by the blackout. The no nonsense delivery of the Governor's message of hope and accountability is refreshing to all who hear it. Unfortunately, citizens engulfed in darkness are fighting for survival as best they can, finding shelter with friends or strangers, or worse, shivering alone in isolated dark places until they can make sense of what to do next. They are unable to hear the encouraging words or see the Governor's compassionate teary eyes and quivering lips, endlessly replayed by all major TV news networks.

Most people will survive. Some will not. No one will pass through untouched the visage of an end-time visited upon modern America. For all the souls in all the communities in each state struggling in pitch black, there are doors left to pry open and miles left to travel until home and safety is in sight.

CHAPTER SIX
HOMEWARD BOUND

Tuesday night, October 15

Standing at my car in the gravel parking lot of the hilltop store, I am resolved to do whatever it takes to make it home uninjured. Before today, I felt confident about my crisis response preparations as well as the thought processes I used when creating my plan. It was all theory less than twelve hours ago. Now I am sure the miles ahead of me will hammer home how much more I should have trained and prepared. Adding to my apprehension is the fact, nothing in my military, police, or personal life proved I could count on anyone else but me when the chips were down. Too often, I found out the hard way, human beings act in their own self-interest during times of crisis and do things they would not ordinarily do if they were not under extreme stress. I resolved a long time ago to protect and defend family, friends, and myself no matter what.

Talking to myself, trying to focus – trying to keep my head present in the moment, and task oriented, "The journey ahead is not a race. There is no need to rush or do something stupid." I am going to suit up and walk remaining miles home. I will camp during the day, and travel at night as quickly and safely as possible, ultimately arriving home injury free. How many days I will be on the road, I have no idea. Relying on my wits and provisions, I will walk in the dark and avoid the open road as much as possible. Walking the open road, whether night or day, would leave me exposed, altogether vulnerable to whomever might be out there lying in wait, intent on taking advantage of the crisis, intent on robbing me of my provisions, or worse. My shoulders shudder with a sudden chill.

Staring down into deep shadows of the open car trunk in front of me, I become overrun with heavy thoughts of what I am about to do. Anxious thoughts of what lies in the unknown dark along miles I am resolved to walk, creep into my bones through cracks in my resolve. My knees suddenly feel weak and my lungs constrict, making it hard to breathe. I am seriously questioning if I have what it takes to do what might be required, even before I have laced up one boot to start down the road. "Self-doubt is normal," the Devil on my right shoulder whispers seductively. The Angel on my left quickly and sternly rebuts, "Right now Cdub, doubt is destructive to your resolve therefore, counterproductive to the mission." Aloud I reassure myself, not caring if anyone hears, "I do have with it takes."

The backpack of provisions in my car and those I have left for the dogs now safe and warm in their penthouse-garage is evidence enough. In the past, I have been tough both mentally and physically. Therefore, I have every reason to feel confident I can be tough emotionally and spiritually, right here, right now. While I talk to myself as my own best friend, I look up from the trunk and marvel at the line of cars on the pass road. They have not moved in the past thirty minutes, most idling their engines in place while others have turned their cars off to conserve fuel. My watch dial glows 9:32 PM in green luminescent numbers. The hands of the dial mock me, "I'm moving. Why aren't you?"

From the main compartment of the metal framed backpack I have leaning against the wall of the store, I unpack the full set of field clothes I stashed away two years ago and place them inside the trunk out of exposure to the drizzle. "This is going to be a wet night for sure," and hurriedly strip off my business casual work clothes. Just as quickly, I suit up in an Army tee-shirt and woodland camouflage shirt and pants. Their musty, ink and glue Army warehouse smell is satisfying, bringing back memories of service to my country and pride in my service ribbons, awards and medals, as well as my eventual honorable discharge. The blackout assures me I am going to rely on those memories as much as I can to bolster my spirits. I need to recall long forgotten military training buried years ago, and do it in a hurry for a successful journey ahead.

"Hopefully a successful one," the Devil on my shoulder mumbles in my ear as I sit lacing up my boots on the edge of the black interior of my car trunk. Suddenly tongue tied there is no rebuttal from the Angel on my opposite shoulder.

Wriggling my feet in my field boots and lacing them up snug, I feel how heavy they are compared to the lightweight athletic shoes now discarded nearby. I am gratified knowing these boots will provide excellent traction and support over the long haul. Stomping my feet, I am feeling more confident now that everything feels comfortable and in place. With my tan golf hat over my damp head, I turn up the collar of my shirt to provide as much protection and warmth to my neck as possible, slip my arms through the handgun shoulder holster and adjust it for a proper fit under my left armpit. The stainless steel .357 magnum revolver in my right hand feels ice cold as I secure it in the holster. I drop three extra speed loaders of 38+P semi-jacketed hollow point ammunition through the top of the pocket on my right pant leg, falling, bulky and heavy to the bottom, mingling with wet wipe packets and chewing gum. Secured horizontal along the front left of my belt is my B. Svoboda, Solingen steel bowie knife I carried throughout my military and police career - the toughest and sharpest blade I have ever owned. I have put the knife through its paces in all sorts of situations and I am very happy to have kept it in my backpack all this time. After suiting up in my field gear, I perform a quick function check of my night vision monocular, and then hang it around my neck.

Having patted my pants pockets, reassuring myself everything is in place, including the friction flashlight and gloves in the left pocket, I lift the loaded pack to the edge of the trunk, allowing shoulder straps to slide firmly into place over each shoulder as I crouch down. With everything in place, my equipment is definitely heavy but manageable. I have hiked long distances with more weight and with less fitting packs than this one, and I am feeling rather confident what I am carrying now is doable for the miles ahead of me.

Keeping my rifle in the shadows as much as possible, I slip into the three-point sling, position the rifle diagonally across the front of my body, military style, and covertly slide in a 30 round magazine until its metallic click assures me it is firmly in place. Wriggling into the poncho, I billow it over me so that it covers the backpack, concealing my body and rifle under a bulky Army-green profile. Lightly stomping my feet in place for a moment, I let everything hang by its own weight, testing feel and distribution of the entire load. Adjusting a few straps here and there, I am finally satisfied it's time to go. I take a deep sigh, slowly crouch, steady myself with one hand on the edge of the open car trunk, pick up my work clothes and shoes from the wet ground, toss them all into the dark interior, and finally close the trunk with a convincing, hollow thud.

My first steps toward home are tentative, and my knees feel tensed, similar to the feeling I've had just before the signal at the start of a 100-yard dash. Walking past the driver door, I lift the handle and shut the door again, making sure it's unlocked. I simply do not want someone thinking something inside is worth breaking my window to get.

With car keys secured in my shirt pocket, I move out toward the pass road, leaving the oasis at the rear of my car. Threading through the maze of parked cars in the gravel parking lot, I am careful to avoid bumping people. As I pass between two idling cars on the pass road, steam from the exhaust of the car on my right envelops me while headlights from the idling car on my left illuminate what surely must look to be a bulky aberration in military clothing. Road pavement is dark and looks to be slick from the drizzle that's been coming down all day. Nonetheless, my boots tread securely on the road thanks to their lug soles and the weight balanced on my body under the green, wet poncho. I walk slowly, reminding myself to pick up my feet. No shuffling allowed. I cannot afford to stumble or fall or worse yet, twist my ankle or break a bone. My trek is not about speed or making time; it is all about moving safely and ultimately arriving home in one piece.

Everyone is under stress whether they look like it or not, therefore I avoid making eye contact with anyone and keep myself walking forward. No telling what the complex human psyche will react to under these conditions. As I steadily make my way down the sloping roadway, I catch more than a few stares in side mirrors of drivers sitting in idling cars. Facial expressions register in my peripheral vision as I walk past, reflecting a look of quiet, frustrated, resolute, weariness, while others have a look of, "Why didn't I think of that," as I move past them, leaving them behind to the fate of their individual plan. I feel good about working mine. I am apprehensive and unsure about what comes next, but at least I am moving.

Along with the old man back at the country store who said he was surprised when the blackout hit, I too was surprised. Along with everyone else, I must respond as best I can. From those two perspectives, I am no different from anyone else. However, in this moment, I am very different in one regard. The backpack I am strapped to is my small Noah's Ark carried for years in my car, to which I added this and that, even practicing with equipment and wearing clothing I am now putting into action. With my life in the balance, I am relying on all this equipment and my planning to get me safely through the miles ahead to Point B. Through all the miles of my journey ahead, there is no doubt; I will discover both the strengths and weaknesses of my preparation. More severely, both my physical and mental ability to carry me home will be tested. I am not eager for the challenge I am undertaking. Nevertheless, I have never been one to duck a fight – even a fight for my life. This crisis is just starting to kick in, and the outcome is certainly in doubt. Regardless, I am here, present and accounted for, loaded up and rolling. By having laced up my boots, strapping on my backpack, and hitting the road with enough self-protection to deter a sustained attempt at separating me from my provisions, I am participating in my destiny as opposed to acquiescing to the momentum of the crisis. "See," talking to myself, "this is an example of the 'surprise element' you bring to life's equation." A soft laugh escapes as I say aloud for my own amusement, "And at your age too. Not bad for an old guy, Cdub." Just at that moment, the sound of a scuffing boot sole on asphalt reminds me to pick up my feet.

Having driven the pass road hundreds of times, I know I am making excellent progress walking. Within a few hundred yards I am approaching the T-intersection of Sheltered Road now jammed with cars facing all directions on both roads, some idling while others seem to have been abandoned where they stand. Nothing is moving with cars completely jumbled together. Beyond the massive tangle of cars, the road is clear. Looking around as I pass through, I cannot imagine how the mass of automobiles will be successfully untangled anytime soon. Quickly threading my way through a growing crowd of people milling around, engaged in heated discussions of how to clear the road and get traffic moving, I hear ideas batted around but no consensus reached. Some strongly urge others to clear the mess by pushing offending vehicles over the embankment. Other voices shout in vehement protest against any such notion, threatening to take matters into their own hands if need be. I keep moving forward, threading myself through the narrow spaces inches apart between people and vehicles. Their situation is not my responsibility, and intervention is not part of my plan. Besides, I know a mob like that can get ugly quick. To hang around here puts me at risk of being mixed up in something I don't intend to get mixed up in. I have experienced firsthand an angry mob when I was a young police officer that was enough for me. At the time, I had more hubris than brains, when circumstances required me to arrest a suspect in the middle of a mob encircling him, protecting him from law enforcement. Looking back on it now, I suppose I had enough of the timidity of the police as well defiance from the mob and summarily waded into the middle of it all with my Remington 870 pump shotgun held high in both hands.

When I racked a shotgun shell into the chamber, it was impressive how the sea of humanity parted. I got my man that day, and he went to jail. I doubt I know how lucky I was. Now is not then, and I certainly am not a young police officer. I am a middle-aged insurance man working in an office cubicle, and all I very much want to do is get home safely. My thoughts are my own as I continue forward, with some people in the crowd following my progress with stern and staring eyes. No one says anything to me, and I am relieved when I am finally free from the palpable tension, angry voices diminishing behind me with each step I take into the quiet dark ahead.

Less than one hundred yards beyond the clogged intersection, I carefully step off the asphalt and onto the gravel road that leads down to an abandoned sawmill straddling a creek, at the valley floor. Railroad tracks run parallel to the creek and I plan to follow those until I reach the river highway where I am determined to cross undetected to the other side. How I am going to do that I don't know exactly. I'll decide that when the time comes. What I do know, a left turn at the bottom and I will be facing home, closer than I am right now but still miles and miles away. Walking several hundred feet more, I pause, turn back, and look up toward the pass road with its mass of cars stuck in place. Muffled voices echo off hillsides that pin us together in our narrow geologic space. Light rain is steadily falling, illuminated in the headlight beams of idling cars. With my right hand under the poncho, I pull back the rifle's charging handle and release it sharply, hearing with satisfaction the bullet seat firmly in place at the head of the bolt and firing pin.

Without having to check, I power on the red dot holographic sight mounted on the rifle, confident the red reticle is glowing in the middle of the glass-aiming window. This particular rifle sight allows me to acquire targets in low light, and provides me the ability to maintain my aim center mass with both eyes open, giving me a wide field of view and less tunnel vision. Having relied on this weapon system in combat, I am completely familiar with its operation and handling characteristics. When I decided to employ a rifle for civilian home defense, there was no question what I would use.

After fifteen minutes more, the sloping gravel road I am walking flattens out. Through the mill yard I make my way at a safe distance past the main building of the sawmill: pungent comingled smells of oil, diesel, and wet cedar wood drift through the air - its dying breath, exhaled from  pitch-black interior spaces. As I warily walk past, the crushing loneliness of the abandoned building, drenched in rain at the dark valley floor, creates a nearly overpowering sinister feeling hovering above my head. Not soon enough I am relieved at last to have moved beyond the mill yard and cross a short, thick wood bridge spanning the creek, its tread worn into shallow ruts by heavy trucks hauling lumber over it. As I had anticipated, I find the railroad tracks I knew would be there. Turning left, I move into deeper shadows of the night making my way down the side of the tracks in the direction of the river highway three miles below.

If for some reason CW had turned right instead of left and had for some reason explored along the creek bank eighty yards into the dark, he would have found a single, disembodied, rhythmically blinking amber light, a prisoner within the black wet woods at the valley floor. Moving closer CW would have discovered the light to be the last functioning hazard signal of a sedan, its grill fatally mangled, its engine cracked and no longer steaming, buried several feet in gravely mud at the creeks edge, the butt end of the car in the air bearing vanity license plates. He would have stood at the driver door and found the driver cold and quite dead at the wheel, barely recognizable as Bryan. If he had stood at the mangled car the many hours it would have taken CW to get there, Bryan's last words to his team would have come to mind; "Don't go anywhere until I get back." If CW had turned right instead of left at the railroad tracks, he would have seen Bryan's lifeless body and would have pondered those things. However, CW did not turn right. Instead, he turned left and never thought of Bryan on his journey home.

While moving into the darkness, my index finger automatically rests itself alongside the trigger guard of my AR15 rifle. As I walk I try unsuccessfully to wrestle into submission intrusive thoughts of the 23rd Psalm, '… *through the valley of the shadow of death…*', and respond by nervously and repeatedly adjusting my right hand resting on the rubber pistol grip. My left hand positions itself more securely around the hard plastic grip-pod mounted under the front picatinny rail, ready to respond with lighting reflexes to the ambush my sixth sense tells me will occur at any moment.

I am living a posttraumatic stress flashback, in the dark, alone and drenching wet - on combat patrol in the Balkans at the very moment I realize my platoon has left me in the dark and are not returning. I have been abandoned and I don't know why. I am fresh meat for Hell's maw. Sweat rolls across my forehead as plumes from my heavy breathing hang in the air. The intense darkness now of the valley floor clutches my heart and squeezes it with the same unmistakable death grip I felt so many years ago, with enemies lurking inches out of sight that I can't see or hear. Adding to my dread are muffled echoes of angry voices from the blocked intersection behind me, followed quickly by unmistakable sounds of cars pushed from the road - rolling over the side of the steep slope, sounds of metal straining and scraping, trees and brush cracking, objects splintering as they come to a sudden stop. Abruptly, silence returns to the night, except for sounds of my labored breathing. Frozen in place, I repeatedly take deep breaths, trying to clear my mind and regain focus. I reassure myself combat in the Balkans and my survival, escape, and evasion episode was a long time ago. "You made it Cdub. You are here now. Present and accounted for. You are on your way home to be with Zeke, Zoie, and Little." A few minutes more and I feel my pulse slowing. I am finally able to breathe more fully again. I look up to the road behind me, what may be happening there is of no concern to me. My only focus is what may be a threat mere yards away, hiding in the dark.

Reverting to combat patrol tactics, I periodically stop, crouch, and scan in all directions using the night vision monocular that provide some ability to pierce the dark. Without it, I would be completely blind, mercilessly ravaged by a vivid imagination adept at convincing me of dangers lurking unseen in the pitch black, mere inches from my face - a threat that does not necessarily exist. Even with the night vision unit, I constantly struggle to keep fear in check. As it is, it would be much too easy to succumb to panic, unable to press forward through unknown dark, loaded gun or not. With the unit's infrared setting, I am able to pick up the heat signature of objects I would otherwise never be able to see. Thankfully, other than an occasional small animal foraging for food, the area is clear in all directions. After the unit is powered down and tucked under the poncho, I remain motionless for a minute to catch my breath, giving my eyes time to adjust to the darkness. Only after details of the night have reemerged do I start cautiously forward again, conscious of how I am walking and how my boots make contact with the ground. Over my shoulder, back through the darkness I have traveled, sharp cracks from a pistol echo off the hill. One, and then another, and then another controlled blast - three shots without any other sound. In the darkness, the pistol shots leave me with only speculation to fill in the blanks of my imagination, testing one shape after another against a pegboard until something seems to fit. How bad the situation must be on the pass road, I do not want to know for sure; glad I am alone in this spot far removed from what surely is madness unleashed.

Two more hours of methodical walk, pause, crouch, scan, straighten, and walk some more, the outline of the intersection where the pass road meets the river highway comes into murky view. From this spot, it is an easy 20-minute drive back to work and a leisurely 40-minute drive from here to my front gate. The time is now 11:20 PM and I have been on the move since 4:45 this afternoon. It seems like days ago I had the energy bar and bottled water at the store up the hill behind me. I have a sudden and nearly uncontrollable urge to find a safe place out of sight to rest and get something substantial to eat. My stomach has already been growling in a fierce way, but I have not wanted to stop, being successful ignoring its gnawing hunger pangs. I'm not going to stop now.

Rain slick railroad tracks I have been following begin curving right toward the city twelve miles east; in the opposite direction I'll be traveling. Therefore, I have to make my way cross-country to the underpass of the river highway. Stepping gingerly over the tracks, I leave them behind and slog my way into the soggy thick field grass with its tangle of low brush, blazing a trail as I move warily along the creek bank toward the intersection clearly in my mind. Progress is slow through thick grasses, brush, and buried slippery tree limbs in this tangled marshland. Several times one of my boots doesn't clear a vine or branch or some other entanglement. I lose my balance and fall awkward with the weight of my gear, muddying my gloves, poncho and pant legs. Each time I fall, I struggle to right myself and get moving again. Luckily, so far, I have not been injured.

After awhile, the full dark shape of the underpass of the old highway bridge comes into view, sitting unused parallel to the river highway. Most of the old highway is  completely gone except for sections such as the bridge spanning the creek I am heading for. Cars don't drive on it anymore, and I suppose it was left in place because taking it out would cost too much money – whatever the reason, it sits and decays a little more each year. It will eventually fall but in the meantime, it is a perfect trellis for vines that grow wild there. I won't know until I get a little closer, but I am hopeful there will be a way for me to cross under the river highway instead of having to expose myself by crossing the open road. Once I am on the other side of the river highway, the railroad tracks that parallel the river will lead me in the direction of home. Moving cautiously closer, I kneel next to a scrub tree, its trunk climbed by blackberry vines. Peeling back the dark void under the old bridge with the night vision monocular, I am relieved to see it is unoccupied. "Thank God." While resting in place a few minutes more, I hear for the first time tonight the whine of a car engine increasing its speed as it barrels down the rain soaked, curved pass road toward the intersection to my front-left. The vehicle comes into view, approaches the intersection at an incredible rate of speed, slows a little but does not stop, making a skidding, wide arcing turn to the left and roars off into the night. It moves like a bat out of hell traveling up the highway toward Holbrook, the next town up the road, small town America with bully cops. "Where are the other cars? How did that one get through?"

I shudder when those three gunshots I heard earlier come to mind. I can't help but recall yet again Kia gunman and the female driver he executed at the crossroad, himself receiving swift justice for his sin. As I rest and recuperate near the old bridge, an occasional vehicle speeds down the pass road. Even more infrequently, a car from the center city twelve miles east finds its escape and barrels toward small town America at break neck speed. I haven't seen or heard a police car since the lights went out. Whatever is causing law enforcement to be unable or unwilling to respond makes this blackout very dangerous.

Having rested in place long enough, I press the off button of the night vision unit and stow it away, take a deep breath, exhale slowly and maneuver my way carefully among the remaining grass, twigs and scrub 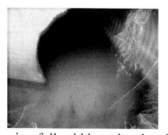 brush to the dank, urine-drenched underpass - its stench becoming stronger as I get closer. With my rifle ready in both hands, I move into the revolting odor under the bridge for a closer inspection, delighted to find a metal pipe full width under the river highway. It will lead me to the railroad tracks beyond. To get through, I will have to wade through creek water because there isn't any high ground to walk on inside the pipe. "God, I do not want to do this." Regardless, my move through the pipe is inevitable, and I locate a flat spot of sand and damp dirt along the creek bank close to the mouth of the pipe to prepare myself. I need to change and move quickly. Right now, I am vulnerable to anyone coming down the valley.

Once on the other side, my goal is to find a place with excellent protection where I can rest and have something to eat. "Just a little further, Cdub. Home is through this pipe," encouraging myself. In spite of being incredibly tired, and in desperate need of something to eat and drink, ideally, I would like to travel beyond Holbrook another ten miles at least in the direction the speeding cars are heading. If I can do that, I will be beyond the reach of their bully cops and much closer to home. Of course, I will have to see about all that after I make it safely through the pipe. The Devil on my shoulder starts to say something but decides I already know and keeps its mouth shut. Kneeling next to the backpack with my knees on the urine drenched sand, I drape the poncho, tent like, over the pack and, when sufficiently concealed, power on the flashlight, hold it in my teeth and fumble around at the bottom of the pack for the waterproof coveralls I know are in there. "In the field everything takes more effort and time," I instruct myself. At last, I find what I am looking for, pull them out and then repack the duct-taped container of food, the small medical kit, and extra clothing I had to remove. With more space now in the main pack compartment, I stow the night vision unit inside. My stocking feet slip easily into the one-piece coverall and snug in the booties. The coverall is a set up more at home in a trout stream with a fly rod than navigating the swift current of a creek in a pitch-black pipe in the middle of the night. I heft the backpack to my shoulders, secure the straps and hip belt, roll my poncho in a bundle and secure it in front of me with the backpack chest strap. After tying my boots together and draping them around my neck, I lift my rifle, thumbing the fire selector switch to safety - the metallic click sounds loud as it echoes off the concrete and metal space under the bridge.

The last thing I want to do is slip and fall in the middle of the creek and accidentally discharge my weapon. Bracing myself with a gloved hand on the side of the rusty, wet, metal pipe and with my rifle over my head in the other hand, I ease my way off the muddy creek bank and into the cold water; the flashlight gripped in my teeth able to shine only a few feet down the black interior. "This sucks." Black water swirls around my stocking feet encased in their protective neoprene booties and its cold creeps up my legs as I inch ever further down into the middle of the creek; the chill adding to my growing sense of anxiety. Through the booties, my feet feel the squish of the creek bottom muck, slippery and dangerous. As long as I shuffle, taking simple baby steps, I should be able to maintain sufficient footing to avoid rocks and other debris along the bottom. Staying dry and injury free is critical. With steps tentative and a bit unstable wading through the cold current, I nevertheless maintain sufficient balance and slowly make my way through 60 yards of pipe.

The flashlight clenched in my teeth illuminates the way with a soft bluish light, more of a reassurance than anything actually bright. Enclosed in the tight dark space under the river road, I imagine the smell of rich black coffee brewing on the other side of the pipe. Imaginary smells of luscious black coffee combined with the flashlight held between my teeth cause saliva to pool along my lower lip and drool out one corner of my mouth and down my chin. I can do nothing about it and let it do its thing, thinking to myself, "I sure look appealing right now." My soft chuckle echoes off sides of the metal pipe.

At last, I am able to take deep satisfying breaths of clean, cold air, grateful to have made it uninjured to the other side. Finding a suitable spot along the left bank, I brace myself and exit the creek onto wet, firm, grass covered ground. Traveling a few feet down a small muddy trail, into a cluster of cottonwood trees that line that section of riverbank, I deploy the bipod on my rifle and gently place it on the ground nearby, unroll my poncho, and cover the rifle to protect it from the elements. Shaking off exposure to the cold temperature of the creek mingling now with light rain falling, I quickly untie my boots from around my neck and peel off the waterproof coveralls, placing those at my feet, being sure I am able to stand in my stocking feet on the dry interior side of the bib. My thick boot socks and pants are still thankfully dry, but I need to dress quickly; exposure to the elements can be a killer if not taken seriously and dealt with appropriately at all times. Ready to move again, boots laced up, bib coverall packed, and the night vision unit around my neck, I sling the rifle in position, and then lift and secure the backpack. Only when my hat and poncho are in place do I begin to notice what had been a growing chill, start to fade. Moving cautiously out of the protective shadows of the cottonwood trees with my rifle locked and loaded under my poncho, I find what I am looking for and set a course along railroad tracks that will lead me home, reminding myself with nearly every step to pick up my feet as I go. Unlike when I first started, every step now feels much more tiring. My spirit and my resolve to keep moving seem to be fading into a fog of exhaustion. Glancing at my wristwatch I find the time is 11:57 PM and my stomach immediately rumbles with fierce intensity.

A sudden nauseous feeling rolls like a wave through me, urging me not to ignore my hunger any longer. Desperately in need of a break to rest and eat, perhaps even take a nap before pushing for home, I nevertheless walk another two hundred yards in hopes of finding a suitably protected place to set up a lean-to. The place I choose is among a stand of tightly packed cottonwood and alder trees, a place where younger trees have toppled over because of water erosion or wind, or both. Just in time too. I do not think I can take another step.

Slinging the pack to the ground, I unzip the bottom compartment, retrieve the tarp and unfold it to its entire 8 x 10 dimension. Laying it over toppled branches, I create a makeshift tent with three sides of the tarp lightly brushing the coarse sand of the riverbank. I spread the poncho on the ground under the tarp, wet side facing the sand. After the backpack and rifle are under cover and lying on the poncho, the aluminum gel-fuel stove is easily set up and firmly planted on a sandy spot in the farthest section of my makeshift shelter. A strong smell of rubbing alcohol wafts free as I pry the lid from a gel fuel can. Soon water in the cup placed over the blue-green flame begins to heat up nicely. The thought of a much-anticipated cup of coffee in a few minutes more makes me smile. For a fleeting moment, while staring at the dancing flames, I feel I am on more of an adventure than a survival trek. Watching the flames heat the cup of water, I remember the glowing orange heating element of my on-its-last-legs toaster, a memory that now seems as if it were a long time ago instead of something that happened before I went to work this morning.

With water about to boil, I exit the shelter and bring leafy branches from the immediate area, placing them around the tarp to conceal my position and cut down on the movement of the tarp from breezes that occasionally blow through. Stepping back to survey my handiwork, I approve and only then do I become aware the rain has stopped for the first time today. "Thank goodness for small mercies." I peer up to a cloudy sky, unable to see anything but outlines of thick clouds. Under cover again and anticipating dinner with diminishing patience for it all to come together, I distract myself and clean my hands, face, and neck with one of the wet wipes I picked from my side pants pocket. The ritual lifts my spirits and makes me feel almost better. No sooner had I finished washing, I hear water boiling in the tin cup and drop in the instant coffee packet, the delicious aroma immediately filling the air around me. In seconds, I have a steamy cup secured by both hands, close to my nose and lips and wonder what is more heavenly: warm dry socks on cold feet, or this hot cup of coffee after hours in the rain and dark. I smile being blessed to have both.

Relishing sips of coffee, I put the metal cooking pot on the stove and pour a fair amount of bottled water into the pot for soup. The first drops of water sizzle for a moment as cool water meets the heated pan. Kneeling, resting back on my heels, watching the water come to a boil, I enjoy the warmth of the hot cup of coffee on my hands and the liquid in my mouth as I savor each sip. Pulling my rifle into my lap, I settle back comfortably under the tarp, and stare blankly at the dancing blue green flames while taking stock of my current situation.

I am concealed among the cottonwood trees along the riverbank, out of the elements; clothed, dry, warm, uninjured and about to feed myself. I do not have a TV, or internet, a working cell phone, computer game, book to read, or an iPod to entertain, distract, or satisfy me. In this rough-hewn world under my tarp tent in the night, my world has been reduced to basic elements, and I am immensely satisfied and grateful for all I am blessed with. Tonight top ramen noodles, cooked over a gel-fuel stove under shelter on a lonely stretch of sandy riverbank, never tasted better or made me feel closer to home. On my journey to this spot, I know I have a long way to go before I am back with Zeke, Zoie, and Little, but I've made excellent progress so far, physically, spiritually, and mentally. "So far so good, Cdub." I am blessed and I say so, with prayers for my friends and family, asking a merciful God to protect them wherever they may be.

With a full stomach, I sit on the poncho with my back comfortably resting against the pack and everything neatly stowed inside again. With deep satisfaction, I enjoy a second cup of hot coffee, now half-empty in the metal cup, clutched with two hands. Having my locked and loaded rifle lying heavy in my lap allows me to relax my body with an assurance I will get moving down the road again in a minute or two. My eyelids are heavy and I close them while lifting the cup to take a sip. Slowly swallowing, feeling the warm liquid run down my throat, I rest my hand on my lap and open my eyes: Daylight. A jolt of electricity goes through my body. I am motionless and awake. That's all I know for the moment.

My tin cup is empty on its side in the sand touching my left hand. Trying to clear my mind, I listen intently to sounds near and far away: birds in the trees and a low hum coming from somewhere I cannot determine and do not recognize. I brush back the sleeve of my jacket and peer bleary-eyed at the wristwatch. I think it says 6:10 AM. "Do I stay or do I walk?" urgently asking myself with no clear answer. Before doing anything rash, I decide it is best to scout the area. I will make a better decision once I am awake and have a good look around. Leaving everything but my rifle and range finder, I exit the tent and head out to the highway, thankful it is not raining and daylight is not yet full.

Low humming sounds up ahead become increasingly pronounced as I cautiously approach, crouching slow and low, edging my body up the side of the embankment, inching forward on my stomach the last few feet to get a view of the roadway. My line of sight breaks through weeds lining the edge of the asphalt under the metal guardrail. I am stunned. The highway is packed with cars heading away from the city, traveling in the direction of Holbrook, with its contingent of bully cops and their peculiar version of small town hospitality.

CHAPTER SEVEN
ENEMIES FOREIGN OR DOMESTIC

Wednesday morning, October 16

Partly covered by grass, weeds, and small scrub brush, I am in a prone position perpendicular to the river road, my rifle locked and loaded at my side on the embankment. No one can see me, but I have an unobstructed, worm's eye view of what's happening in both directions up and down the highway. From my vantage point under the guardrail, I see vehicle tires slowly rumble past not more than three feet in front of me. In spaces between cars, I see the intersection of the pass road has a solid line of cars spilling out, merging with the larger stream of traffic rolling past me. "Seems the pass road is moving again." Edging backward off the embankment, I make my way to my brush-covered tent, having decided on the way the best thing to do for now is get water boiling for breakfast.

Having breakfast will restore my strength for the road ahead and give me time to decide what to do next. Fog has formed on the lens of my wristwatch but I am able to make out the time through the blurry dial - 7:15 AM. Less than twenty-four hours since the blackout hit. I have seen two people shot dead, heard gunshots in the night, and I can only speculate about vehicles pushed off the road. Now this morning looks to be a never-ending mass of humanity fleeing the city. "What's going on?" I ask urgently.

With black coffee in hand and hot instant oatmeal in my blue metal bowl, I know this is a good start even though I was surprised at having slept until daybreak. My next decision is a critical one, and I have to think this through - I am concealed in a tent out of the elements but I am now in daylight. If I move, I will be exposed to whatever might happen out there. If I stay, I will be extending the time it takes to get home. Moreover, the longer I stay here the more I increase my chances of being discovered under the cottonwood trees. If I had actually planned to be here during the day, I would have found a location with much more cover; but that is not possible now. If I am discovered, there is no telling what will happen, and I simply do not believe anyone will act civilized. I hope my cynicism is unfounded, however I do not want to have it tested either. Trying to keep my imagination in check, I busy myself with trying the hand crank emergency radio I bought awhile back. After a minute of cranking I can tell the unit is working, the light is on but every channel has only static – the same noise I heard from my car radio yesterday.

After having finished my coffee and wiped clean the cups and utensils, I store them, the radio, and the tarp neatly in their assigned spots in the backpack. In the process, I find I have made my decision: I am going to move down the road in daylight. Having weighed my options, I decide this seems the best choice in a bad situation. Dressing in less than military garb and keeping my rifle hidden by slinging the poncho over my shoulder will definitely help lower people's anxicty when they see me walking the road. The old adage, "there's safety in numbers" comes to mind, and I hope it's true but I am not very confident. "Why would anyone today act any different than what I saw yesterday?" I have a bad feeling about what I am about to do. Nevertheless, I trust this is my best decision and I set to work making it happen.

Quickly changing out of the Army woodland camouflage jacket and pants, I stow them in the pack and slip on clean black field pants that compliment the muted green color of the zip up jacket. With my hat pushed down over my matted hair, this combination is the best I can do not to look like GI Joe marching down the road in broad daylight. After settling the backpack in place and buckling myself in, I sling my rifle across my shoulders, at an angle along my right side far enough where I can control it by the pistol grip and still keep it hidden. After positioning the poncho over my right shoulder and looking it over, I am confident no one will notice the rifle underneath. Before moving out, I quickly swallow an energy drink, and after two gulps, put the cap back on and return the empty container to my left side pants pocket.

Taking a deep breath and looking around the area that was once my makeshift home, I set off down the railroad tracks that parallel the road crammed with a streaming mass of humanity in every type of vehicle imaginable. Surprisingly, I am actually feeling in a better mood than I thought I would, given the circumstances. Perhaps this will be a good day after all.

After a short while, the railroad tracks and river highway become nearly level affording me an ideal location to leave the tracks and make my way on flat, firm asphalt. No one seems to pay any attention to me, and I make good progress heading toward Holbrook. Vehicle traffic is slow and steady: moving in an orderly fashion. So far everyone is behaving. I slow the pace of my walking and remind myself this is not a race. It is all a matter of getting home safely. "Remember, pick up your feet, and don't shuffle." Right at that moment I stumble hard, nearly toppling over face first but catch myself with a few awkward lurches. I recover and catch my breath, "That was close." While taking my hat off and wiping away the sweat from my forehead, I turn and look down the line of oncoming cars, seeing for the first time an indication of why people are leaving the city in a mass exodus: columns of thick black smoke reach into the morning sky from areas of downtown and surrounding neighborhoods. Multiple thick black oily columns have begun fanning out as they catch the wind at various altitudes above the city.

For several minutes, I alternately watch smoke rising skyward, then stare again at the streaming line of cars, and then back again to the burning city. "How can this be happening? Has everyone gone completely crazy?" Urging myself onward, all I can do is shake my head and think of home. "Zeke, Zoie, and Little are waiting for me. When we're together, everything will be ok." Surely, the madness unfolding in the city won't touch us at "Stanton Mountain," a nickname my friend Max likes to call my place. "I hope my friends are doing ok," I say aloud.

Not having walked much further, I hear a couple of motorcycle engines closing in behind me. Thumbing the selector switch to fire, I place my finger on the trigger of my concealed rifle and turn to face two Harley Davidson's on a slow approach along the tight space between the roadside and the endless line of slow moving cars in the right lane of the highway. Both motorcycles have large American flags flying from their backrests. The lead hog has chrome ape hanger handlebars, an all black paint job, and huge tires with white sidewalls that surely must have come from a small car. I love an all black and chrome bike, and if I could choose one, it would be the one slowly coming up to me now. The second hog following black beauty is ok too; a Fat Boy with buckhorn handlebars and a green and gold metallic flake paint job. "Too each his own," I think dismissively with a slight smirk turning the corner of my mouth. Confidently, I stand my ground at the side of the road as the two Harley's pull up close. The big guy with the ape hangers slowly steers into position in front of me, stops and rev's his V-twin a few times, letting loose unmistakable thunder from unobstructed straight exhaust pipes.

While I am eyeballing the details he offers, 'Wanna lift?' from under his black and white skull and crossbones bandana tied over his mouth and nose bandit style.

Having quickly sized up the situation, I feel comfortable enough to say, "Yeah, sure. Thanks. I could use a lift." He sounds friendly I assure myself. I am wary and keep myself alert for any sign of danger. "I know a little about Harley's but is this bike gonna take me and my gear too?" I ask.

"Sure no problem" Big Biker says from behind the scarf. "I once had an old lady bigger than you and your gear combined. This bike'll handle us fine. No worries."

"What do you want me to do with the flag?"

"Can you carry it 'til we get into town?" he asks.

"Sure, not a problem," I reply enthusiastically, happy to have a ride and be off my feet for a change.

I remove the large cotton stitched American flag attached to what looks to be a long broom handle and release it from the Harley Davidson backrest. Big Biker says to toss the broom handle and with a shrug, I toss it to the side of the road and fold the flag in my arms. Steadying myself, I lower my weight on the back fender, feeling the cold metal of the bike fender under my butt. The entire bike sinks a bit lower on its springs as I settle in.

I like this guy; he has one padded seat and that's for him - same as I had on the Harley Springer I rode cross-country after being discharged from the Army. *'Sit on the rail or don't ride at all.'* I laugh aloud as my heavy boots find foot pegs meant for rail riders as the biker revs the Harley engine a few times. I think he understood why I laughed although I didn't say anything. Before he starts moving, he asks over his right shoulder if I am all set and ready to ride. "Just a second," I say toward his grey beard floating over his shoulder. "I need to reposition something," and then bring the rifle out from under the poncho and lay it across my lap, covering it with the poncho and American flag on top.

He is surprised seeing the muzzle come out from its hiding place along my right side, arcing across his back into my lap and says, "Whoa. That's some serious shit my Man."

"It's not meant for you. We ok?" I ask Big Biker.

"Hell yeah Dude. Let's ride."

The bike growls and we move swiftly in the open air, followed at a safe distance by the metallic green Harley with buckhorn handlebars I think look stupid. Both bikes move easily down the right side of traffic, eventually weaving through the right lane into the narrow space between the left and right columns of slow moving cars. This is the safest spot for us. No one is going to merge left or right since everyone is traveling in the same direction and at the same slow speed.

Having the Harley rider stop and offer me a lift is a generous act of kindness I very much appreciate. Riding is a heck of a lot more enjoyable than walking too. Makes me feel good to be alive; and being on the back of a badass hog with badass exhausts announcing our approach makes me feel badass too. Sure enough, just as Big Biker said it would, his hog handles the added weight as if I weren't even there.

In less than five minutes and not more than ten miles down the road, Big Biker notices what looks to be a problem up ahead.

Turning his head over his right shoulder, "Cars are stopping; something up ahead."

Leaning slightly over his left shoulder, I try to see what he is seeing but I can't tell much sitting on the back of the bike. Nonetheless, I reply "Ok". The throaty bike engine rumbles as Big Biker shifts to a lower gear and slower speed. Our party continues up to the front of the line with people standing outside their vehicles making way for us. Coming into view is a mass of flashing emergency lights the likes of which I have never seen in one place before. Blue, red, white, and yellow lights flash and blink from the tops of emergency vehicles stretched the entire width of the river road. In some places, there are vehicles two and three deep. "An accident?" I ask toward the bikers left ear.

"Dunno," he says over his right shoulder.

We proceed forward until we cannot go any further. A crush of people stand in the space in front of us, their attention turned squarely toward the blockade. Both Harley's shift into neutral and we idle to a stop behind the crowd in our lane. From my vantage point on the back of the bike, I have a clear view of state police, city police from several if not all the small towns in the area, sheriff cars, fire trucks, and ambulances. They have laced themselves into a blockade of the public highway. It is obvious no one is being allowed to pass, and at this point, no one is saying why we can't go through. Law enforcement and fire personnel stand behind their vehicles passively looking at the gathering crowd of cars and people in front of them. Police officers and Sheriff Deputies in various uniforms have shotgun's and AR15 rifles resting on their hips with rifle muzzles pointing upward. Reminds me of a news report during the aftermath of Hurricane Katrina when law enforcement from a small town in Louisiana blocked a road over a bridge between their town and New Orleans. For unknown reasons, refugees from the flooded city were not allowed to pass through. A one sided gunfight erupted from what had been a verbal

confrontation. If I remember correctly, an unarmed man in a wheelchair was shot in the back and killed by police. A shiver of cold shakes my body with the thought. Turning back, I see the progression of vehicles  slowing to a halt further and further down the line, quickly stretching into the distance as far as I can see. Drivers and passengers ahead of me are exiting their vehicles, and moving forward toward the barricade, adding to the tightly packed mass of people already at the front.

Up and down the blockaded width of highway, I hear people asking law enforcement, "What in hell is going on here?" The only response I hear comes from individual officers relatively close by saying no one can pass, the road is blocked; "Please return to your vehicles."

The crowd around me has grown considerably larger in the last few minutes with some even sitting or standing on their cars, vans, or pickup trucks. We are pinned together along lanes of parked cars facing the barricade of emergency vehicles to our front; however, beyond the barricade, the road is clear. I stay seated on the fender of the bike with my rifle concealed across my lap under my Army-surplus poncho and Big Biker's American flag. "Waddya wanna do?" I ask Big Biker.

Lowering the bandana from his face he says, "Nothing to-do just yet," and then quickly adds, "This is bullshit."

That's a reasonable response if I've ever heard one. Right then the other biker walks up and stands next to me as Big Biker remains straddling his idling Harley. Grey-blond split ends tumble out as she removes her Wehrmacht replica helmet. When the pink skull and crossbones bandana is lowered, she smiles a toothy smile in my direction without making eye contact, turning her attention immediately to Big Biker. As they discuss the situation, I get a close up view of miles and years etched into the face of a hard living and hard riding woman, thinking with every confidence, "She could kick my ass all day long without breaking a sweat."

Big Biker and Biker Woman agree they are going to go up front and see if they can get an answer for any of this "God damn bullshit." Big Biker turns the engine off, settles the bike on the kickstand, and leans it left, amply able to hold my weight. As he lifts himself free I remark, "If it's ok with you, I'll stay here."

"Sure thing Brother. Don't let anyone mess with our rides though," he says commandingly.

"Count on me. I got ya covered" and watch as they aggressively make their way through the press of humanity to a position as close as they can to the nearest emergency vehicle blocking our lane of travel. Turning slightly in my seat, I am able to look back down the road again and marvel at what a mess it is, thankful the sun is out and it isn't raining. Columns of black smoke rising skyward from the city center 20 miles behind me have multiplied. "This is not good. Not good at all," I mumble under my breath.

The kid beside me, buckled in his car seat, stares at me with a passive face, his bright blue eyes at first fixed on me, then down toward the American flag and poncho, and then back to me again. He does it again. I look down to see what he's staring at: the butt of my AR15. It's exposed and clearly visible as a six position collapsible stock anyone with any knowledge about such things would know. The corner of the poncho and American flag covering it must have been kicked up when Big Biker got off the Harley.

As nonchalant as I can, quickly looking left and right, I drape the poncho and flag over the stock and reposition myself again on the fender ensuring there is nothing else of the rifle exposed. Looking toward the kid with the blue eyes, I find he has turned his attention to some sort of electronic gizmo he's thumbing furiously. A guy I assume to be "Daddy" is in the driver seat of the polished Starfire Pearl Lexus RX hybrid 4x4, drumming his fingers on the top of the doorframe with his left elbow resting out the window. Leaning forward and looking toward the front passenger seat, I see what I expect to find - a blond thin faced pretty woman fiddling with either her hair or makeup in the vanity mirror. "Must be Mommy," and notice both the man and woman take great pains ignoring one another in their confined space. Mommy, Daddy and the blue-eyed kid thumbing the gizmo, all look completely bored. "Jeez, what a life."

A bullhorn screeching to life from the Fire Chief perched on the chrome step at the rear of the fire engine parked at an angle behind two other police cars abruptly calls my attention away from middleclass America. "Hello," he says haltingly in the bullhorn he is holding directed at the mass of cars and growing crowd of vocal citizens that have exited their vehicles. The bullhorn screeches, and he fiddles with something on the back and tries again.

"Is this on? Can you hear me?"

The volume of the Fire Chief's voice is close to ear splitting causing the crowd to stop what they are doing, lower their voices, and turn in his direction. The Chief with his annoying bullhorn now has our full attention. The blue-eyed kid in the car next to me is sticking a finger in each ear. "Smart kid. I should do that," I think to myself, but I don't.

The Fire Chief continues, "The highway is blocked. There is no entry beyond this point. You are advised to return to your homes or to other areas of sanctuary."

With that, the collective howl of the crowd is nearly as loud as the volume coming from the bullhorn with "bullshit" this and "bullshit" that up and down the line.

Mr. Fire Chief continues his speech into the bullhorn, "Excuse me. Your attention please! Power is out area wide. This blockade is a precautionary emergency action intended to ensure the safety of our citizens and businesses within the county. I am confident authorities are working diligently to get power restored, but when that will be, I do not know. Please return to your vehicles and vacate the area."

My fellow Americans are not accepting the message well and show their growing displeasure by leaning over hoods and trunks of police vehicles, shouting at cops standing out of reach. A few officers in my vicinity begin advising civilians to step back from police vehicles.

I notice a few lawmen are nervously looking up and down the line, taking several retreating steps from the massive, angry crowd in front of them. Not all officers have their weapons pointed upward now. Some have their guns in the "port arms" ready position: a sure sign to me they anticipate trouble that may include the use of deadly force. Sitting on the back of the Harley, I put my right hand under the poncho and flip the selector switch of my rifle to the fire position. Looking straight ahead, and by feel alone, I ensure the 30 round magazine of penetrator ammunition is securely in place. Thankfully, I have another 90 rounds of the same ammo ready in my backpack if I need it, hoping with all my might there won't be trouble. Once again, my senses scream otherwise. With a round chambered, I am locked, cocked, and ready to roll, no longer feeling anything close to badass on the back of a badass hog.

In a former life as a police officer, I have stood where those cops are standing. Having experienced similar situations, I know things can quickly get out of hand. All I want to do is get home; nevertheless, glad I am armed in case the unthinkable happens and forced to defend myself or someone else. People around me shout to the cops and to the Fire Chief that they live in Holbrook or other places beyond. Others shout they have relatives up the road who are counting on them for assistance; "We need to get home. Please let us pass." Citizens plead their case into disinterested faces of cops who have black guns on their hips, standing their ground beyond the blockade.

Collective voices of grown adult's sound remarkably like a chorus of children pleading with mommy and daddy, promising they will be good children if only mommy and daddy cop will let them pass. A growing number of people verbally pelt cops with vain attempts at logic to "see things from our point of view" without any visible affect on the situation. The one sided cacophony goes on for 5 or 10 minutes, perhaps more, until a half-full plastic water bottle is thrown from somewhere behind me in a trajectory poorly aimed at the Fire Chief standing at the back end of the fire truck. The plastic bottle strikes the side of the engine with a plastic squishy thump, and falls harmlessly to the asphalt. Mr. Fire Chief nonetheless dutifully ducks at the sound of the thump and then bellows in the bullhorn, "People, please stay calm. Please return to your vehicles and vacate the area." No one is listening, not at that moment any way. Realizing he is wasting his time bellowing into the bullhorn, the Fire Chief steps down, and in his place, a man steps up wearing the green and tan uniform of the Sheriff's Office. Using the same bullhorn, the Sheriff with a shiny gold star promptly and authoritatively identifies himself to the expectant and agitated crowd stretching out in front of him that he is indeed the Sheriff of the County we are all now occupying.

"As Sheriff I have authority to declare a state of emergency and enforce martial law in this county in times of crisis," which he informs everyone he has, "so ordered earlier this morning."

Through the bullhorn aimed at the crowd of citizens, he goes on to say he is enforcing the blockade as his duty to protect the citizens of the county against all "enemies, foreign or domestic." Those four words "enemies, foreign or domestic" roll through the mass of people like a hot wave. For a moment, there is only silence. The crowd stands transfixed, unable to comprehend what the Sheriff just said. As for me, I smirk. The oath Mr. Sheriff misquoted accurately uses the word "and" not "or". I comment aloud but mostly to myself, "It's enemies, foreign 'and' domestic, Schmuck." I laugh and look around to see if anyone else agrees, but no one is paying attention to me. Sitting on the fender of the Harley Davidson in the sunshine of the chilly morning air, I accept the faux pas as a minor slip. However, to me, his slip up is not unexpected from a public servant with little more than a high school education, a badge, and more authority than linguistic precision. "Being precise is never wrong," I mutter under my breath with a chuckle. In a moment of self-important superiority, I think I am likely the only one within earshot that caught it. Then, for the second time in less than 24 hours, all hell breaks loose.

The impact on the massive crowd of citizens of the Sheriff's poor choice of words, "enemies, foreign or domestic" has the effect of unleashing an enraged tidal wave of people bent on crushing themselves against the police barricade. I once try stepping down off the bike, to back away somewhere to the rear, but the rush of people has pinned me in place. Throngs of angry, frustrated people stream past me. I can do nothing but sit back down.

In the process I catch a glimpse of Big Biker and Biker Woman at the very front, and like many others in the crowd, they too are delivering their point of view with fists pounding on the now well-dented hoods of blockading police cars. Up and down the blockade, taxpaying civilians scream, pound, and kick any vehicle in front of them. A few clusters of people try to flip several police cars onto their sides but can't quite get the leverage they need. Police stand their ground and all point their rifles, shotguns and a few handguns toward the crowd of frustrated and enraged citizens. Firemen and ambulance personnel back away.

Incredibly, the voice of Mrs. Middleclass from within the interior of the Lexus cuts through the noise of the crowd. She is barking orders at Mr. Middleclass to "Do something!" I think with derision, "Buddy, I'll bet you've heard that more than once," and looking at the back seat of the Lexus I can't see the blue-eyed kid. He probably ducked down as Mommy and Daddy fight again. Mr. Middleclass responds to his wife's command by forcibly shouldering his driver door open against the crush of people, exits, and with nowhere to go, stands along my side with nothing else to do. "Cunt," he mumbles. I hear his weak defensive epithet only because the angry crowd tightly presses us together. I'm sure he's hoping "Mommy" didn't hear him. Sheepishly, he darts his eyes in my direction. We exchange an uncomfortable glance, and quickly turn our attention toward the blockade with a riot unfolding around us, the worst of its energy a mere fifty feet away. With nothing else to do, I remain seated on the back of the Harley with Mr. Middleclass standing in the roadway slightly forward of my right shoulder.

I cannot be sure what "Mommy" Middleclass is doing, but I am confident she's fuming seeing him there in the road, doing nothing - a clear violation of the order she delivered moments before. "Oh yeah, you've got a nasty punishment cooked up for 'Daddy' when you finally get him alone," I think sarcastically. With nothing else to do but people watch, I really notice Mr. Middleclass standing next to me. I mean, I take a good, hard look at him and judge him to be better outfitted now, perfectly dressed with his pressed shirt and pants and perfect hair while fleeing a burning city, than what I would be on my best day. My judgment of this stranger is immediate, harsh and visceral - the epitome of all my deep-seated self-pity of everything he represents that seems to have eluded me. "Look at him, nothing's out of place with this guy; long sleeve sky blue button down cotton shirt neatly pressed by his favorite drycleaner, I'm sure." He has perfectly fitting flat panel khaki pants down to expensive Italian leather loafers I cannot quite identify, and the belt exactly matches the color and stitching on his shoes. "How perfect is that?" I am sure if the wind were to blow; his hair wouldn't dare move out of place for fear of being sheep-sheared by "Mommy". Sitting on the Harley fender I notice my butt is nearly numb. I squirm, repositioning myself, holding onto the rifle under the poncho and flag, trying the best I can to find a position that will restore circulation.

Isn't it odd how time has the ability to stand still? We don't even know it has until sometime later, when if we're lucky, our mind replays each frame of the movie over and over again. Sitting in the sun "bitch style" on the fender of the Harley parked at the front of the rioting crowd, I blink once and I'm instantly mesmerized by the sight of a small bulge building under the skin behind the left ear of Mr. Middleclass at a point where his perfectly trimmed hairline meets his perfectly tanned neck. Amazingly, the tip of a tightly wrapped red rosebud pokes through, effortless, in slow motion, rotating itself free. With pedals fanned outward a fully formed rose blossom has emerged on the back of his neck. From within the beautiful flower a furious hornet instantly disgorges, buzzing angrily past my right ear, over my shoulder, and into the distance behind me. Mr. Middleclass is altogether unconcerned by this miraculous event, and continues standing beside me, passively facing forward, staring at the riotous scene with what, I'm sure, is the same pout he had when mumbling the C-word under his breath as the ineffectual, impotent man he is.

How mysterious, I blink once more and, although I am certain he doesn't mean to, Mr. Middleclass can't help spray his DNA full in my face through the rose blossom on his neck in volumes I have no way of avoiding. Unceremoniously, his neck wound spews volumes of 98.6-degree sticky blood, misty bubbly white saliva, bits of soft tan skin, and splintered hard bone. Mr. Middleclass instantly drops dead to the pavement below, and I somehow miraculously drop or am pulled left off the bike and onto the asphalt, wedged there between the Harley and the car parked next to it.

I don't know who fired the shot that killed him and nearly killed me, but surely, it came from the front. "Why him? Had a gun toting police officer noticed the butt of my rifle and meant to kill me?" What I do know is gun shots immediately multiply. People rush away from the police blockade, charging back down the lane of travel toward some other place they hope will provide safety from bullets being fired into them. Lying with my nose pressed to the dirty pavement, I hear, in the distance Ms. Middleclass screaming something from within the Lexus. "Ain't life grand?" I remark derisively as her screams register as an auditory blur in the horror above me. I have no idea what she is saying or if she is trying to say anything at all. Her hoarse screams mingle incoherently with hundreds of others doing the same thing at the same time.

What seems to be a never-ending number of people stumble over my backpack and me - my rifle is pinned beneath me, wrapped in the poncho and American flag. At this moment, I can do nothing but cover my head and hope for the best as shoe soles glance off the side of my head, nearly crushing my fingers with each glancing blow delivered unwittingly by terrified citizens running for their lives. I don't blame them. If I could run, I'd run too. Loud gunfire grows steadily from behind the police blockade, shooting into the fleeing crowd with their black guns, unleashing swarms of hornets furious and vengeful, buzzing in all directions mixing now with answers from civilians with a voice in the matter, firing their own weapons from behind their cars and trucks packed together on the road.

The fury of the gunfight grows in intensity as I try to low crawl down the line of cars to get out of the area and to safety, but I cannot seem to make my legs move. In terror, I look over my left shoulder and see my right calf crossed over my left, both pinned by the combined weight of Big Biker and Biker Woman lying one on top of the other, face down, not moving. Big Biker is a big man and Biker Woman is not exactly slim and trim, and their combined dead weight pins my legs tight beneath them. Bullet holes seep blood onto their leather jackets at the base of their skulls. They were shot in the back as they ran away. I feel sad for them. They died together alongside their Harley's and that says something. In this moment, I am determined to make it out of here alive and do it safely. After strenuous maneuvering with a good deal of kicking and wriggling, I finally free my heavy boots from the weight of the two bikers who had me pinned into position, as if their lifeless bodies were holding me back, screaming for me not to leave them. I can do nothing for them and disentangle my rifle from the poncho and flag that had been concealing it and low crawl as fast as I can for a long way down the line of cars. Overhead, bullets continue smashing themselves with deadly force into windshield glass, car metal, soft bodies of police and firefighters, civilian men, women, and children among the mass of cars on the river road. It is a raging gun battle the likes of which I never thought possible in America, an embodiment of insanity that seems endless. Through it all, I wriggle on my belly over bits of glass and spots of blood until I come to a space between two parked cars wide enough to make good my escape. Before scurrying away, I look back over my shoulder and catch a glimpse of the flag tied to the back of Biker Woman's hog.

Stars and stripes jump spastically from the strike of bullets passing through. The flag flutters in the breeze created by bullets flying around it from all directions. I am angry because of the senseless killings but do nothing more than turn my attention to making my escape. Crawling through the space between cars, to the littered roadside, with my belly to the ground, I slide down the embankment, making my way to the railroad tracks that lead to the river beyond - to home and safety somewhere away from here. While crawling through the wet grass to the gravel of the railroad bed another thirty feet beyond, I repeatedly vow never again to move during daylight.

Sounds of the gunfight on the roadway behind me rage in full force and effect. Out of immediate danger, I pause to catch my breath and quickly inspect my rifle determining everything is in order. My heart feels hollow, but there is no time to do anything more than flee the area. To do otherwise puts me at risk of being butchered by law enforcement intent on protecting and serving the way they are doing to my fellow citizens on the road behind me. Before moving, I unfurl the battered, blood stained flag I had released from Big Biker's Harley, and quickly roll it in my poncho for protection. Carrying the roll secure in my arms, I crouch and run as fast as possible across the railroad tracks and into the grassy field beyond, toward the riverbank, desperate to put the firefight behind me, hoping I can make good my escape undetected. Unfortunately, that is not to be.

A couple of Holbrook's finest bully cops see me make for the riverbank. Unbeknownst to me, they disengage from the firefight at the blockade and make their way in a direction they hope will intercept me. I don't see them coming until it is nearly too late. At the riverbank, I begin making my way toward home when several unmistakable thuds strike wet ground around me; instantly two more bullets pass through twigs in the brush close overhead. I fall to the ground and claw furiously at my pack, unbuckling myself, letting it roll off to one side while dropping the rolled poncho with the flag inside, and then low-crawling as fast as I can several yards in the direction of trees along the riverbank, with my rifle cradled in the crook of my arms. As I hit the ground when the second round of bullets were fired, I caught a glimpse for the first time of two police officers in the far distance coming my way. On the ground and undetected by the cops, I back into tree roots along the river's edge. In the distance and getting closer, I hear the officers have spotted my backpack. They laugh and joke and fire a couple more rifle shots at it or in the vicinity, perhaps thinking I may be lying next to it. Whatever they are, they are clearly in a mood to shoot first and ask questions later. Both officers of the law make their way toward my abandoned pack lying on the ground, passing close by my hiding place in the soft sand under the riverbank. As they do, I hold my breath and strain to hear their every footstep above the sound of my heartbeat, unable to hear anything more than someone laughing followed by the words, "Yeah dude."

The cops pass by and I use the opportunity to look up in their direction through the tree roots I am hiding in, able to catch a glimpse of dark colored uniforms walking cautiously away from me. Their backs are to me, and I watch from my concealed position as they realize I am not lying with my pack. Having worked side by side with badge heavy police officers in the past, I am confident these two are thinking, "Good thing the Pussy ran away. No way could he have stood up against a righteous hail of bullets from two outstanding lawmen." To be on the safe side they both immediately swing muzzles of their AR15's in several hasty 360-degree turns, scanning the area around them, eyes darting in all directions, never losing the grin plastered on their faces. I am nowhere to be seen. They let their guard down, turning their full attention to what my backpack might offer them.

From my hiding place at the river's edge, I become aware the distant gunfight on the river highway sounds nothing like a firestorm of angry hornets and more like a bag of popcorn half done popping. There are kernels left to pop in the bag and the timer has seconds left to count down, but the popping, although steady, is noticeably diminishing. My would-be killers and soon to be robbers in dark blue police uniforms are approximately twenty-five yards to my front and without a concern in the world. Using the situation to my advantage, I silently back myself from under the eroded riverbank full of exposed tree roots, through the soft sand, and out the other side. Bringing my AR rifle up with the butt comfortably in my shoulder, I kneel in the sand at the base of the tree.

Taking a quiet deep breath while slowly leaning low around the base of the tree, I watch as Bully Cop 1 slings the rifle to his shoulder and heads toward my backpack with the rolled up poncho nearby containing Big Biker's flag. Bully Cop 2 stands a few feet away, holding his rifle casually in front of him. He alternately looks down at his friend and then to the surrounding area and then back at his cop friend getting ready to riffle the contents - both cops casually talk about how "badass" they are with their guns and what they think this "Fucker's pack" might have inside.

I have seen enough and I have had enough. My body in motion is fluid as I assume a modified standing position with my right knee resting firmly on the soft grassy bank at the base of the tree. My left leg is planted in the sand, and my rifle is supported against the tree trunk, completing a stabilized three point firing stance from a concealed position at the rear of my enemy. Damn I am good and not surprisingly, I feel the edges of a sinister smirk curl the right corner of my very dry mouth as I effortlessly acquire the correct sight picture down my rifle sights and bring my aim to bear on Bully Cop 2 standing holding his rifle in front of him. He chuckles in response to something Cop 1 said. I let him finish his laugh and then kill him. Squeezing my rifle trigger three times in rapid, controlled succession, three 65-grain bullets head down range and slam themselves slightly lower than center mass into the body of my would-be killer dressed in a police uniform.

It is a fact 5.56 caliber bullets tumble when they strike their target. That peculiar characteristic means they take all sorts of interesting paths as they make their way through flesh and bone. My mind registers the strike of each bullet as would-be Killer Cop 2 contorts with my three shots - one actually tumbles its way through his body and out his belt buckle. My bullet releases its energy into the hand guard of the AR rifle he was carrying, splintering the plastic and flinging the now useless weapon into a rotation in mid air in front of him. The rifle drops to the sandy, leaf strewn ground a fraction of a second before its prior operator does. While Cop 2 is twirling his rifle like a drum major's baton leading a 4th of July parade, my aim is already settling on Killer Cop 1. He is kneeling at my backpack, ready to roll it over and pilfer its contents - a frozen look of surprise on his face. I notice he had tossed to one side my poncho roll not realizing its contents are infinitely more valuable than anything in the pack. Cop 1 is beginning to turn his head in my direction when my bullet tears into his left thigh, exactly where I had aimed. It tumbles through his femur and hipbone, shattering each one in jagged splinters, immobilizing muscle and nerve. From my position at the tree, I allow the trauma to sink in; watching him scream in agonizing pain on a blanket of multicolored fall leaves covering the ground beneath him. He valiantly tries to position himself in such a way as to grip his shattered thigh and gushing leg wound. He is much too fat for that to happen in this lifetime - perhaps in the next. Holding a steady aim down my sights, I slowly come around the tree and approach him at an easy pace. Popcorn popping in the microwave on the river road is almost done; hardly any kernels are left in the bag and the microwave timer is about to ring: I can feel it.

The pallor of would-be Killer Cop 1 has turned ashen, a sure sign he is going into shock. Along his forehead, large beads of sweat roll down to a pock marked face and sting his eyes. He grimaces and blinks repeatedly. I wonder, "Why doesn't he wipe any of it away?" In what sounds like a far off voice I remark aloud, "I don't know you" interrupting him the moment he began to say something. I do not care. Stone cold, I shoot three bullets one at a time, methodically into his chest at point blank range. He receives each warrant without protest and immediately dies - forever. I did not give him time to beg, moan, or twitch. This killer deserved each bullet I gave him – the same as his friend, lying dead nearby. A satisfying aroma of cordite drifts from my hot rifle chamber causing me instinctively to thumb the rifle's selector switch to safe. Without remorse, I turn and leave both dead officers; one with his face in the sand, and the other on his back: mouth agape with glazed grey unseeing eyes, searching the late afternoon sky for something he will never find.

Fallen leaves blanketing the sandy riverbank shuffle under my boot steps as I return to my backpack and poncho roll. Unfurling the American battle flag from its protective poncho covering, I do the best I can to quickly fold it into a ceremonial three-point shape, stars facing out, a sign of respect, if for no one else than for Big Biker and Biker Woman lying dead on the highway alongside their Harleys. Placing it reverently in the main compartment of the backpack, I heft the pack over my shoulders, and strap it on. With my rifle in position, I secure the poncho over my head and shoulders, covering the pack and the rifle. Dabbing at a tear in my eye, I leave my two impromptu color guards where they lie.

Picking up my pace, I maneuver through the outskirts of town along the sandy riverbank in the direction of home a long way off, noticing the late afternoon light is fading fast, grateful for approaching dark. The only sounds now are river water lapping at the shoreline and the creaking sound my backpack makes as it strains against its metal frame while I walk the sandy shore. As fast as I can, with each step forward, I put the carnage behind me. Finally on the far side of town, I am fortunate to find an aluminum boat with its oars nearby under the deck of a house. Having set my backpack down in the bottom of the rowboat I back myself as far as I can into the shadows under the deck boards over hanging the rocky shoreline to wait until dark before making a move. Cradling my rifle in my arms, I am hopeful I will remain undetected, my dark green poncho helping me blend with the shadows. Checking my wristwatch, I am surprised to find the day has flown by; it is 4:04 PM. It has been a long and terrible day. With a great deal of relief and satisfaction I think, "It'll be dark soon."

Patiently waiting in the shadows, I listen to the rhythms of the water countdown seconds that seem to tick by in slow motion. My loaded rifle is at the ready with a magazine count light by seven rounds. My nerves are raw from everything that has happened today and adrenaline pumps through my veins. Any notion of dozing off is far from my mind. Within the closed space covering me, I smell the rubber poncho and feel warm and secure. I know its smell and feel that much more protected because of its familiarity.

Quietly adjusting the hood of the poncho to cover my head and face more fully, I attempt to create a sense of solitude and safety among the shadows under the deck while I wait a while longer before it will be safe to move down river under the cover of night.

Lyrics from a favorite song come to mind again for a second time today, from a song on "OPUS69" produced by an obscure band from Amsterdam I discovered quite by accident while on a business trip a long time ago. My fragile emotional state and the songs poignant words bring tears to my eyes. In the privacy of my hiding place and alert to any danger, I cry warm tears that stream to my chin down cold cheeks, *"I'll do what it takes, I'll shoulder any burden, protect, and defend family and friends. I love my God, my family and my country, I'm a man living my days in America."* Those lyrics had come to mind as I ceremonially folded the battle flag laid out on my poncho along the riverbank. "I'm a man living in America," I repeat to myself. Yes indeed. "Heimlich Maneuver of Amsterdam, Netherlands, I could not have said it better myself." It is several minutes before I wipe salty streams from my cheeks and tears from my eyes. Never in my wildest nightmare would I have ever dreamed of combat on the streets of America as I witnessed today. Involuntarily, more tears come and I let them roll, after awhile crying without them.

Not soon enough, darkness has closed in sufficient for me to push from shore and float with the river current away from dangers that might be waiting to ambush me in the darkness somewhere inland along the road. The bottom of the aluminum boat scrapes against stones on the shoreline until I am able to force the boat into enough water for it to float freely.

In those few seconds it takes me to move it, I'm afraid the sound of metal scraping over rocks will alert everyone in the immediate vicinity to grab their guns and shoot the thief to death, no questions asked. My pulse is racing hard. The sound of it pounding in my ears doesn't go away until the rowboat is positioned in the middle of the river, floating at a good clip centered in the current and taking me down river in the direction of home. In the past month, when driving to and from work, I have seen channel-dredging equipment in the river a few miles from here that will ultimately block my progress. Therefore, floating to the boat dock two miles from my house is not to be. "That would be too easy," I grumble to my backpack resting on the bottom of the boat at my feet.

I am making good progress, and that allows me a moment to pull from my pack a water bottle and a couple of Cliff bars to eat. Between periodic adjustments to the alignment of the boat, I have dinner in the middle of the river and for dessert, splash river water on my arms, neck, and face, doing my best not to give thought to the grime, and bloody hardened bits I am washing off. It takes more effort than I thought it would. All the while, I cannot avoid the fact it is flesh and blood in the wastewater my boots are resting in. Disregarding the gore, I am thankful for cold water to bathe with and how good it feels to be at least halfway clean. Looking up to the sky, I try to find the moon, but the sky is nearly black with only an occasional indication the moon is there behind thick and unyielding clouds. I smile when at times I detect a fragment of its silver light in thinner areas of the cloud layer. Makes me feel Hope is nearby.

After nearly two hours of floating with the current in the stolen aluminum rowboat, my departure from the river is coming up soon. In preparation, I position the boat in a line of river current closer to shore and then row onto Trestle Beach. "Perfect," congratulating myself having landed exactly where I wanted. With great relief, I jump ashore, pull the boat further up the gently sloping beach, and then crouch along one side of the boat, scanning the immediate area with my night vision unit while my mind focuses on next steps for the journey ahead. Without realizing it, I doze off and moments later, wake up feeling the cold aluminum metal of the rowboat pressing across my forehead. That scares me. Shaking myself awake, I believe the area is safe and move forward through the soft sandy beach and quickly up the dark trail toward the road beyond. With each step, my vision grows progressively more blurry. Natural night vision techniques no longer work and fail me. I never think to use the electronic NV device. Suddenly, I realize I can't feel my feet in my heavy boots I know are down there somewhere. A nauseous wave rolls over me - I think I'm going to puke. I am frantic to pull over somewhere although I know I'm not driving my car. "Where am I?" The only thing that seems right to do is sit down. I do, hard enough to rattle my teeth.

Exhaustion inhibits panic from ripping CW's fragile mind the instant he becomes aware he has no clue where he is or which way to go. He's blind, alone, and with a loaded gun. Unable to see, he feels familiar hands pawing at the backpack somehow now in front of him. Floating out of body CW passively wonders what the man on his knees is looking for.

CHAPTER EIGHT
POWER STRUGGLE

Thursday, October 17

In 2003, the Northeast blackout affected 30 million people, resulting in 11 deaths and 10 billion dollars in damage over a four-day span of time. The official government investigation spelled out forty-six mandatory corrective actions to prevent or limit the effect of another massive blackout and over time, those had been implemented with good effect. However, as with most things, after the initial rush of government mandated oversight had come and gone, grid operator training lapsed and protocols slowly became outdated. Strict attention was no longer paid to keep training effective and protocols current in the face of new software and new hardware coming on line, as well as the ever-increasing demand on the grid from a modern techfotainment society with an insatiable appetite for electricity.

Time cuddled with persons responsible for remaining vigilant, providing each employee a warm, dependable routine if not a false sense of security. Sure, there were isolated but quite small blackout events since 2003, but those were acceptable when managing the world's largest and most diverse electrical grid. There was comfort in knowing all power outage events paled in comparison to all other cascade failures. Slowly but surely, mandatory quarterly training meetings became perfunctory: an opportunity to socialize with team members on other shifts, more so than for conducting actual training such meetings were designed to accomplish. Before the current blackout crisis hit, Power Station A5 meetings consisted of roll call, kudos all around and assurances of paid overtime for those who qualified, with usual grumblings by those who did not qualify for the extra pay. On each occasion, ample quantities of black coffee was provided that perfectly complemented pastries purchased by the team leader everyone admired: a quirky, likeable fellow known for talking your ear off about technical aspects of ham radio and the sense of community being a part of it engenders. Maple bars were always the first to disappear from the pink cardboard donut containers. Glazed and chocolate covered donuts were second, and the rest picked over, one by one, until the only thing left were disappointed faces from expectant technicians lifting the lid one last time, only to find telltale rings of icing and stray bits of multi-colored sprinkles lying on the bottom of the empty box.

Mr. I-Don't-Give-A-Shit grid operator about to retire piped up again with the same flawed premise he always piped up with at some point during meetings, "What's the point of these meetings anyway? We have implemented everything the Federal Energy Task Force recommended and we should be left alone to do our jobs. It's been years since the big event and that's proof enough the system works, it's reliable, and it's safe." Mr. I-Don't-Give-A-Shit sounded reasonable, especially to rookies in the group and to those with a penchant for believing anything they want to hear. However, his premise was woefully flawed, but no one investigated. Perfect check marks in spaces on required training and preventive maintenance forms in well-organized three-ring binders along one wall of the lunchroom supported Mr. I-Don't-Give-A-Shit and dulled any wayward interest in looking further.

In logical minds of each grid operator, IT staff and Operational Crisis Management Team (OCMT) member at Power Station A5, the gravity of their current blackout event simply should not be happening. Nonetheless, problems no one comprehended now compound one on the other with undeniable effect. With a catastrophe now upon them no one ever imagined possible, each attempt to bring generators on line without Emergency Management System (EMS) server software having been thoroughly debugged, cause transmission lines to overheat from the tremendous amount of energy trying to pass through - with no ability to shed excess load.

Overheated lines repeatedly trip breakers. Each failure burns circuits, wire connections, and damages internal parts of generator units in critical roles - generators vitally needed for a successful recovery. Each time a failure occurs, more generator parts have to be repaired or replaced from a diminishing supply of spare parts too few to begin with.

With little choice left, the commander of the OCMT issued orders to cannibalize some generators for their parts to repair other generators. It is a logical decision at the time. However, the strategy ultimately prolongs the blackout in a sector of the state with people in desperate need of power. Training for personnel at station A5, as well as other stations in their sector, and region wide never contemplated a scenario that included not enough generator spare parts during a blackout. IT staff never considered storing entire servers, with EMS operational software, that could be deployed en masse. A resource like that now would completely alleviate the need for IT staff to debug each line of code in the dark by flashlight beam.

Grid operators and IT staff, panting and sweating in their confined space, scurrying here and there, toiling through endless hours in the dark, have become the proverbial dog chasing its tail. They have no choice but to chase it. Reality crashes heavy against their once inexhaustible self-esteem familiar with fixing insolvable problems. Not this time. This time their struggling failure in the dark is a sad inescapable fact.

Against seemingly insurmountable odds, in heroic effort, if through sheer will alone, they find the strength to run faster and faster and faster, holding on for dear life to the belief their redemption is within reach, if only they are smart enough and fast enough to catch their tail. As technicians move hurriedly here and there, flashlight beams cut through thick layers of humid darkness within the windowless cinder block confine of Power Station A5, splashing light effects on walls and ceilings giving the place a child like feel, as if the work being done there is more a game of flashlight swordplay than something deadly serious. Controlled chaos reigns as engineers and IT staff try fix after failed fix in their efforts to restore power to the station. If they can stabilize power here and connect to the grid, they will springboard their connection to other stations. Restoring power sector by sector, will reverse the blackout that is, unbeknownst to them, vastly larger and incredibly more devastating than the 2003 Northeast cascade event.

Operational Crisis Management Team members have commandeered the power station lunchroom, spreading grid maps and control books over every inch of the two aging folding tables at the center of the room. Chairs are pushed against walls, a few occupied by staff members stretched out and comatose, unable to give anything more. They are willing but unable to stay awake any longer. Cold remnants of coffee sit at the bottom of the glass orb on the now useless warming plate, a cruel reminder of better days behind them. Phones aren't working and will not be working until backup generators can be restarted and stay operational.

If they had an outside line or some other form of reliable communication, they could coordinate their restart activities with another station nearby. A coordinated effort between stations would ultimately replicate capacity for energy load bearing along transmission lines to other parts of the grid. If only they had a "God damn foothold" and a little luck, both evidently unobtainable regardless of their herculean attempts to the contrary.

Daisy chained contingency backup generators along an outside wall of the building start up and run for short durations but never long enough, nor with enough energy, for the Emergency Management System (EMS) to go live and stabilize with the power grid. In spite of their collective IQ and passionate want of success, they are unable to establish a foothold. Technicians pour over schematics and outdated protocols in the humid lunchroom full of flashlight beams while other personnel rush back and forth, to and from the control room, trying one protocol step after another; each one more disappointing than the last in its failure. A living dread born of failure hovers in the darkness unseen, inches below the ceiling, unwilling to be ignored. If some small success cannot be gained to bolster their spirits, grid operators will suffocate in their humid, windowless space with nothing to show for their effort but failure upon failure.

The OCMT plan, put into motion some time ago, sent two engineers home to gather individual ham radios in a desperate effort to create some form of reliable two-way communication. One operator was to return to A5 with his equipment and the other operator to set up his equipment at a power station across town several miles away.

With ham radios connected to individual portable power equipment, communication could be established between stations and a synchronized recovery effort begun. A connection to the outside world would also mean no longer being isolated. That alone would be a tremendous relief to everyone working in the dark. Sending two engineers home to gather ham radio equipment was a logical strategy, although having two grid operators out of commission even for a short while was a hard idea to swallow for OCMT members. Nevertheless, swallow hard they did and both engineers were sent on their way across town in separate vehicles. As they left their brethren, neither one turned back to report fires burning throughout the city a short distance beyond the station. With only thoughts of their critical mission in mind, they both rushed headlong to their cars and sped away into the night and into dangers they did not know existed until too late to turn back.

All that was countless hours ago. Now the two grid operators are well beyond overdue without anyone knowing they are incomprehensively separated from any safe route of return. Chaos reigns within a cityscape foreign to anything resembling an ordinary life before the blackout. They should already be in place with one of them in the lunchroom at Station A5 with his ham radio equipment calling to the other operator across town - failing that, calling to any other ham radio operator they can raise. Within the isolation of the power station, how could technicians, valiantly laboring within their windowless box, know the world outside was on fire around them, consumed as they were in their downward spiral? Even if they did know, they would not have been able to stop it.

With an engineer's precision, a thin pencil line is drawn smoothly, almost effortlessly, along one edge of a three-sided ruler through but not obliterating the emergency start up protocol typed neatly on the page in 12-point Calibri font. Another failed protocol has been crossed off the list. Palpable dread undulates overhead, thickening as willpower weakens and their tail inches further out of reach.

CHAPTER NINE

TRESTLE BEACH

Thursday evening, October 17

CW came out of his exhaustion-induced coma, curled up on the ground under a tarp he had somehow tucked around him like a blanket. Opening bleary, sleep drugged eyes, it takes a minute or two for his mind to register where he is exactly. Yes, Trestle Beach. As he regains full

situational awareness, engrained training keeps him from making a sound or any sudden movement. Lying motionless on the ground, the feel of the pack he's spooning and the rifle clutched in his arms reassures him. He doesn't recall how he came to be lying down, concealed as he is with the tarp around him. The last thing he remembers, it was dark and he couldn't see, so he sat down. Now he's awake and it's still dark. His mind registers it's not raining and he silently mouths, "Thank you" while raising his eyes to heaven in a prayer.

Slowly, bringing his wrist to his face, the calendar window on the watch displays "17", 9:15 PM. A new day. He had been unconscious nearly 24-hours. "No wonder I feel like shit," he grumbles softly to himself without moving. Looking up, he sees the top flap of the main pack compartment lying open above his head. His tin coffee cup is off to one side on the ground. A thought comes to mind of the cup the morning after crossing under the river road through the pipe toward Holbrook. Again, raising his head slightly, he looks at the pack compartment, saddened having caught glimpses of white stars from Big Biker's folded American flag secured inside. After a few minutes more listening to the night sounds, the area remains quiet and he feels safe to move. Breathing deeply CW disentangles himself from the tarp, rolls to one knee and stands on trembling legs, scanning the darkness, the red dot sight on his loaded rifle floating in front of him with each sweeping motion. All clear.

CW stretches his exceedingly aching back and legs, strips off the poncho and rifle, and adjusts damp field clothes that seem to cling to him for dear life. Other than feeling better from having slept, seems the only real accomplishment was the date change on his wristwatch. One thing he is sure of Zeke, Zoie, and Little are Point B and he's on his way to point B. Having secured the tarp and cup, he shoulders the pack, straps himself in, adjusts the rifle in its three-point sling along his chest and wriggles the poncho over him, finally pulling the hat down over his matted hair. Muscles tense as CW steps forward toward the train trestle 10-yards away. Loaded gun or not, each step seems inconsequential compared to the obstacle of dark miles left to walk.

Toward palpable dread, CW pushes forward to embrace the unknown - heavily at first, through the brambles and then along the sandy narrow path between overgrown brush and trees on one side and the steep, rocky embankment of the train bed on the other.

As CW begins moving, he is finally able to recall fragmented memories – only glimpses really of having slept a deep sleep, miraculously concealed among blackberry brambles off to one side of the trestle. Evidently, after escaping the carnage of Holbrook, and having pulled the rowboat on shore, he fell to the ground asleep, although he doesn't remember doing it. He knows he is lucky, having escaped being detected by anyone that might have come along during those long hours. Miraculously, he is safe, uninjured and sufficiently rested to push on toward home: home – first through darkness hovering among creosote-laden timbers of the trestle; a structure that feels as if it had once inhaled a breath, and is content now to hold it forever.

While he scans toward the river road with the night vision infra-red unit, ghosts of struggle and death aggressively project themselves on the dark curtain under the trestle. Ignoring his tormented thoughts, he decides it is safe to move. Facing his "cap forward" CW picks up his feet and begins plodding up the road toward home, drinking from a fresh bottle of water pulled from his pack and another oatmeal energy bar – same meal he had at the hilltop store two days ago.

A mile further on, he crosses over to the right side, to walk in the dark, narrow clear path that runs alongside the tracks. If anyone comes by, CW will be painted black against the dark, thick stand of trees. Everyone else will be silhouetted against the roadway, down his rifle sights. A brief flurry of wind brushes his face as Depression flies in from a perch somewhere in the night and rests heavily on the backpack carried across his aching, blistered, slumping shoulders – shoulders responsible to help carry him home.

CHAPTER TEN

SHELBY GALES

Thursday night, October 17

Gales Country Market is burning. That much is sure. The store is the only large structure up ahead that could cause flames to stretch above the tree line and make the clouds glow with its light. How extensive it's burning I still can't tell but I only have a short distance to walk before I know for sure. Pushing forward through the darkness I make steady plodding progress past trees that line the highway and railroad tracks, along a route of travel that will bring me to a position directly opposite the store. Whatever caused the  store to burn might be waiting for me too. I have to be careful and go slow. Bypassing the store is not an option. Not only must I pass it, I have to do it safely to get home.

"Home" with Zeke, Zoie, and Little seems a hundred miles away, somewhere in the night, fading away, a vision in my imagination, out of reach tonight and perhaps the next. My muscles ache and my shoulders sag from the weight of my gear, but I push myself along the railroad tracks toward the flames. As I do so, I realize I now have a blister on each heel instead of just one. "Well, isn't that special," I mutter sarcastically in the dark to no one but me. Unable to defend against weary thoughts, my spirit has become exceedingly sad. I am tired and hungry, and everything I have seen so far piles the weight on and nearly defeats me. In spite of it all, I slog along with my gear and heavy boots, talking to myself to keep my spirits up, repeating, "You're doing good Cdub. You're the Man! You'll make it." It's a weak attempt at being my own best friend out here in the dark. I know it but I do it anyway. For short durations, it has the desired  effect of helping me stave off growing depression about making it home. Regardless, my imagination edges itself to the abyss, leans over into the inky blackness as torments, specter like, spring up from the cold ether far below, brushing my face with their icy chills. Everyone in the world has disappeared. I am doomed to walk these railroad tracks alone at night, forever afraid of an ambush by unseen predators at every turn, tortured for eternity by the horrors chiseled in my memory that lay along miles behind me.

My thoughts are tormented by what seems an unanswerable question, "Am I dead? Was I killed with Big Biker and I don't know it?" The Devil on my shoulder standing over the Angel it just slaughtered, assures me Hell is walking these tracks for eternity toward a home I long for but will never reach: with Zeke, Zoie, and Little wondering why I abandoned them, each one calling my name to come save them as they slowly, excruciatingly waste away and die. In reality from exactly where I stand looking toward the fire column in the distance, home is only another ten miles, past the burning store up ahead. "I'm going home. I'll be home soon," I mutter repeatedly as a mantra, talking to myself to bolster my spirits while following railroad tracks that parallel a road black and wet for as far as I can see. There are no cars or movement of any kind on the road - nothing what it was a couple of days ago before the blackout when the highway was filled with cars, trucks, and life.

Arriving as planned across the highway from the store, I am awestruck by the sight of hungry flames licking every inch of its wooden

structure. My mind, spirit and weary body need rest, and I heavily settle myself on the ground, still strapped to my backpack, to watch the incredible spectacle of fire burning the building down. The heat of it on my face, even at this distance, is uncomfortable and causes me to move further back into the shadow of the woods.

With my backpack against a nearby tree trunk, I sit and try to recall all the many times my field boots clopped on those wood floors, up and down aisles looking for this or that, but more times than not simply having twenty bucks worth of gas put in the tank on my way to work.

My sense of awe vanishes when I see what is lying on the pavement out front. I am unsure from this distance who they are, but even without binoculars, I can tell those two lumpy shapes on the pavement are bodies; lying face down, twisted, and awkward with their clothes steaming from the heat of the fire a few feet away. Pulling the compact binoculars from a side pocket of the backpack and with the light of the raging inferno, I cannot mistake seeing one of them has a blond ponytail that lies lightly to one side, falling over the collar of her dark blue and steaming jacket. I remember a cute twenty-something girl with a shy, friendly smile who pumped gas in my car on my way to work two days ago. She had a ponytail like that. I always wanted to ask her name but never did, and I cannot help feeling a renewed surge of sadness, nearly causing me to break down and cry from all the grief. No one deserves what she got, and yet there she is, dead. As horrific as the scene is, I am unable to put the binoculars down. Toward the two people lying on the pavement I say aloud "I'm sorry," in a voice soft from weary grief and a spirit nearly defeated.

Out of reach of the reflection of the flames, I sit in the shadows watching the store burn. Heat chases away the damp that has collected on my clothes over the miles I have traveled. For a moment I feel safe enough to close my eyes and embrace the warmth of the fire, trying not to see the two bodies when I open my eyes again - their hair and clothing starting to show signs of flames spreading along parts of their backs and legs. I simply cannot look anymore and turn my attention to the wood school built in the 1930's situated on a large lot across a side road separating it from the fully engulfed store. Light from the conflagration dancing along the nearest wood plank wall of the school, as if alive, sends the old school a sinister message, "You're next". I am sure it will burn sooner than later and burn fast and bright too because of all the wood fuel. Sure would be a sight to see and I wish I could convince myself to sit here and watch it. I won't because I need to get myself up and moving; but oh, the warmth feels so good. It has been a very long day and I'd love to rest, but not now and certainly not here. Nevertheless, I hesitate a few minutes more to savor the light and warmth before pushing further down the road toward home. Happy faces of Zeke, Zoie, and Little come to mind but I don't smile and their faces quickly fade from view.

Almost unnoticed in the distant dark beyond the store, I catch a glimpse of a lone figure running in a crouch as fast as it can go from behind the burning store, disappearing into the shadows behind the school across the street. A minute more and the first gas pump ignites with an explosion so forceful it takes down the front portion of Gales Market and blows out glass from every window.

The blast sends shrapnel ripping in all directions with bits of metal flying into the trees over my head, causing pine needles and splinters of branches to shower down to the ground around me. When the pump explodes, I immediately roll over and tuck in, hitting the ground face first: covering my head with my hands. A split second later pump 2 erupts in a fireball bigger and more forceful than the first, boiling, rolling dark red and brilliant orange gasoline fueled flames high into the night sky. The ground trembles under my outstretched body as I pray frantically for protection from flying debris. The total effect of sight, sound, and smell is incredible. Everything within a 30-yard radius is on fire or steaming in earnest from the inferno caused by the flaming gas pumps and store. Gales Market is burning down to its foundation with a heat so intense even at this distance I am forced to hurriedly crawl on my stomach further back into the protective coolness of the clump of wet trees and scrub brush I've been occupying.

At a safe distance, while pulling myself upright to a kneeling position, I see the lone figure I saw a minute before now scurry across the river road from around the corner of the old school. The figure makes its way onto my side about 100-yards away. Perhaps I have been spotted and I am being out flanked. I am not going to let that happen. Immediately turning away from the reflection and warmth of the flames, I maneuver through the cluster of trees and tall grass until I am standing in the dark alongside the railroad tracks, pausing for a moment to make sure the area is safe.

Stepping across the tracks, my mind barks orders as my own worst drill sergeant, "Pick up your feet Mister! I don't care how tired you are or how heavy those boots feel". Exhausted, I somehow dutifully respond – picking up my feet, crossing the tracks toward the riverbank. Turning to face the shadowy cluster of trees, I take a concealed prone position with my back to the river. Flickers of light from the burning store pierce the dense stand of trees in front of me as flames cast a glow on the clouds above the treetops in a muted, smoky grey, orange color.

Whoever attempts to out flank me will have to pass in front of the light and will be silhouetted in the window of my holographic rifle sight. If something goes wrong I am confident, whoever it is will be on the receiving end of a losing proposition. In less than five minutes, I hear someone approaching off to my left, walking in my direction down the center of the tracks. At this distance, I am just able to make out the dark outline of the person I saw running from the old school. I can't be sure but I think I hear muffled sobbing. While watching the dark outline of the lone figure, I slowly and quietly lay my pack on the ground and try to flatten out more among the short weeds and scrub grass thirty feet from the center of the tracks. Instinctively, nervously, I thumb the rifle selector switch a couple of times making sure the weapon is ready to fire. The shadowy figure comes closer and I discover this person, alone out here in the dark is a female. She's not paying any attention to her surroundings and she doesn't seem to present a threat to me so I let her come.

Concealed by dark shadows of the night, I watch and listen without making a sound. In a few minutes, she is nearly in front of me in the center of the tracks. Flickers of flame from the burning store silhouette her ponytail, dark jacket and jeans with heavy boots, similar to the girl burning out front on the pavement of the store. I hope she passes quickly so I can be on my way and get my life back. Suddenly approximately sixty yards further down from where the girl first made her appearance, tree branches part and brush cracks, giving way as two dark figures force their way through the brush from the river road, bounding as they do into the shadowy open space along the railroad tracks. They pause to get their bearings, one looking left, and the other looking right. Hearing the distant sound, the girl instinctively does a half turn looking down the tracks and then takes off running as fast as she can in the opposite direction. As she runs, I hear her mumbling in soft, panicked tones, "No! Oh God Please No!" One of the dark figures backhands the other on the chest and both turn their attention to the girl running away. Darkened shapes slowly and then ever more

quickly pick up the pace at a full run down the center of the railroad tracks in hot pursuit; their boots hitting hard the wood ties and kicking up gravel as they run by. I am completely unnoticed and watch it all unfold in front of me. Not far distant to my right I hear the girl frantically pawing at brush, and then a wood door being forced open and then shut with not much authority.

Boots of the two men close in where the girl is now attempting to hide in a shed with peeling white paint that is nearly buried by overgrown vines and brush, among deep shadows of a dense stand of trees.

The men are now far enough away from me that I cautiously make my way in their direction, stalking these two guys under cover of dark. The only items with me now are my rifle with one magazine of ammunition, my bowie knife horizontal along the front of my belt, and the revolver in the shoulder holster under my left arm. Having quickly sized up the situation, I anticipated making this move and had quietly emptied everything from my pockets and from around my neck and covered it all with the poncho lying in the shadows in the scrub grass. No matter what's going on, my experience tells me this will not end well for someone; I just hope it's not me. As I move forward slow and low, the moon attempts to break through a cloud-filled sky. Seeing it, I find myself praying the moon stays hidden for a while longer. When I hear the men reach the shed another 50 feet directly ahead, I crouch to one knee and listen intently, hearing one man go right while the other goes left along each side. Several minutes pass then sounds break the stillness of vines and brush being drawn back and a shed door being forced open. One of the men has found the entrance and is attempting to force his way to the girl trapped inside. Hearing his partner's progress, the second man quickly retraces his steps and reaches the corner of the shed near the door at the moment a shotgun blast explodes from inside with a split second flash of flame.

The first man has been surprised to death by a load of buckshot from a shotgun I didn't know she had. The impact of the blast propelled him back through the door and onto the wet ground. He groans and the night is silent again. The second man now frozen at the corner has my full attention. From where he's standing, I am sure he clearly sees his dead friend, arms splayed outward from his side, lying on his back on the ground among the tall grass, weeds, and berry vines that have grown wild there. At the corner, with his back to the shed wall, Killer 2 pulls a lock blade knife from his pants pocket and with its ominous metallic click locks the blade in place.

He calls out over his right shoulder to the female somewhere in the ink black interior, "I'm going to cut you Bitch. You're gonna bleed real good."

If I am one thing, I am methodical - combine that with being trained and, under the right set of circumstances, I have been known to be deadly. There are a couple of Serb soldiers dead in the Balkan woods that know this when, hunting me, they never considered I was hunting them. Suddenly an overpowering scent of Plumeria blossom envelops me. The eyes of the dead woman in the Mercury Sable at the crossroad appear as an apparition, inches in front of me, keeping me frozen in place. She condemns me again – "Why didn't you save me?" My thoughts softly, reverently respond, "I'm sorry. I wasn't the man I am today." Her sad black eyes no longer full of condemnation slowly fade away. With strength restored, I am able to move forward.

As the second attacker makes his way cautiously toward the door, I follow quick and quiet to the corner where he stood a moment before, leaning my rifle gently against the peeling paint of the wall, not more than 15 feet separating the two of us at that moment. I watch as he quickly peeks around the door and see him very nearly eat the girls second load of buckshot intended for his face. Perhaps when the girl let that second blast go she had a glimpse of his silhouette coming through the door. Regardless, the trapped girl inside was a little too quick on the trigger and I don't blame her. She is alone in that dark shed in the middle of the night, hunted by killers, albeit one of them dead outside and one remaining intent on finishing the job. She has a double-barreled shotgun. I am sure of it. I haven't heard the slide of a pump action forcing another shell into the shotgun chamber: Bad for her. Good for him. The same realization has probably registered with her killer because he leans his head more slowly a second time into the interior from his vantage point at the door but cannot see the girl inside. The interior on a night like tonight is pitch-black. Being overly confident, he steps inside the doorway and is hit hard across his left shoulder by the shotgun barrel swung with all her might, hard at his head. If she had been taller, or perhaps stronger, she may have been successful in connecting the cold steel barrel with the side of his head. A blow delivered with a force like that would have knocked him unconscious or at least to one side long enough to allow her to escape.

Unfortunately for her, the man was not knocked unconscious nor off to one side. Nevertheless, as soon as she swings the shotgun she bolts with everything she has toward the exit. The man cries out in shock and pain but swiftly spins and grabs a handful of the girl's hair. His prize is stopped dead in her tracks - brought slowly, kicking and screaming, within inches of his face to look deep in his murderous eyes. Lifting her with one muscular arm, her boots nearly leave the ground.

"You are gonna die and I'm going to enjoy it," and then puts his knee swift and hard in her left side.

The force of the sudden blow takes her breath away and she gasps for air. She stops screaming and wriggling and falls limp where the man throws her, into a dark corner of the forgotten shed. She is without salvation from the inevitable assault and death minutes away. The knife-wielding killer reaches down and violently grabs a clump of her sandy blond hair in each of his fists, the cold metal of his knife pressing against her right temple, a potent visual of the implement of terror he will kill her with. He straightens up and she can do nothing but come up with him, locking eyes, nearly nose to nose. She cries without tears or sound. Her killer studies her, smiling an evil grin that curls around tobacco stained teeth as he licks cracked lips in anticipation of what he is about to do to her.

I hear him spit each venomous word slowly in her face, "You are gonna fucking pay."

I never met B. Svoboda of Solingen, Germany however; I have always admired his craftsmanship. He is the blacksmith who decades ago handcrafted the Solingen-steel bowie knife I hold in my right hand. Jerking the attackers head back with my left fist entwined with clumps of his greasy, shaggy hair, I force his eyes, wide with shock, to stare into the pitch black of the ceiling of the abandoned shed. Instantaneously, razor sharp steel easily separate flesh, sinew and muscle as I drive the 8-inch ice-cold knife blade to the hilt through the soft spot where his neck connects with his right shoulder. My knife can go no further – its blade tip licking the top of his heart. His body seizes up, registering the trauma - every muscle excruciatingly taut in painful, cramping spasm, unable to respond to any command of the mind other than to instantly open his paws with fingers splayed outward. The lock blade knife, once so menacing, now falls harmless to the floor, out of sight and out of reach. In an instant, his would-be prey also falls away and pushes herself backward into an interior corner, hidden from view, crying uncontrollably. In our slow motion dance in the seconds before his death, my hot, quick breath comes back to me off the nape of his sweaty neck. We are so intimately connected I can practically taste his salt. I desire nothing more in our seconds together than for each centimeter of burning steel embedded in his body to be his everlasting torture; relived again, and again for eternity in Hell. "How precious," I softly whisper with lips that lightly brush the hair on the back of his neck, as a nearly inaudible girlish whimper escapes his throat the moment I slightly twist and pull B. Svoboda's masterpiece out of his fatal, gushing wound.

In one smooth arcing motion, I bring the knife around and bury it to its hilt in his right side, cleaving his liver: he grunts and his body shudders, unable to do anything but buckle at the knees when he receives my second insult to a body already racked with unspeakable pain. My knife blade pulls free from his side only when I allow him to crash to the floor with a thud onto moldy paper; crushing unseen rusted metal cans and rotted wood discarded on the floor of the abandoned shed. As he comes to rest, he exhales one long sigh, and soon his muscle twitching dies with him. The interior of the shed is quiet but for my heavy breathing and disembodied sobs of a terrified girl unseen somewhere in a dark corner. I kneel down, wipe the bloody blade on his nearest pant leg, and then secure the knife in its holster along my belt.

Magically, slivers of moonlight fall around the entrance of the shed, allowing me to see the dead man out front the girl blasted with her shotgun. He is lying on the ground, a massive dark wet hole in the center of his chest; the toes of his black soled boots point to the moon. Picking up the sawed off shotgun the girl used, I open it and release two spent shells that spring free and land in the vicinity of the man I knifed to death. The girl hasn't moved, sobbing unseen in the interior a few feet from me. To the darkness, and in as soft and casual a voice I can muster I ask, "Are you hurt?" No response. Soft sobbing continues mixed with gulps of air breathed in an attempt to regain composure.

I kneel down in the open entry with the hope more light will show me to her. As I do so, I face her direction but I cannot yet see her: "I'm here to help, obviously. However, we are not safe. We have to leave. I live up the road about another ten miles. That's where I was going when I saw these two follow you here."

Silence passes between us, but then a halting, "Thank you," comes from the pitch black of the far corner in front of me.

"We have to go," I reply urgently. "Now," I insist.

In response, there is only silence for a short while until from the blackness a soft pink hand and then wrist slowly appear into the sliver of blue moonlight in front of me. I take her hand and pull her to me. We stand in the entrance bathed in thin shards of light that play more fully outside among the shadowy, wet woods in their attempt to pierce the interior of this place. She hugs me strong for a full two minutes, burying her head in the corner of my chest, crying with deep sadness and relief as I hold her close, safe and warm in my arms. When she regains composure, we step together through the door into the world outside and away from the dull-white peeling paint of the rotting shed nearly buried in vines, scrub brush, and moss. We make our way past the outside corner of the building where I retrieve my AR15 rifle, thread my right arm through the sling, and position the rifle across my chest. I give back her sawed off shotgun. She takes it without looking at me. "Got more of those shells with you?" I ask.

"Yes," she says in a quiet voice.

"Good. Keep it loaded. I know you know how to use it, but," I say in what I think to be a light hearted tone, "just to make sure, keep it pointed away from me". My attempt at lifting the heavy space surrounding us goes without notice and she simply assures me she will as we walk the short distance back to my original spot and retrieve my backpack, poncho and the rest of the things I had left there. In no time, I have everything secured and turn us to face the path along the railroad tracks in the direction of home. "This way," and I start forward. She follows without saying a word, her head bowed low.

The glow from Gales Market reflects on the dark clouds above us. Glimpses of its flames break through thick dark woods as we move past. I notice the girl doesn't look toward the store while I can hardly keep from not looking. Walking in silence, the girl follows me, but several feet behind. Neither of us acknowledges the shed as we pass it and its two new occupants. I begin wondering who the girl is. She looks familiar but I am not sure. I'm guessing she's probably in her early twenty's with the same youthful face and light colored ponytail as the girl at the burning store. I don't say anything and we simply walk in silence, listening to the night, and our breathing, and the sounds of our boots as we make our way along the railroad tracks.

After a while, I figure it's about time for formal introductions. "My name is CW. Actually Charles William Stanton but I prefer Cdub." The sound of my name hangs in the air. She doesn't say anything, just keeps walking with her head down. After awhile more I ask, "What's your name?"

"Shelby," she replies meekly without further elaboration.

"How is it you are out here in the middle of the night and chased by those two dick-heads?" Dead dick-heads I think to myself with a good deal of satisfaction; although we are lucky it isn't the two of us lying back there with our toes to the moon.

"When the electricity went out, we kept the store going to help people that needed it," comes her soft reply.

"You worked at the store?" I ask with a bit of surprise in my voice. "I used to come in the store practically every day, at least to get gas on my way to work."

She replies softly, "Yeah I know. I've seen you. Never knew your name though. You were friendly but you did your thing and left. Not like some folks who want to tell their entire life story every time they come in."

Shelby stops walking and does not hold back long streams of tears falling down her cheeks. She presses her hands to her face and mouth in silent agonizing grief. I almost walk back the few steps that separate us, to put my arms around her, to hold her close, to reassure her it is good to be alive, and let her know she is safe. However, I don't move. She stands alone in the dark and weeps while I stand waiting patiently for her, scanning the dark for any danger that may be approaching, trying as much as possible to listen more to the night sounds than to her heartbreaking sobs. In a minute or two, we resume walking.

As I have been doing since being on the road, ever so often, I pause and scan the area with my night vision monocular. Eventually she asks why I do that. My explanation makes sense to her, and she begins scanning the night, using the natural night vision technique I teach her. Off to one side of the tracks, down in a small depression where it is extra dark, I stop and set up the gel-fuel stove. While the water is heating, I teach her how to operate the night vision monocular, nodding with approval she is a fast learner. With a cup of coffee in our hands, we rest for a while and munch on energy bars we retrieve from an outside pouch of my backpack. We also take the opportunity to clean our face, neck and hands with a wet wipe. When we are done with it all, we stuff everything back in my pack and head off down the tracks again. I ask as gently as possible, very curious to know, "Was that your people back at the store?" There is a long pause where our breathing, our boot steps, and the creaking of my backpack are the only sounds that fill the space around us, making me feel, and rightly so, how stupid of me to ask.

"Yes," she softly replies when she is finally able to say the word.

I turn and look toward her face bowed low, covered as it is in grief and shadows of the night, "I'm sorry for your loss. Can you tell me what happened?" After a momentary pause, Shelby begins telling me how her Mom owned the store.

"Mom bought it when the old couple that had originally built it was ready to retire. I guess it was too much for them. Mom bought it with the insurance money she got when Dad got killed in a logging accident five years ago."

Shelby and her two sisters helped at the store. "Even our dog Skipper helped out. Everyone liked him and I think it made him feel good being with us, especially being around Mom all day." Her oldest sister, Sheri was 27 years old and 6 weeks pregnant at the time she was murdered. "Her boyfriend, the only boy she's ever known, dumped her right after he found out they were gonna have a kid. Ran off and joined the Army. They'd been living together, so when he left, Sheri moved in with us in our two bedroom, single wide trailer."

Then there is Shelly, her twin sister: "Shelly is 24, the youngest by an hour, so I guess that makes me the middle child. Anyway, we all helped run the store, you know, pumping gas and tending to the register."

My heart is about to break hearing all she is telling me, completely at a loss of what to do or how to respond. I say nothing as Shelby talks in quiet tones, the two of us slowly and cautiously walking along the gravel path at the side of the railroad tracks.

"After lights went out, Mom decided to keep the store open as long as we had daylight and groceries lasted. People in the area appreciated what we were doing and folks would come and go without trouble. We figured we were all in this together.

Not having a generator for light we shut the place down when it got dark and camped inside with the shotgun kept hidden behind the counter for protection. I think the gun actually belonged to my Dad."

In a voice weak with grief Shelby says, "Camping in the warehouse part of the store again tonight, we heard pickup trucks race to a stop out front, their tires screeching, and engines revving. We all looked through the window glass that's part of what used to be the wooden mechanics garage door and recognized one of the trucks from times before: a late 70's or early 80's model Ford. I think it was rusty orange and definitely beat to shit. Either it didn't have mufflers or they were rusted through 'cuz it was really loud. The thing I recognized most was the huge confederate flag flying from a pole stuck on the back right side of the pickup bed. I'm from the country too but I've never understood why rednecks like some of the stuff they do."

"Through the glare of the headlights Shelly and I recognized a couple of the boys in the group as twin brothers we went to high school with. Those were the two that chased me to the shed. We didn't recognize anyone else out front. All the guys milled around together and we watched them mess with the gas pumps. They were trying to figure out how to get gas but we don't have a way of pumping gas manually. No-one could get any. Unable to get gas made the gang out front real mad. A couple of them started kicking pump number one as if they were about ready to kick it over. Mom told us to stay put and went outside with Skipper following close at her heels. One thing led to another, and a big guy with a flattop haircut walked up and slapped Mom hard, causing her to fall to one knee.

Sheri told us to be quiet and tried to leave us and go outside with Mom, but my sister and I wouldn't let go of her arm. Shelly and I were shaking and couldn't stop, pleading with Sheri to stay with us and not leave us alone."

Shelby describes how Sheri made her way to the cash register, got the shotgun from under the counter, and brought it back with a crumpled brown paper lunch bag of shells. From their hiding place in the store they watched as their Mother got up, rubbing her face while angrily talking to the agitated group of men. Skipper kept barking, unable to do anything more than stand his ground between Momma Gales and the man who hit her.

"Someone grabbed my Mother's arm and spun her around, walking her into the store followed by most of the group while a few others stayed with their trucks out front. Once inside the store, the group started tearing the place up, taking what was left in the cash register and trashing the place. They overturned display cases of food, stomping on bread and cereal and one even tried to break the cooler glass. The guy couldn't break it so he turned his attention to the stuff on the counter at the register and ran his arm along, spilling everything to the floor. Everyone was laughing and carrying on and Mom started shouting, 'Stop it! What do you guys think you're doing? Damn you. Damn you all!' Skipper stood his ground barking in front of Mom. Then the guy with the flattop grabbed Mom, 'Shut up Bitch. Shut your mangy mutt too!' and slapped her hard again, laughing as he did it."

"Shelly and I moved further back into the dark recess of the store, shaking and holding on to one another as Sheri turned around, handed Shelly the shotgun, telling us to stay put, 'Be ready to use the shotgun just in case.' I could see my Mom try to slap the man that slapped her, but got pushed backward, stumbled and fell to the wood floor next to Skipper, still barking at the group of men now gathered in a half circle around the two. By that time, Shelly and I were nearly in a panic and said so in urgent whispers to Sheri but Sheri said she is going to help Mom. Right at that moment someone in the group, I didn't see who, shot Momma while she was on her knees in front of the cash register. They shot and killed Skipper too - neither of them made a sound. They must have died instantly lying together lit by pickup truck headlights between racks of spilled groceries."

Shelby is crying streams of tears, trying to catch her breath and cannot talk again for a very long time. My heart has broken and there is nothing left to do but mourn the shards. Sounds of our boot steps on the gravel path alongside the railroad tracks are interrupted when Shelby describes how Sheri was already on her way to help when her Mom and Skipper were killed. Sheri then tore through the store, followed a split second later by Shelly doing the same thing, dropping the shotgun as she left.

"I was so scared I couldn't move. I wanted to be brave like my sisters and my Mom, but I wasn't. Like a coward I hid, watching as my sisters angrily confronted the group - everyone shouting and cussing each other. At one point Sheri knelt down and cradled Mom, stroking Mom's dark brown hair while Shelly stood by and cried."

Shelby pauses, buries her face again in her hands, sobbing deeply, with shoulders hunched over and shaking. When she regains composure, she tells me how she watched from her hiding place at the back of the store as the group of guys took her two sisters and gang raped them on the deli tables inside the store, located along the front windows near the entrance. Headlights of pickup trucks outside illuminated the horror while laughter from the rapists mingled with her sister's cries of pain and torment. The bell on the front door of the store gleefully jingled each time men came and went.

"I hear that damn bell in my head and I can't make it stop. I want it to stop."

When the gang finished raping Shelby's battered and abused sisters, her sisters were pushed through the front doors toward pickup trucks waiting to take them somewhere for more of the same. Seeing where they were headed, her two sisters fought back hard.

"My sisters did everything they could not to get into those trucks. They either broke free or were let go. As they turned to run back into the store, both were shot in the back. They died where they fell on the pavement out front. One of the men even flicked his cigarette butt onto the back of one of them. I tried to scream but nothing came out. I wanted to jump up and run to be with Sheri and Shelly but I couldn't. I was frozen in place. I was chicken and I'm ashamed."

The twins from high school came into the store and poured gasoline over everything, including Momma Gales and Skipper too. As they were leaving, they threw a match down one aisle. The place exploded in flames. When Shelby saw the fire, she turned and ran out the back. The two guys noticed her because they started shouting, "Stop! Hey, Hey you! Stop!" and shouting to their friends she was getting away. For some reason everyone else left and those two stayed. When she ran out the back, Shelby ran straight for the woods behind their trailer located near the back of the store.

Shelby explains, "I know those woods. My sisters and I used to play there all the time when we were kids. When I ran into the woods tonight I hid and felt safe for awhile."

Shelby tells me how she watched the store explode in flames and their house trailer being close to the store didn't take long to catch fire too.

"Everything we had, which wasn't much was in that trailer and in that store. Now everything and everyone is gone."

From her hiding place in the woods, Shelby watched as her would be killers wouldn't give up looking for her. They raced back and forth in their pickup truck, using a spotlight on the driver side, running up and down the highway and side streets, even around the back of the store and through the grass and field. Eventually they parked the truck and started looking for her on foot. She could see they were heading for the woods to search there.

At that point, Shelby got scared and made the mistake of leaving her hiding place instead of hiding herself more deeply. She explained how she thought the coast was clear and ran as fast as she could across the street to the old school.

"That's when I first noticed you, crossing from behind the store to the back of the school - then a while later running across the road to the railroad tracks."

Shelby nods her head a few times in silence, exhales a deep sigh and says, "That's everything before you came along." After a long while of walking in silence Shelby says, "Since we seem to be going in that direction anyway, I'd like to see if my Aunt and Uncle are home if that's ok with you? They live at Big Meadow. It's only two miles up the road from here."

"Big Meadow?" I ask. "I know that place. Lynn and, uhm?"

"Right," she says looking at me. "Lynn and Roy."

I remark how I take my dogs to Big Meadow when I go out of town on business. "Nice people. So they're your Aunt and Uncle huh?"

"Yes," not elaborating further, deep in thought.

"Sure. We'll stop."

"Thanks, Cdub."

We walk in silence along the gravel path beside the railroad tracks that parallel the river road. With each boot step the miles and days on the road constrict themselves around the muscles of my legs and shoulders, making it more and more difficult to walk the closer to home I get. It feels a lifetime ago I pulled the stolen aluminum rowboat onto shore at Trestle Beach - a break to renew my strength and get my wits about me makes Big Meadow sound like the perfect place.

"Shelby," I repeat silently in my inner voice; that's a nice name. Instead, I say aloud, "Glad to have you with me Shelby.

"Thanks, Cdub. I'm glad to be here," she says with a smile and deep sadness, her face veiled in shadows of the night.

Big Meadow is coming up fast. Walking together in the dark, we find our way to the dirt road leading to the wooden porch of Lynn and Roy's 1940's farmhouse they've called home for more than thirty years. In the kennel across the yard from the house, dogs howl and bark, pacing and making their fence clang against metal fittings. It's obvious we've arrived. Shelby calls out to the darkened interior of the house, identifying herself to her Aunt and Uncle hopefully inside. Almost immediately, we hear the front door lock being fumbled with, accompanied by friendly voices from inside calling to Shelby. Lynn and Roy quickly smother her with hugs and kisses, thankful knowing Shelby is safe.

After a moment, Shelby introduces me. Lynn squints and a smile of recognition brightens her face.

"Sure. Yes, Yes. CW, it's good to see you. You have those three beautiful Great Danes don't you?"

"Yes I do Ma-am, three goofballs that's for sure: Zeke, Zoie, and Little."

"Come in, the both of you." Lynn and Roy guide us into the black interior of their spacious old home as Lynn asks how the dogs are doing.

"I'm sure they are doing ok but I haven't seen them for nearly three days."

Even in the dark, I feel the history of their home surround me, immediately familiar with smells of an old home full of memories. Using my friction flashlight, I provide our group a weak light to see by as we make our way from the front door, and then immediately right into the living room. A clock is ticking on a wall somewhere in the dark, giving the space an intimate feel. In the living room, there are two overstuffed chairs and a sofa that look old, well cared for, and comfortable. As my bluish flashlight beam sweeps the room, I catch a glimpse of a well-used moderately sized brick fireplace painted white with a mantel full of family photos and a display case of military medals on a backdrop of a folded American flag. Roy helps me remove my backpack and I place it gently against a wall near the sofa that runs between the windows that face the porch and the dog kennel somewhere unseen in the night.

I ensure my rifle is on safe, extend the bipod on the foregrip and place the rifle on the floor near the pack - ready for easy access in case of trouble. Lynn asks Shelby to go with her to the kitchen down the hall to help get us all something to eat and drink.

"Shelby," I say, "go ahead and leave that thing with me," pointing to the shotgun she has in one hand. She pauses, looking down absently, having forgotten she is carrying it.

"Good idea. Here's the bag of shells too."

She gives me the gun and paper bag and follows Lynn down the hallway into the dark kitchen. In less than a minute, I see the soft glow of a candle flame flicker to life and spill some of its light down the hall toward Roy and me. Opening the breech of her shotgun I find it is loaded. "Good girl," I say to myself and set the sawed off shotgun down on the fireplace hearth along with the bag of shells. I caution Roy, "That things loaded; be careful."

"I will," he replies without saying anything more.

Muffled voices in close conversation from the kitchen echo down the hallway over heavily waxed and polished wood floors, as Lynn and Shelby discuss the tragedy at the store, hugging tight to one another and crying deep sighs of grief into each other's shoulders. After a while, familiar sounds of cupboards being opened and a teakettle being put on an open flame burner make the old house feel that much more welcome and secure.

My stomach involuntarily growls in anticipation of receiving something substantial to eat and drink. Roy takes a seat in a cushioned chair nearby me as I arrange my belongings. At one point, I offer him a can of gel-fuel as appreciation for their hospitality, but he declines, saying thank you but they have their own supply.

"Living in the country, the lights go out from time to time. We make do. Thanks though," and leans toward me on the edge of his chair asking in a low, quiet voice, "So, what have you heard? Heard anything about what's going on?"

"I've been walking the road for nearly three days having come over the pass from work. I've seen things on the road I don't think I'll ever forget, but as for any real news, I can't even get a signal on my emergency radio. I have no idea what's happening out there. If you ask me, electricity being out this long, and the way people are acting, makes me think what's going on is real bad; might go on for a lot longer than we're used to."

Roy agrees, adding, he and Lynn have lived in the house, "for thirty years and haven't experienced a blackout lasting more than a day at most."

"How are you set for food?"

"We're ok. Not great but we're ok for now." I see him smiling as he says, "We're in our 60's but we're tough old birds. We'll be fine. Thanks for asking."

Soon, Lynn and Shelby make their way from the kitchen to the living room. When Shelby enters the room carrying a tray of cheese and crackers in one hand and a lit candle in the other, the glow washes over her in soft, golden light. This is the first moment I truly see Shelby. Enchanted, I cannot help but stare at this lovely young woman. Captured by her soft features, brown eyes, and tender lips that part in a shy smile, she easily reads the look of instant wonder and attraction on my face and does not look away. Lynn, passing close by carrying tea and cups for each of us, smiles approvingly having noticed the exchange between Shelby and me. So thoroughly caught off guard by my reaction when Shelby entered the room, I grin and blush warmly. Completely awkward in the moment and unable to think clearly, I reach out and help Lynn set the tray down on the coffee table that needed no assistance from me. I feel flush for quite awhile after. Our little group eagerly clusters around the coffee table in the living room and enjoys a little bit of home, cheered by light from the candle secured by melted wax to a plate. I check my watch. It is 12:34 AM: a new day.

Shelby places a hand on my knee, "What time is it?"

"A bit after twelve," I reply, flush with warmth again coursing through my body now from the touch of her hand.

In silent communion, we eat cheese, crackers, bologna and sip hot peppermint tea from Lynn's dainty porcelain teacups. The silence that accompanies our feast is both welcoming and comforting.

We do not need to say aloud how good it feels being together in a warm dry house, with food, candlelight and new friends. In less time than one would think all the food and tea are consumed. After everyone has finished eating, Lynn offers an upstairs bedroom for Shelby and the one across the hall for me. Shelby says that will be great for her. I however decline, although I am deeply grateful, preferring instead to stay in the living room for the night.

"Bedroom's all made up and it's yours for the night," Lynn kindly repeats the offer.

"Thank you. I'll be ok resting down here for a few hours. That way I can push off before daylight. I'll try not to wake you when I leave."

Roy and Lynn both reply almost in unison I am welcome to stay for as long as I want, and very kind to make the offer. Staying here for a while longer has its appeal but I politely decline, "Zeke, Zoie and Little are waiting for me and I promised them I'd come back."

Roy says, "When you're ready, let me drive you to your house. It wouldn't be a problem at all."

"Thank you Roy. I wouldn't want to wake you and I don't want anyone in the area knowing I am arriving home. I'd rather arrive anonymously just in case someone is already there.

"Yes of course. We completely understand," Lynn says. "I hope you sleep well and don't worry about waking us. Come back soon."

They gather the tray of cups and plates and pause nearby as Shelby retrieves the candle. She then turns and extends her hand to me. Giving her my hand, hers feels warm, small, and surprisingly strong as she pulls me to her. Standing together, Shelby hugs me tight for a long, comfortable, satisfying moment. With my arms wrapped tight around her, I try to memorize every detail of our embrace, knowing it will likely be our last. My heart begins beating faster and I take a deep breath, realizing I don't want her to let go, followed closely by a strong reminder to protect my heart. It has been years since I felt wanted and appreciated. The honesty of her embrace makes me feel strong, tall, humble, and altogether vulnerable. Locked in our tender embrace, we are for a moment safe from the night outside, with its trauma and bad memories. Nothing can touch us as we hold onto one another by candlelight in the living room at Big Meadow. As I stroke her hair softly, Shelby turns her face to me, the light from her brown eyes melting the impenetrable wall around my heart.

In a whisper meant for only me, "CW. Thank you for everything."

Her voice cracks and tears well up in her eyes but she does not yet let me go. For what seems a lifetime I look deep in her brown eyes, gently wiping away a tear that begins to fall down her blushing cheek. Intimately close, I whisper, "I am so very glad I was there to help. You were brave tonight. Now you are warm and safe. As you should be."

"Yes," she says while sniffling back growing emotion.

Shelby snuggles in closer with her head buried in the crook of my arm for a few seconds more, and then turns and leads Lynn and Roy down the hallway to the dark kitchen, the single candle flame guiding them, as they make their way slowly up creaky wooden stairs to their beds above me. Squeaking floorboards from muffled footfalls on thick wooden floor planks in bedrooms upstairs softly echo within the darkened interior of the old house until everyone settles in. The house becomes quiet but for the ticking clock on the wall and my wildly beating heart. Surely, it is my imagination gone wild, but I cannot shake the feeling that half of me has walked out of the room.

Alone in the living room with my gear and rifle, refreshed from having something to eat and from being out of the elements, but mostly from having my heart warmed by Shelby's comfortable embrace, I am unable to rest. The interior layout of the house is unfamiliar and I busy myself conducting a quick security survey before I lay back down to try and rest. Starting first with the room across the hall, I find the space identical to the living room, each with a small side window on one wall and two windows facing the covered wooden porch. "I guess this would be the dining room," I remark to myself. As quiet as possible in my heavy boots I move down the hallway and through the kitchen to the back pantry with its locked door leading to a small porch and yard beyond. Satisfied I have a good layout in my mind and that all points of entry are secure, I return to my bedroll on the floor, positioned between the sofa under the living room windows and the coffee table the four of us had clustered around in our silent feast.

Setting the alarm on my wristwatch for 3 AM, I am confident I will be able to get my gear and be on the road quickly to make my way the remaining five miles to home. I am excited to get going but desperately in need of rest. My plan is to be in position on my property before daybreak, concealed and protected from anyone coming to the property, or from anyone that might already be there. My head sinks softly into one of the sofa cushions I have commandeered as a pillow as I mull the possibility intruders may have set up residence in my home. I need to be very careful when I arrive. If someone is there, more than likely my food stores have been ransacked and the cache of rifles and ammunition have been discovered. "Just don't hurt my goofy dogs." Exhaustion from enduring the miles and horror behind me help push anxious thoughts from my mind. My body begins to relax in spite of the awkward feeling of the weight of my heavy boots on my feet, laced snug and altogether clumsy. It will feel heavenly to go without them for even a little while. However, not just yet. With that thought slipping out of my mind, I relax and quickly drift off to dreamless sleep.

CHAPTER ELEVEN
HEAVEN'S GATE

Friday, October 18

In the stillness of the early morning, I am awakened by the feel of Shelby lying next to me, snuggled as close as possible, holding me tight, asleep with her head on my chest. I don't know how long I've been sleeping and I never heard her come in. While lying together in the quiet dark, I listen with deep satisfaction to the soft rhythms of her breathing as she sleeps. I dare not move. I don't even want to breathe too hard, not wanting to disturb her. "God, please a few minutes more." Closing my eyes again, I relish the closeness of our bodies.

Not lifting her head, she begins gently caressing the side of my face with the palm of her hand. The stubble of my beard grown these past few days must surely feel like sandpaper to her soft hand. Regardless of all I want to be, I am inadequate, wishing I were younger and perfect and certainly with a face washed, clean-shaven, and smooth for her caress. As if reading my thoughts, she lifts her head, positioning herself on one elbow and more fully traces with her fingertips my eyebrows, my nose, and then my lips. Surely she will not see the obvious, moving on to my graying hairline along my left temple. Shelby lightly brushes my hair back. I open my eyes and look into hers. Her beautiful brown eyes radiate confidence and longing. Time stands still with the taste of her mouth as passion of her lips on mine transport us to another place. She is young, sweet and wondrous and I am lost in bliss, our bodies tight together, senses aroused beyond measure. We yield ourselves fully to our passion and miraculously I become a man reborn with a heart resurrected from the dead.

Soon we are fast asleep in a tight embrace. Suddenly the alarm breaks through my dreams. I don't want the dream to end, not now, not this soon. I must get moving. Shelby, sleeping soundly, continues to snuggle as close as possible. I am delighted to find her kiss and taste of her skin lingering in my mouth as I slowly rise from my bedroll on the floor.

Murmuring sweetly, without opening her eyes she says, "No. Don't go yet. A few minutes more."

Easing myself from her embrace, I kneel close and kiss her cheek, "Gotta go, but not for long. You'll be safe here," I whisper. "I promise I'll be back soon," kissing her mouth again.

Trying not to walk heavily in my heavy boots on Lynn and Roy's wooden floors, I step toward the front door carrying my rifle and backpack. when I hear Shelby sit up sleepily and lean back against the sofa, rubbing wonderfully pretty sleepy eyes.

"You promise?" She says in a tender whisper that floats in the air like a mist in front of me. Standing in the early morning dark of a new day, I don't know what to say. "I promise. I will be seeing you again soon Shelby Gales."

Sitting on the floor, arms crossed over her chest, she smiles and turns tender sleepy eyes toward me again, "I'll be looking for you CW."

As I step out and greet the cold morning air, the smile on my face radiates warmth to the deepest recesses of my soul, flowing through my body like sweet honey, all because of Shelby. I heft the backpack over my shoulders, cinch the straps into place, and hold my rifle firmly in both hands, checking my watch: 3:20 AM. I have plenty of time but I need to get moving. I offer Shelby a quick wave and strike my boots against wood stairs leading from Lynn and Roy's large covered porch. Gravel crunches under foot along the path that leads me away from the comfort of the house, and away from the gentle kisses of Shelby Gales, watching my progress from inside the house on the other side of the window glass.

Walking in the early morning darkness toward home, a wide smile breaks across my face remembering again, "I'll be looking for you CW."

It is 5:15 AM and I am surveying my property from a secluded spot among dense vegetation, along the hillside across the road from my house. I am in the final stages of deciding where my concealed position will be to wait for daybreak and perhaps a bit of sun too. Quickly crossing the road, I easily traverse a section of my overgrown field fence at a far corner and make my way over the creek that runs the full length of my property. The creek starts somewhere in the hills and flows past my place on its way to the river two miles further on and can get full quickly. Thankfully, I find this time of season it isn't yet swollen and make my way across it without much difficulty, not needing to suit up in my waterproof coveralls although my boots do get wet –there are dry ones in the house waiting for me a short distance away.

On the opposite bank, I conceal the pack and non-essentials in tall grass at the base of a dead cottonwood tree. Removing a few pieces of hard candy and a Cliff bar for breakfast I leave everything else with the pack and poncho. I secure the silencer to the rifle muzzle, "Better safe than sorry," and heft the rifle, a magazine of ammunition, and range finder and make my way cautiously along the left side of the creek, crouching low, pausing frequently to listen to sounds of early morning. The last thing I want is for the dogs to alert to my presence in their pen now an acre away.

The best I can hope for is to get into position without being observed. If I can do that, I will have control of my surroundings. If trouble starts, I will have the element of surprise supported by a loaded AR15 rifle.

Twenty minutes pass and I am in position on my stomach in the thick brush with a clear view of the house and any approach to the property, including anyone coming through the front gate over the railroad flat car bridge thirty yards to my left. I retrieve the range finder hanging inside my jacket, on its cord around my neck, adjust its focus and conduct my first indepth, slow scan of the area - an activity I will conduct many times before I am ready to move from my concealment to take control again of my house and property. All quiet. After another thirty minutes, daylight begins peeling back the darkness, providing detail to what had been shadowy outlines of a quiet landscape surrounding my house. Resting the range finder in my hands, the weight of it is replaced by a memory of Shelby's soft hand in mine when I first pulled her up from the darkness of the shed miles away, and when she pulled me to her, as we embraced not many hours ago at Big Meadow. On my stomach on the wet ground, with my rifle locked and loaded, I watch daylight firmly dispel stubborn shadows from around my home. In my concealed position, I smile with thoughts of Shelby Gales washing over me.

Sucking on butterscotch hard candy to help keep myself alert, I give thanks for all my blessings. I say a prayer for Shelby, Lynn, and Roy, and for all my friends and family where ever they may be.

I reposition my feet in their wet, heavy boots, blisters on my heels reminding me of the many miles I have labored getting to this spot, in my concealed position on the wet ground. All things considered, so far so good.

"Be patient," talking to myself. No telling who might have invaded my home while I was away or who might be watching my house right now from their own hiding spot. I am home after having traveled 43 miles over three days, and that doesn't mean I'm safe. It simply means I have walked too many miles and gone through too much to throw caution to the wind, regardless of how much I want my life back. Nestled in my hiding place it takes all my willpower not to lay my head down and succumb to badly needed sleep. Repeatedly scanning the house, barn, and dog pen to my front using my range finder helps keep me awake. "Stay focused," I encourage myself quietly.

It has been two hours peering through the lens of the range finder. I'll give myself another 30 minutes before moving out. Ten minutes go by when suddenly there is movement up ahead on my right, along the field

 fence approximately eighty-five yards away. A few seconds later, movement again shakes the tops of the tall grass where an old post makes a 45-degree angle at a corner of my property. Quickly scanning other areas, I return my focus to the spot near the post. The pervasive feeling of weariness my body wallowed in moments before is now completely gone as grass stalks shake more vigorously.

Slowly, a dirty black baseball cap with a faded yellow "Papé" logo embroidered on its front rises from the brush and comes into full view.

The man under the cap stands with little care for safety and concealment, obviously feeling safe where he is because he gives no indication of being concerned. The magnification lens on my range finder allows me to zoom in close and confirm he is not anyone I have seen in the area before today. He looks to be in his mid to late 40's, if his scraggly growth of salt and pepper beard is an indication of anything other than he hasn't shaved for a while. He is wearing a well-worn, dirty, faded, green plaid coat with tattered seams, giving him a look of having lived most of his life on the poor side of things. As he attempts to untangle himself from the brambles and blackberry vines, his scoped bolt-action hunting rifle carried in his right hand comes into view.

"Did he sleep out there all night?" It's a reasonable question without a reasonable answer coming to mind. I've have been in position before daylight and didn't hear anything, unless I dozed off and didn't know it. I congratulate myself for being cautious, for not rushing into the house this morning – taking extraordinary precaution to avoid an ambush, or an encounter with a group of armed men, by lying concealed for hours, low against the ground. The hair on the back of my neck bristles knowing I have achieved the element of surprise. I see him and he does not see me. In most armed encounters, the element of surprise makes all the difference when the shooting starts.

Free from his entanglements he braces a foot on the sagging, poor excuse of a fence, testing its strength. Satisfied it will support his weight; he slings the rifle over his shoulder and steadies himself with his right hand on the weathered cedar post. Metal wire strains and stretches with his weight, threatening to break as he bears down and crosses over the fence.

 He is standing on my property, my land, my home. Legally at that moment, he is trespassing. He knows he has crossed onto someone else's property and he does not belong there. On my side of the fence, he pauses to pick a few remnants of blackberry vine that stubbornly cling to his clothing and then takes the rifle off his shoulder, repositions it in front of him, casually looks around, and makes his way toward the well-house 30 feet away.

With that rifle and the circumstances we are enduring these days, I consider him a threat. A surge of adrenaline raises the hair on the back of my neck again. My breathing comes quick, as the word "threat" crosses my mind. Perhaps he will simply pass through and that will be the end of it. I can only hope that will be the case because I don't want trouble, and he does not need the kind of trouble I can give him. The intruder leans over the side of the well house, pauses to peer down into the interior past the antique water bucket, and moves on toward the barn as if he hasn't a care in the world.

Making his way right to left, toward the barn directly in front of him, the digital display in my range finder counts down 80, 75, 70 yards. When he passes behind the barn out of sight, I take the lens away and watch for movement coming from either corner of the barn, not having to guess very long. The outline of the baseball cap he's wearing peeks around the corner at the far right side. I see him crouching, and scanning the area to his front in a quick sweeping motion with his riflescope. I am confident he will not be able to focus on anything using the scope that way. Nevertheless, military training takes over and I flatten myself even more until my chin is nearly resting on the damp ground with my eyes fixed in his direction. Lying there, the smell of dark wet earth takes me back to summer days when the dogs and I lay in the pasture and napped together in the sun after playing all day. Those are precious memories I hope to relive.

Believing he is alone and it's safe to move from his partial concealment, the man in the Papé logo baseball cap stands and cradles his rifle in his arms. He moves around to the front of the barn, toward the house where Zeke, Zoie, and Little occupy the enclosed dog pen located between the house and barn. He cannot see them from where he is, but he will soon. Unknown to him, Zoie appears from the garage, walking lazily into the covered enclosure surrounded by a tall fence I built to keep the dogs secure. Likely, she is curious to know what the sound is she has detected. She presses her nose into the corner of the enclosure nearest the side of the barn. I imagine Zoie has that curious, expectant look that is all her own.

As soon as Zoie sees the strange man, she erupts with furious, deep, bellows. The man nearly jumps a foot in the air, completely surprised by the sudden and unexpected encounter with a huge, barking dog showing him its large teeth. Instinctively he jumps back several steps sweeping the muzzle of his rifle back and forth. Little Zeke, and "Biggie" Zeke bolt from the garage and stand with her, shoulder to shoulder - all three barking, standing their ground. Their combined voices full and with authority reverberate off wooded hills that surround my acreage. In another time, I am sure I would have laughed seeing him jolt from the initial surprise of it all, but this is no laughing matter. The rifle carried by this man trespassing on my property is now pointing at my three dogs. The best move he can make is immediately turn around and leave. He's not listening to my thoughts and instead, stands his ground, realizing they do not have a way of getting through the fence to attack him. Having regained his composure, he concludes he is not in any immediate danger, backs away from the pen, and turns his attention to the front door of my house. Nevertheless, as he leaves the dogs, he periodically turns around to ensure they indeed haven't gotten loose to attack him. None of the three stop barking, bouncing and turning in place, with hair raised high on their backs, doing what they can to make the man go away. I know what they are saying; "How is it he doesn't know, or doesn't care?"

Papé Cap shoulders his rifle, approaches the front door of my house and knocks. When he doesn't hear anything, he puts his ear to the door listening intently for any sound from inside, and then knocks again even louder and more forcefully than before, putting an ear again to the door. At one point, he tries to see inside but without luck - I have the curtains drawn shut. When I see him turn away from the front door, making his way back to my dogs, I extend the bipod on the foregrip of my rifle and rest it securely on the ground among the tangle of field grass in front of me, thumbing the selector switch until I hear it click into the fire position. Adrenaline again surges through me in earnest, my heartbeat throbbing in my ears and shortening my breath. Snuggling the butt of the rifle into my right shoulder, I settle myself and sight down the red dot reticle center mass on the intruder. Instead of backing away and leaving, the man makes a move toward Little at the gate, stretched full length with big paws draped over the top. The man carries his rifle loosely in his right hand, its muzzled pointed toward the ground. At the approach of the stranger Little backs down and stands next to his brother and sister while Papé Cap studies Zeke, Zoie, and Little for a moment. Retracing his steps to the front door of the house, he bangs on it harder than ever with his fist, calling out loudly, "Is there anyone home? Hello! Is there anyone home? I've been injured and I need help."

"Liar," I mumble as I watch his every move. He pauses with his ear to the door and finally satisfied no one is home, backs up a step and then kicks open the front door with a heavy boot, breaking it violently open. The door explodes inward, embedding the doorknob in the drywall.

With his rifle pointed in front of him, he enters my house and in less than five minutes returns carrying a can of beer from the refrigerator, gone only long enough to have made sure no one was home but not long enough to have searched and found my cache of weapons and ammunition hidden away. Standing on the deck, he looks out over my front lawn and down toward the gate, casually drinking the beer as if he owns the place. After a few deep swallows from the can, he leaves the deck and heads in the direction of the dog pen. Just when I start to raise myself from my concealed position to confront him, he whistles and waves toward the neighbor's field. I instantly hit the ground, undetected, and watch as two men in their late 20's or early 30's climb over the fence at the spot Papé Cap trespassed, each of them carrying a rifle. "That was close," muttering to myself. Having difficulty reigning in my racing heartbeat, I settle myself against the ground with my aim once again down my loaded rifle pointing at Papé Cap.

I am too far away to hear exactly what the group is saying, but one of them enters the house, comes back out with a beer, and stands again with the other two in front of the dog pen, the tight group staring at three loudly barking dogs. Papé Cap makes loud kissing noises as if trying to convince the dogs he is a nice guy. Zeke instinctively backs a comfortable distance away toward the back of the enclosure. "Good boy," I remark to myself, while Zoie and Little alternately charge at the hand Papé Cap has extended over the top of the gate. The dogs are doing their best to scare him away, but all three intruders stand together, talk, and laugh for a few minutes more.

I slow my breathing anticipating trouble, and steady my aim, keeping my sights center mass on Papé Cap. He seems to be the leader. My right index finger presses against the cold, slender metal of the trigger, taking up the slack, watching with growing anxiety the scene unfolding, "It's come to it, Cdub." I ready myself for the armed encounter I know is coming, but hope it doesn't. I don't have to wait long to find out.

His two friends go inside my house and while alone, watching my dogs, Papé Cap finishes his beer, crushes the can in his fist and throws the empty onto the metal roof of the dog enclosure. The can lands with a light clinking sound. One of his friends comes to the front deck carrying a bulging white plastic bag that was stored in a bedroom closet and yells out, "Hey Dude! Look at this!" Papé Cap walks over and starts poking through the contents of the emergency food bag containing peanut butter, road flares, hard candy, merlot, rice, gel-fuel. A moment later, the second guy joins them, dragging the entire large plastic container onto the deck, out into the sunlight.

Zeke, Zoie, and Little are raising the alarm in the only way they know how, making it clear, the intruders are handling property that belongs to another –'Leave Now'. Evidently, Papé Cap has had enough of the dogs mouthing off. He leaves his friends and heads toward the pen, while his two friends are seriously preoccupied with my provisions.

At a position several feet from the enclosure, Papé Cap pulls back slightly on his rifle bolt, checking to ensure a loaded bullet is seated in the chamber ready to fire. He locks it in place. Aiming down the sights of my rifle, I watch him reposition his feet – and settle his rifle in the pocket of his right shoulder. With the first sign of the muzzle rising at an angle aimed toward my three corralled and defenseless dogs, his time on earth has run out. I inhale slightly, exhale a little, hold my breath, and squeeze the trigger straight back in one smooth, well trained, motion.

Gently squeezing four pounds of trigger pull until the hammer fell seemed to take forever. Inevitably, I shot him dead where he stood with a single 5.56 caliber armor-piercing bullet. When it hit between his shoulder blades, below his neckline, his head jerked back, causing him to spray a mist of blood as if he had a mouthful of strawberry milk when surprised by a laugh he could not contain. Shooting from a distance of sixty yards, I am sure he never heard it coming. Of course, having the silencer screwed to the muzzle of my rifle muffled the sound dramatically. Hardly feeling the recoil from the shot, I breathe fully again. Being on the business end of my rifle is a completely different story for Papé Cap. He collapses like a sack of bricks and doesn't move, his rifle falling with him, the lens glass of the scope shattering as it strikes the concrete walkway nearby. As muffled as my shot was, the two boys on my deck vanish, taking their weapons with them, leaving behind everything they had taken out of the emergency food container. The would-be killer in the Papé baseball cap deserved what I gave him. I would have killed his friends too if they hadn't run off.

"Take things slow. Think things through." Remaining concealed, I continue scanning the area, motionless in my position in the tall grass and thick vines. When I made the shot, the dogs abruptly stopped barking and backed themselves into the far side of the pen, looking intently in all directions. They don't move from that spot for a long time.

Lying motionless after killing Papé Cap, I contemplate how remarkable life so quickly and definitively changes a person. After the lights went out, I have done and seen things that have stained my conscience with a memory so deep, I am afraid they will never fade. Time drags by excruciatingly slow. All the while, the entire area has remained perfectly quiet. There is no sign of his two friends or anyone else for that matter, just another ordinary country morning. Finally, Papé Cap is 40 minutes dead. I am satisfied it is safe to move from my concealed position and my adrenaline rush has subsided as well.

Zeke, Zoie and Little start barking furiously when they first see a figure rise from my hiding spot. Their tone changes from alarm to recognition and complete delight only when I am within a foot or two of them. Although I am grimy and weathered from days on the road, they quickly recognize my face and scent, and then all three bounce around wanting to regain their freedom. Instead, I offer them my left hand as reassurance. I am home at last. Three days ago I put them inside the garage, giving each one a dog treat, patting their heads before closing and locking the door and then driving away to work. Now I have a dead man at my house, and stains on my heart I fear will never go away.

As I walk slowly around the outside of their pen with my left hand running along the fence line, the dogs follow me, alternately licking, and sniffing as much as they can through small openings in the wire mesh. At the rear of the house, I crouch, scan the length of the backyard, and up into the wooded hillsides beyond until I am confident the area is safe. Looks to me, other than my front door, the house is intact.

Retracing my steps, I make my way back and let myself into the dog pen, closing the gate behind me, and herd the muscular gaggle into the garage out of sight, where I hug and pet them and rub their ears the way they like it. Zeke is whining and barking for joy. Little is bouncing up and down more like a rabbit than a Great Dane, and Zoie is panting and wagging her tail furiously back and forth with eyes locked on me, watching my every move. Within the concealed space of the garage, I am overjoyed to have been here the moment they needed me the most. This is home: dog tails wagging, tongues hanging out of big dog mouths, and the four of us safe in the cool space and half-dark of the garage. I pat them on their heads, wipe dog kisses from my face, and stand up. It is time to take control of my home. Retrieving the house key from my shirt pocket, I unlock and push open the door from the garage that leads into the TV room. Zeke and Little burst through followed by Zoie. I am pretty darn confident no one is in the house, given all the commotion we've been making and the fact Papé Cap and friends went through the place.

For my own peace of mind I have to check it out thoroughly, room to room, and closet to closet. Who knows, those two yahoos that did the disappearing act might be trying to conceal themselves inside somewhere. Unsettled memories rear their ugly heads as I contemplate the task at hand, having conducted enough clearing rooms one at a time while a police officer years ago. Close quarter's combat can change a person and it has certainly had an effect on me. Regardless, my task is necessary, and I am very thankful the dogs are with me bouncing, prancing, room-to-room, and closet-to-closet. As the dogs look on, I climb into the attic and even squirm my way down into the crawl space under the house. Assured at last the house is completely clear, from top to bottom, I now breathe easy and send the dogs outside, all three clamoring onto the front yard, happy to be free, acting as if it is just another day for them. From their carefree antics, I wonder if they have even now forgotten about the dead man lying in a heap on the ground outside. While I inspect the extent of damage done to my front door, I find myself envying their short-term memory. Looking up briefly, I smile seeing Zoie and Little chasing each other in circles around Zeke who is exceedingly annoyed. From the volume of his commands, he is telling them to knock it off. Chuckling to myself, I look back at the door and conclude it can be repaired with a few nails and scrap wood that will hold as a temporary fix when I get around to it. I step into the living room and draw back curtains at the picture window. Sunlight instantly bathes the interior of the living room, spraying itself on the walls, tempting me to stay awhile and enjoy the comfort of the home I worked so hard to return to.

"You have to keep moving Cdub" encouraging myself. Reminding myself. I need to get the backpack where I left it in the far pasture and I have a lot of work to do before this day is done.

When he sees me walk out of the house to the edge of the deck, Zeke heads for the creek, his usual routine once the dogs are free from the garage when I arrive home from work. Little follows close behind,  running full speed down the sloping front yard to join whatever his big brother is doing. Zoie walks beside me, her tail wagging in earnest, seemingly unable to be as close as she wants to be, all the while brushing her strong body against my legs and occasionally touching my hand with her cold wet nose. Soon, all three are in the water standing together, periodically checking to make sure I am still on the bank nearby watching them wade in the creek. Sunlight is breaking free from cloudy skies and blessing the wet ground and surrounding woods with wide swaths of its precious golden light, gloriously illuminating hillsides packed with tall trees that surround my home. I am seeing fall colors for the first time with new eyes that once were blind but now see. In vivid detail, the entire scene spread around me is a magnificent painted display of orange, yellow and rusty red leaves of all shapes, and sizes. As my reward for having safely passed through the many hardships I endured getting here, it is as if we now have the world to ourselves.

Feeling safe, I turn my face to the sun and close my eyes, unable to do anything other than grin from ear to ear. The dogs and I are together again. We are safe and uninjured. Nothing ugly from the world outside will ever penetrate our invisible, impenetrable shield created from my sheer want of it to be. This is my home and my soul is immensely satisfied. Dogs splashing happily in the creek, unseen birds in the trees lightly calling to one another from places far off in the woods, and water talking its way over stones in the creek below, all assure me life is good and meaningful and worthy of my best effort living it. Keeping my eyes closed for a moment longer, I feel the comfort of home embrace me, intimately whispering a sweet promise of rest and renewal, cuddling my weariness in a feeling of warmth reminiscent of my favorite blanket on a cold day. I am fully content and gratified by it all, aided in no small measure by a deep sense of security that comes with hands firmly embracing my loaded rifle. I turn toward the far meadow and make my way along the path at the foot of the hill that follows the creek. All three dogs see the movement and immediately rush ahead to lead the way, bouncing out of the creek with a great deal of splashing, charging past, up the footpath, each one occasionally pausing, looking back, making sure I'm following. As we crest the rise, wiggly bodies in a jumble around me, bounce around, each performing a canine version of a happy dance. They each get a pat on the head and I slowly scan the area all around with the range finder.

Satisfied it's safe to move, I make my way to the furthest point on my property to the dead cottonwood tree where my backpack is, finding it as I had left it hours before, albeit now with dew on the top flap. "It's been in shade all this time. Interesting. We're gonna get wet this year."

Setting my rifle down, I lift the pack and position its familiar full weight across bruised shoulders and my exceedingly aching back, "Gosh you're heavy." After adjusting the hip belt and shoulder straps, I retrieve my rifle and begin the short walk back to the house. Each step recalls the miles I have traveled, increasing my awareness of how utterly exhausted I am. Muscles I had long forgotten now cry out for individual attention. My legs are heavy and my feet feel like lead weights, each with blisters on my heels and perhaps on the outside of each little toe as well. Every ache and pain deserve much needed and long overdue care and I assure myself, "In a little while," each one will have my full, undivided attention, but not right now. If I were not so weary or so anxious to be settled in, trudging down the trail into the middle pasture toward the house would not take as long and require as much effort as it is now taking me. The sound of my heavy boots crunching along the gravel the few remaining yards to my front door remind me of walking miles upon miles along railroad tracks in the night, grateful now beyond measure knowing those miles are behind me. Approaching the house, I lift my head and the sight of Papé Cap reminds me of work to be done before nightfall, coming in less than five hours from now.

The four of us make our way through the busted front door of the house. I kick it shut and prop it closed with a nearby chair; finally wrapped in the quiet of my home with my happy and healthy dogs. Exhilarating relief at having achieved this goal contrasts sharply with images from my journey, flashing one after another in rapid succession on the big screen in my mind. Memories hit me with a force of clarity more urgent than the last. Powerless to deflect the onslaught I am driven into submission to the floor on my knees where I cry deep sobs of sadness and relief with my face buried in my hands. After a while, against all odds, I fight and keep moving forward, reminding myself repeatedly, I made it home, I actually made it home - my three dogs are healthy and safe, and the ugly death and trauma forced upon me lay along miles of road behind me. For a moment I had somehow forgot I still wore my backpack. Disengaging from it is a fabulous feeling of relief. With great pleasure, I set it down in a space where sunlight is shining through the picture window, brightly reflecting off my wood laminate flooring.

Engrossed in thought and the activity of off loading his belongings, CW does not hear or see the vehicle on the road out front, speeding along in a direction away from the hills on his left, down to the river road a few miles in the distance. If in that moment, the sound of that lone truck on the road had registered, he would have followed its high-speed travel as it passed his property.

CW would have caught glimpses within spaces between the trees that line the road of its rusted orange color and its large confederate flag flying from a pole stuck to the right side of the pickup bed. He did not hear or see the pickup truck because it traveled on a road outside his conscious mind.

All living things need food, water, and shelter to survive, and with that in mind, priority number one is clean water. I raise toilet lids to allow the dog's access to the water contained in the bowl and use a coffee cup to take water from the toilet tanks and pour that into their water feeder until the water feeder is full. If they need more, the creek will provide all they need. Under these circumstances, I remind myself to ration all good water for drinking and cooking, everything contained in both the 50-gallon hot water tank and 150-gallon well tank. Bathing will either be accomplished using wet wipes or from any of the multitude of handy-wipe containers I have stored away. An alternative is using water I will capture in buckets with linen sheets attached that will filter rainwater through downspouts. During my hasty activities around the house, Zoie wanders with me. I smile when I hear the other two dogs crunching their dry food from their self-feeder bowl I relocated to the laundry room at the entrance to the guest bathroom.

Now that we have sufficient water and food, I locate a suitable spot and dig a slit trench in the backyard at a safe distance from the master bedroom window using a spade shovel retrieved from the garage, finding the ground soft from the rain we have been having.

Nevertheless, I start huffing and puffing, and breaking a sweat in no time, muscles aching, threatening to seriously deplete what precious little energy I have remaining. Finally, the latrine is complete, and I lean the shovel against the house and turn my attention to Zoie standing at the edge of the trench as if admiring my handiwork. Patting Zoie's head and stroking her back a few times, I realize we will regain our happy home one small gesture at a time. She and I make our way through the muddy backyard to the sliding glass door at the back patio where I kick off as much clumps of grass and mud as possible from the lugs of my boots, unlace them and set the boots off to one side to dry.

Cool air surrounds my damp stocking feet as I step inside the house and lock the sliding glass patio door behind me. As we walk through the house, Zoie and I find both Zeke and Little curled up together on their mattress in the front bedroom, sound asleep and snoring. Life is good and now that I am inside, Zoie joins her brothers in bed for a nap. I stand in my quiet living room at the picture window and survey the front lawn, this time of year is so beautiful, even when daylight, when we get it, fades too quickly. "Celebrate what you have," I say aloud. Thoughts intrude of dead Papé Cap, waiting for me to bury him, and the blisters on my feet crying out for much needed attention. All that will have to wait awhile longer. Instead of attending to the dead man, or my blisters, or the aspirin I promised to take but promptly forgot until just now, I walk out on the deck and pull the lid off the plastic food container my three intruders had begun rummaging through. I drag it and the plastic bag of food supplies into the living room.

After fumbling around in the bag, I'm soon smiling with a can of tuna and sleeve of crackers in my hands. Merlot is quickly recovered the yahoo-brothers reminded me I had. After a mouthful or more, savoring its aroma and heavenly taste, I begin to relax. Savoring large mouthfuls from the bottle, I set to one side the can of tuna and sleeve of crackers and take deep breaths that wash through me with satisfaction beyond description. "A few minutes more." Shortly, but not soon I shake myself awake. "I have things to do." Thankfully shelter is crossed off the list. "Generating power?" and then creating a secure space for the night are next. The model 6000 generator starts easily but is really loud, echoing into the quiet countryside. With each passing minute waiting for it to warm up, my apprehension about announcing I'm home can't be ignored and I shut the generator down – the remaining fuel in the line not burning through fast enough until it finally is off. Fiddling with the electrical connection from the generator to the panel I finally get it to fit properly. "Could'a done that better" a weak voice shrieks in my mind, disembodied from a life it was once connected to. "Who used to say that all the time?" I chuckle while standing up. A vague recollection slips away easily, back to the place where moments in life are no longer memories. I turn my attention to filling the generator tank with gasoline, reminding myself I do not have enough to keep the unit running for extended periods. As with food and water, I also have to ration the generator. I retrieve ammo and set the scoped 30.06 bolt-action rifle resting on its bipod in the living room - feels good. Only things I seem to have plenty of are time, hope, and ammunition.

With security arranged, I gather up a few blankets from the hall closet and toss them into the dog's room thinking I might stay with them for the night. Not one of the dogs lifts their head as I throw in the blankets. They are sound asleep. "Thank God." Pausing for a moment, I survey the work I have accomplished over the last couple of hours and conclude that if all goes well, I will be comfortable and safe until the lights come back on. When that might be, I do not know.

For the first time in a very long time, I sit down and sink into my favorite upholstered chair positioned alongside the picture window. The bottle of merlot resting in my lap between my legs is now more than half-gone. I am relaxed, likely due in no small part to the merlot but certainly from sitting for a time in the quiet of my home with my dogs safe and snoring in the adjacent room  nearby. I have forgotten all about the aspirin I assured myself I would take, and I no longer feel any of the many blisters on my feet. My thoughts drift in a daydream, floating with the sunbeams streaming through my window into my quiet home. For the few moments I spend alone time in my chair, the dead man in the Papé cap is out of sight and out of mind.

CHAPTER TWELVE
ALMOST HOME

Friday afternoon, October 18

Shelby is waiting for me at Big Meadow and I am going to keep my promise to return soon. Before I can do that, I have to bury Papé Cap in the dirt somewhere, as far away from the house as possible. Pausing a moment more, I gaze out my living room window with a heart full of thanksgiving for fresh air to breathe, ears that hear my dogs snoring, and eyes to see my living room fully lit by sunlight on a mostly cloudy, early fall day. My mind cycles from one thought to the next, of things I must do, should do, or perhaps should have done already. The half-empty bottle of merlot I have been sipping tempts me to sit back a while longer and lose all track of time. Regardless, I stand on my two aching feet, make my way to the back bedroom and strip off my wet, dirty field clothes that have protected me so well during my travels. After brushing my teeth and wiping myself down with a damp cloth followed by a soft dry towel, I hurriedly change into a clean tee shirt, blue jeans, thick, warm socks, and well-worn field boots. Lastly, I pull the tan golf hat over my matted hair, and throw myself into my well-worn light brown farm jacket.

All three dogs are in their bedroom cuddled together on their king size mattress once claimed by my ex-wife. It's fitting they have it. My ex never let Zeke or me near it, as if that thing were more precious than both of us combined. When she moved out, one of the first things I did was donate the mattress to him. Zoie and Little Zeke weren't part of my family back then and thankfully spared the melodrama that came with living with her. Stepping softly away from the living room, I peek in on the three in their bedroom and find them snoring soundly. Zoie somehow still hears my footfalls and as she does, half-heartedly thumps her tail on the mattress in acknowledgement. Zoie knows I am there at the door and she is happy because of it. "Good girl Zoie," I whisper with a smile seeing her tail stop wagging as she runs toward dreamland to catch up with Zeke and Little. Life would be perfect without want, complete in the simplicity contained in our quiet world, if I could capture this moment, savor it forever, keep it bottled, not let time intrude. The air I take deep into my lungs as I stand at their door is cleaner and more refreshing than I recall it ever has been with the knowledge memories of bad things haven't pierced their innocent spirits: I'll do my best never to let bad things intrude. I may be overly confident, but I believe I can wrestle into submission those that have pierced mine. Standing quietly at their door, listening to their heavy breathing, watching their chests rise and fall in rhythm, I am satisfied beyond measure.

Impatient thoughts of Papé Cap intrude. He is easily brushed off as I move quietly to my backpack lying on the floor in a corner of the living room at one side of the picture window. Reaching into its main compartment, I retrieve the dirty, bloodstained battle flag I hurriedly folded into a three-point configuration at the river's edge, its stars facing outward. The cloth of the thing seems heavier, more likely than not from the weight I impart to it, remembering where it came from and what we have been through to get here. Stepping onto the deck, I squint into the sun's blessed rays. Pausing, I take another sip of wine, happy none of the dogs have jumped up to follow me outside as the door squeaked on its hinges when I opened it, so glad they are sound asleep and able to rest. At the corner of the deck by the  stairs I built leading to the front lawn, I unfurl the battle flag, clip it to the lanyard of the flagpole, hoist it half-mast, and as I secure it in place, it somehow catches a breeze I cannot detect from my position below. The Stars and Stripes come alive with the breeze, as if the flag possesses a will of its own - testifying to the world it is alive, it did not die at the blockade on the river road outside small town America along with so many others that did. Seeing it flutter I say a prayer for Big Biker and Biker Woman, offering thanks for the kindness of the ride they offered me a lifetime ago. As I stand quietly and swallow the last mouthful of wine in silent toast to those two, I suddenly realize we never knew each other's name - nonetheless we are bonded in a way only a brother or sister in arms can truly be.

Papé Cap is calling again: "You sure are pushy for a dead guy," I say aloud with some amusement. Glancing up one more time at the flag gently flapping on the flagpole, I turn and enter the house, retrieve the barn key from the basket over the refrigerator, make my way out the sliding glass door through the backyard patio, and unlock the metal door to the barn located near the dog pen. Papé Cap and I finally agree on one thing and one thing only; he has been waiting long enough for me to carry him to a place out of sight of everyone but God. I am in the mood to oblige. My diesel tractor coughs to life and backs out easily through the large door at the back of the barn as I make my way to give the dead man the full measure of attention he deserves. Approaching his lifeless heap, I lower the bucket near his back legs, inching the tractor slowly forward, the lip of it briefly scraping its metal on the gravel with an edgy, grinding sound that sends chills up my spine. Standing over the dead man, I push his right shoulder with my booted foot. The man rolls onto his back, face up, mouth open in a silent yawn. Various pieces of ¾ minus driveway rock cling to his scraggly bearded face, nestled into his cheek and forehead as his body cooled, relaxing like putty into the ground. The path of the bullet that killed him tore his mouth and broke his teeth into jagged edges. I am surprised to see he didn't bleed much. Cocking my head to one side, I stare into his hazy unseeing, unblinking eyes – they are filmy, like eyes of a dead fish. There's only a small pool of dark red blood on the gravel from the exit wound. "Prick, you could have left. Now look at you, fucking ugly dead and me having to clean up your sorry ass."

With the edge of my boot, I kick dirt and gravel over the small dark pool of blood and cover it, being careful not to get any on my sole, "That will do until rain comes and washes the spot clean." Reaching down, I pick up his rifle, throwing back the bolt, ejecting from its chamber the .308 caliber round he would have used to kill one of my dogs. It falls to the ground. I pick it up and put it in my pants pocket thinking it might come in handy, although I don't own a .308 rifle. "Well," I correct myself, "I guess I technically do own one seeing as how Papé Cap no longer needs his." Inspecting the rifle further, I see the cheap scope is busted and useless, its lens having landed on the cement walkway when he collapsed. "Oh well. It's a piece of shit rifle anyway," a disappointing offering of some model or other I'm not interested enough to confirm.

I toss the rifle to the bottom of the tractor bucket - it settles in with a loud clanging noise while I turn my attention to the dead man's pockets. I find a bit of money, a car registration and a gas receipt. "Jack Stram. Well, well. Mr. Papé Cap has a name." Looking more closely at the receipt I see it's from Gales Market, earlier this month. "Lots of people go through there," I tell myself. "Doesn't mean anything. Doesn't mean he had anything to do with the Gales murders." This guy was probably another faceless man in a stream of faceless people that stopped in at one time or other, that's all. Taking a deep breath a memory of Shelby's soft touch settles in, embracing me, renewing my spirit. Quickly stuffing all his papers and money back in his jacket pocket, including the bullet cartridge I ejected from his rifle, I leave undisturbed the remaining .308 rounds in his pocket where he put them.

"God damn you," I mutter aloud as I look down on him in disgust. "You better be praying I don't see you on the other side of eternity, 'cuz if I have anything to do with it I am going to kick your ass again and again for wanting to kill my dogs." With my boot, I flip him on his stomach. As he rolls over his baseball cap falls off a balding head, revealing shaggy, dirty, salt and pepper hair with what looks to be too much hair product in it. Maybe I am feeling powerful given what this man did to deserve what he got from me. Whatever it is, he isn't heavy when I pick him up and unceremoniously toss him in the bucket of his orange colored hearse for the short ride to his hole in the ground. The dead man's arms and legs, hanging over the sides, bounce awkwardly in time with the movement of the tractor as I steer along the gravel drive. I can't help wonder where his two buddies ran off to when I killed their friend. Over the engine noise, I say aloud, "If you know what's good for you, you won't come back, you God Damn Pricks!" sincerely hoping they don't.

The gravesite I have chosen is between my wood chip pile and rifle range. It's a spot where the grass will easily grow thick and green come spring and summer. He will be out of the way of usual traffic on the property, away from any water supply, as well as a good distance from the creek: a spot where the earth should be easy work for the small trencher attached to the PTO at the back of the tractor. As Papé Cap lies in the bucket for added front-end weight, I swing the machine around to work the trencher, glad to know my prediction is right; the ground is soft from days in a row of rain.

Stretched out and gouging big scoops of dark, rich dirt, the hydraulic arm is alive, clawing at the ground, digging deeper with each scoop, unafraid of the morbid task it has been set to accomplish. In no time, I have a neatly dug and adequately proportioned trench, home sweet home for Papé Cap. He can keep his rifle too. He and his possessions, including the baseball cap, tumble in the ditch. With the front bucket, I scrape the dirt and grass down on top, pushing it all into place over him, packing it in by running my tractor tires back and forth over the length of bare earth, leaving the entire affair crisscrossed with patterns of tire tread. Satisfied with a job well done, I return the tractor to its place in the barn, making it ready for the Machio cutting deck when it's time for spring field mowing. After closing and locking the barn, I retrieve my pickup truck keys, in preparation to return to Shelby Gales, discovering a sudden surge of energy and desire for her that both surprises and alarms me. I try, but not very successfully to calm myself, evidently not having quite perfected emotional self-protection I had been working on prior to Shelby. She is vulnerable, and in many ways, I am too. I do not want to leave my heart open to painful rejection. I have been there and done that. More importantly, I do not want to hurt Shelby. We are both in a fragile emotional state right now and yet my heart nonetheless draws me near to her in leaps and bounds.

Standing at the guestroom door, I jingle the truck keys. All three dogs immediately jump out of bed and stretch their long muscular bodies in front of me, yawning in unison. Jiggling the keys again, while heading for the front door of the house and saying, "Let's go for a ride," causes near pandemonium.

A collective 425 pounds of dog twist and turn, nearly beside themselves with excitement. Going for a ride, eating, and getting their ears rubbed must be their favorite things in life. Sure enough, as soon as a crack of daylight shows at the opening of the door, they explode through it to the front lawn, to take care of their business, while I close the busted front door behind me, hoping it will stay in place until I get back. The truck engine starts easily. As it warms up, I secure my AR15 in the passenger seat and then all three dogs pile in the crew cab. It's a tight fit for the four of us but we make it work. They're funny. They have never enjoyed riding in the bed of the truck although I have encouraged them several times to do so. No matter what I try, they simply refuse to go along with the program.

Within ten minutes of locking my front gate, the four of us are rolling down the driveway of Lynn and Roy's house at Big Meadow. Evening is approaching quickly, with a sky that looks like it will be clouding over and raining again tonight. Daylight I estimate will be complete for this day in a little more than an hour and I remind myself, "I have a lot to do before I bed down with the dogs, so I need to hurry". Dogs in the kennel kick up a storm as I pull the truck to the front of the house. My three dogs in the cramped space of the truck cab dutifully and forcefully reply with their own deafening noise. Edging myself out of my seat, I close the truck door as quickly as I can - allowing Zeke, Zoie, and

Little only enough room at each window to stick their big barking heads out, crying lustily back to their caged compatriots.

Almost as soon as my truck tires push to a halt on the gravel drive, I see the screen door of the house fling open. Shelby bounces through it and down the wooden steps, seeming to walk on air as she glides to my side, instantly wrapping her arms in a tight embrace around me, turning her beaming face up toward me with a wide smile, eyes gleaming with joy. That wonderful smile of hers transcends all the beautiful sunrises I had ever seen. As we embrace and kiss and sway in each other's arms, standing together, not letting go, foreheads touching, eyes riveted on the other I say, "I promised I'd see you again Shelby Gales."

"I've been waiting for you CW, each and every minute since I watched you walk away. I missed you terribly. Please, don't ever leave me again," burying her face, flush with tears of happiness into the protection and comfort of my chest and arm.

"I promise," silently wondering if she really means what she just said. Doubts be damned, my heart is transformed into a songbird, albeit with clipped wings, out on a limb, singing a gay song at the top of its tiny lungs, oblivious of what could happen if it fell, simply singing a new and altogether wonderful melody. Somehow, we become aware of Lynn and Roy watching from the porch. They too are holding each other with big grins on their friendly faces.

"Come in Cdub," Roy calls out waving us to the house.

Shelby and I walk together and she bounces as we go. At the wooden steps to the house, I pause and try to kick off any dirt or mud that may have been clinging to my boots, but Lynn and Roy both tell me not to worry about that.

"You're not gonna hurt anything. Come on in here. Do you want something to eat?" they say invitingly.

"Sure, but only if you are, then I'll take a little something," and quickly add, "Oh, I'm sorry I didn't bring anything to share. As soon as I was done with things around my place, I jumped in the truck and came here. It won't take me long to go back and get something."

Upon hearing my suggestion of leaving, Shelby pulls me closer to her and holds me even tighter.

Roy quickly says, "No such thing. We've got plenty," and with that Lynn and Roy set plates of sandwiches on the kitchen table for the four of us. Shelby sits next to me, holding my hand in both of hers as if guarding a precious treasure.

In no time, we are enjoying once again the comfort of our companionship as we had several hours before. We talk about better days and the delight of seeing the sun today. I don't speak of having killed and buried Papé Cap or of my intent to deliver a similar outcome to the other two intruders who ran away before I could get my rifle settled center mass on either one of them.

I figure in this quiet and peaceful place there's nothing to be gained by sharing that ugliness with these kind people. The food and company is good, but daylight is fading fast and before too long I am restless and evidently show it without meaning to.

Shelby turns to me, puts her hand on mine, and says, "It's going to be dark soon. I know we are welcome to stay here, but I figure we should think about going home."

Hearing her use the word, "we" makes my heart leap in my chest and instantly my life changed forever. If I had ever been sure of anything, I know now I don't ever want a life that doesn't include Shelby. The wall that had been so high and thick and completely impenetrable around my heart has dissolved. Swallowing hard before I say another word for fear my emotions will get the best of me right there in front of Lynn and Roy, I softly reply with eyes fixed on her, "Yes Shelby. It's taken me quite a journey to get home and there's a lot to do before nightfall. Infinitely more important than any of that, I don't want to leave you and I don't want you to leave me either." Sitting in my chair at the kitchen table, I watch tears stream from Shelby's happy eyes.

Placing soft hands on each side of my scruffy face, she looks deep into my eyes and without saying a word, draws her lips to mine with a loving kiss, and softly says, "It is everything I desire."

I am an imperfect, middle-aged, unshaven sinner sitting in front of Shelby in the quiet of Lynn and Roy's kitchen, and yet within the space between breaths, my heart has spoken in tongues of divine poetry proclaiming the wonders of her touch on my once barren heart. After brushing back a lock of her sandy blond hair and gently wiping away tears from her soft and blushing cheeks, I sound stupid. The only words stumbling out of my bumbling mouth are, "Thank you, more than you know." She responds with a radiant smile and a kiss with lips I cannot live without, effortlessly cleaving the dark veil that had cloaked any hope of love in my life.

Turning to Lynn and Roy who have been holding hands and watching quietly, Shelby and I try to help with the dishes but Lynn and Roy will have nothing of it. They quickly shoo us on our way with bright smiles on their faces saying, "You two get going before it gets dark. We'll be fine."

Reassuring them, I reply, "We'll come back soon and check on you."

As I point the truck down the gravel drive, Shelby from the passenger seat, looks back and happily waves out the window to her Aunt and Uncle standing on their large wooden porch at their front door, holding tight to one another, waving sincerely, with smiles that look as if they might become permanent fixtures. Zeke, Zoie, and Little instantly take to Shelby and her to them.

Turned in her seat toward the dogs while I drive, she pets their large heads and laughs a lilting child-like laugh as she lets them enthusiastically lick her face with their big tongues and soft dog kisses, thumping their tails in earnest against the cab walls, signaling total acceptance and appreciation of Shelby Gales. Our drive home is glorious high-octane energy within a closed space. This is our world and it is very, very good. My heart opens up wider than I ever imagined it could, thirstily drinking in everything this moment is offering, including hope for love I never thought I would see again in my lifetime.

Back at the house, the dogs jump from the truck and run off to the creek to do their usual exploring and wading in the water. From the front lawn, Shelby and I watch them splash and chase one another, happy to be home and happy we are there with them. While we are holding hands, standing shoulder to shoulder, partly leaning on each other, I use the opportunity to tell her all that happened when I got home this morning. I explain how I waited, concealed in my spot along the creek in the tall grass; how I saw Papé Cap and his two buddies trespass and break into my house - finally how I had to kill him before he killed the dogs.

"Sounds to me, Papé Cap got what he deserved."

I chuckle aloud and smile when I hear Shelby say, "Papé Cap," and privately think to myself, "Yes he did. Yes he did indeed."

We leave the dogs outside while I show her around the interior of the house. As she settles herself in, I clean my boots and place them in the storage closet with my other farm wear and turn my attention to getting us some light for the night, as well as unpacking my night vision unit, checking it to ensure it is operational for security watch. Once we are all in tonight, no one is going out again, not even the dogs. We discuss the idea of staying together in one room while the dogs have the run of the house from their bedroom. Shelby likes the idea, and we set to work outfitting the back bedroom I use as my office into a combined sleeping and living space. It's not a large room but will accommodate our needs well and won't take much to keep comfortably warm. As important as those considerations are, the bedroom is on the same side of the house as the dog's room, both having a window with a clear view to the front of the property and the length of the road. Anyone driving up has to come through the gate and then cross the bridge, clearly visible from either window, including the picture window in the living room where I previously positioned my bolt action 30.06 along the far wall.

Into our living space, I bring the storage bin Papé Cap and his two friends had riffled through and leave it with Shelby to organize as she sees fit while I attend to bringing my pack, rifle, and other equipment inside our room. Shelby sets to work immediately, organizing food in one corner and outfitting the desktop as the platform for our gel-fuel stove.

Blankets, pillows and camping pads are gathered and spread on the floor along a far wall that will do nicely as a comfortable bed. Her double barrel shotgun is loaded and lying on her side of the bedding along the wall. My 870 pump shotgun I carried as a police officer a long time ago is loaded with layers of military grade double 00 buckshot and rifle slugs, and placed standing in the corner near my side for easy access. The AR rifle remains  loaded and resting on its bipod on the desk with its muzzle pointed toward the front gate. With security and bedding in place, Shelby boils more water for a sponge bath while I sip a cup of coffee she provided when water first came to boil.

With the cup in my hands, I exit the house and make my way up the grassy slope in back to find a good spot to string a trip wire with metal cans attached along what I believe would be a likely access point for anyone attempting to surprise us. With the trip wire set up outside and the dogs free to roam the house inside, and the window in their room slightly open, I am confident we will be alert to anything coming onto the property, real or imagined. Back in our living quarters, I also open the window slightly in our room to ensure we are able to hear any sound from outside, while also making sure Shelby and I have enough warm clothes to keep us comfortable for what we both hope is a good night's sleep.

I strip off my clothes and fold them in a corner, preparing myself for a luxurious sponge bath. Soap and warm water on my skin makes me feel alive and new as Shelby washes my neck and face with a hand towel. It takes awhile, but I clean up well and after a shave and clean hair, I actually feel civilized again; much more so now than after having changed into comfortable blue jeans, tee-shirt, and warm dry boot socks before I drove to Big Meadow. I am now painfully aware of every blister, bruise, and aching muscle but do my best to put those discomforts out of my mind while concentrating on the fact I am home, unharmed and with the lovely Shelby. Clean and shaved and with Shelby making us something to eat, life is wonderfully complete right here in this one room of our blacked out house.

As I watch her doing this and that, busying herself making our room comfortable and homey, I sit with a smile on my face thinking to myself how it is so right to use the word "our" when describing home. Shortly, she sends me out the door while she cleans up and gets ready for bed and I take the opportunity to double check the interior perimeter of the house with all the dogs following my every move. Zeke, Zoie and Little receive one of their favorite dog cookies and I bed them down without effort on their king size mattress in their room next door to Shelby and me. By the time I return, Shelby has cleaned up and has a small bluish light from the emergency radio welcoming my arrival in the nearly dark interior. We enjoy a quick dinner of soup cups, crackers and bottled water, with small talk and a piece of butterscotch hard candy for dessert.

After we brush our teeth, we rest our weary backs against the bedroom wall and cuddle under covers with warm clothes covering our clean bodies. Fairly soon, we slide down and stretch out under the blankets for the night. With a click of a button, the bluish light goes out, and we are comfortable and warm in a new world we are creating for ourselves. Holding her close, I kiss her left ear and whisper, "Good night Sweetie."

Her whisper is intimate and close in the dark, "Good night. See you in the morning."

Shelby spoons her body closer into mine and morning arrives much sooner than expected.

CHAPTER THIRTEEN
REFUGEES

Wednesday morning, October 24

Gasping to catch my breath suddenly awakens me. My body is ramrod straight, ice cold, naked, stretched out at the morgue on a coroner's stainless-steel autopsy table. From somewhere deep inside me a shudder rumbles up and down my body. Drops of sweat from my forehead sting my unblinking eyes as steam from my panting breath floats lazily in the dark coldness of the morning inches in front of my face. Feeling the warmth of Shelby Gales, our bodies lying close together under the blankets, instantly reassures me I had only been sleeping. Relaxing tense muscles and breathing more fully, I notice the sound of Zoie, on her side in a shadowy corner nearby begin making soft, snuffling, mumbling barking noises as she dreams. It's quiet and dark in our room. I feel safe and nearly wide-awake. "I guess I'm done sleeping."

Lying motionless a minute more, I will myself fully awake. Finally, with my wits about me I ease myself out from under the warmth of our bed. Shelby moans and rolls to her side as I tuck my covers around her. With my face nearly resting on the cold window frame, fresh cold morning air fills my lungs as I breathe deeply. Breathing fresh air again at the small opening in the window pushes off last remnants of sleep. "Feels good to be alive."

Kneeling and resting back on my heels, I survey the scene spread out in front of me. It is amazing to comprehend it has been only six days since Shelby and I have been at the house, hunkered down with the dogs. We have so quickly fallen into a close, comfortable routine it is difficult to imagine my life not ever being as complete and satisfying as what I now enjoy. Peering out the window to the dark landscape outside I know for a certainty, before Shelby, my spirit was lost - miraculously, her arms and gentle kisses have guided me home. Shelby begins moaning, nearly talking in her sleep. She settles down and returns to her dreams while I remain quiet and aware of the sounds of early morning in the country. "Nothing out of the ordinary out there – unlike our nightmares in here," I mutter softly.

Several nights in a row I have been awakened when hearing her cry in her sleep. Not knowing what else to do, I snuggled her closer to me and that seemed to help. After awhile, sleep returned each time and morning returned soon enough. Regardless of any other distractions or concerns, Shelby's grief is never far from my mind.

Occasionally she talked some about her painful thoughts. Far too many times, Shelby simply doesn't talk about the emotional torment she carries inside her. We have begun randomly interrupting one another during the day, to give or receive a hug, sometimes a little more. It's our way of encouraging one another without talking about painful memories all the time. We love our warm embraces, and holding her close in those moments are always sweeter and more satisfying than the last.

Sliding to a sitting position under the window, my back against the wall, the cold air begins to chill the top of my head. In the stillness of the morning I reflect how it has been a good week, even without power restored. We have ventured away from home and visited Lynn and Roy, making sure everyone is doing ok, all things considered. At our house, Shelby and I have been able to run our generator a few times but it sure is loud, echoing off quiet hillsides that surround us. Using the generator, we powered up the kitchen stove, and even turned on a few lights for a short while. Having hot water and electricity again lifted our spirits immensely - although we can't use the generator often or for very long because gasoline is in short supply. Television, internet, and phones are still not working. The emergency radio also has no signal and we have no way of knowing what's going on in the outside world. Despite the lack of information, we make do just fine, taking things one day at a time while camping in the house waiting for the lights to come back on. At night, on the lookout for intruders, Shelby and I have taken turns at the picture window in the living room. Security detail is more my idea than hers and I'm thinking it's probably not needed anyway.

Other than Papé Cap the morning of the first day home, we haven't seen or heard anything since we've been here. Even the sound of our generator is the only one we've heard. Our secluded country home and the road out front have remained quiet. Although yesterday morning Shelby said she thought she saw someone on the road walking past the front gate a couple of times during the night. She said she couldn't be sure, concluding she was probably "seeing things" the way the night can play tricks on you. Nonetheless, we reviewed principles of natural night vision, as well as operating the night vision unit to assist seeing in the dark. I tucked her information into a back pocket of my mind, reading anxiety between the lines, and taking seriously what she thought she saw.

I have been awake now for several hours and finally daylight begins to break through the night. Steady rain for a third day in a row arrives with dawn. After breakfast, the dogs are fed and let out to roam the property. There's no need for Shelby or me to go outside for anything so we again settle ourselves in our makeshift living quarters in the back bedroom to pass the day and wile away long hours playing card games. Eventually the dogs are on the floor with us, curled up nearby and napping, completing a deeply satisfying feel of home. This is our family and it feels very good. Over hands of cards we share stories of our past and what we want from life in the future. These are precious moments for the both of us - endearing ourselves to one another in ways that make us feel "this" was all somehow meant to be. "Look what it took to bring us together" Shelby would remark with playful pragmatism punctuated by one of her wonderful smiles. She and I agree it feels we were meant for one another.

At about the time Shelby is ready to lay her cards down and call "Fish" on me for the umpteenth time, all three dogs are startled and stand up quickly with their ears up and eyes darting around. Instinctively I reach for my shotgun and Shelby retrieves hers. Soon we hear the noise of a car in the distance, skidding, swinging right onto the road out front. Merely hearing the car is unusual let alone the sound of its incredible rate of speed. Clearly, its engine strains for more power and whines in protest against the abuse its gears are taking at the hand of the driver. At any moment, I expect to hear the sound of a horrendous crash. Leaving Shelby at the window in our room with her loaded shotgun and Zeke by her side, Zoie and Little follow me to the window in their bedroom. The five of us look down the road to our right in time to see a black passenger car screaming down the road. Very soon, I know it's headed toward the gate.

"Get ready," I shout, raising my shotgun and aiming it out the open window in the direction of the oncoming car.

As the car approaches the front gate, the driver brakes hard, skipping tires on the wet road, grey smoke pouring from brakes locked up tight, its backend fishtailing nearly out of control. Amazingly, it doesn't spin off into the creek or crash into the hillside to the right. Instead, it makes a high-speed crashing entrance headlong into the metal gate, exploding it open with a loud crash of metal and wood post cracking, sending large splinters flying in all directions. The black BMW sedan driven by a madman flies across the top of the metal bridge spanning the creek and nearly loses its right rear tire over the edge as it crosses. At that moment, I first recognize the car and then the driver and passenger.

At the wheel is my friend Max West. His wife Mia is slumped in the passenger seat, holding a hand to one side of her head. Max has a frozen frantic look on his face and their car is beat to shit: dented, scraped and muddy up and down its sides with its back window severely cracked but not completely broken. Miraculously, Max brings the car to an abrupt, sliding, rock-spitting stop, diagonal to the garage.

Yelling, "They're friends. Don't shoot," I race out to the car, with Shelby following close and the dogs even closer. She does her best to keep the dogs back as Max and I gingerly remove Mia from the passenger seat. Slowly picking our way up the steps and into the house, with every step we take, Max reassures a nearly comatose Mia. Blinking repeatedly through a stream of tears from bloodshot and puffy eyes he says in a hoarse, gravelly voice, "We made it. We're here. You're going to be fine. We made it Mia. Hang on." We seat Mia on the sofa in the TV room as Shelby quickly locates the medical kit. Max settles in next to Mia while I corral Zoie and Little in the garage. They are a bit too interested in things right now and we can do without them getting in the way. Zeke is no trouble and lies down quietly in his spot nearby, content to watch silently everything that's going on. I stoop down and scratch his ear before I stand to one side and survey the scene.

Everyone is clustered tight together, sitting on the sofa in the TV room as Shelby, speaking softly, directs her attention to cleaning Mia's head wound. Both Max and Mia are pale and shiver uncontrollably although I do not believe it's from cold inside the house. I am puzzled and gravely concerned.

"What terror have they endured? Clearly, Mia is in a state of shock. That deep gash on the side of her head has something to do with it, that's for sure." Blood has dried in streaks down her face and matted her hair. She has a right eye nearly closed, black, blue and bloodshot. Adjusting a blanket around Mia's shoulders, Max sits even closer, continuing to comfort her, "We're safe, Sweetheart. We made it. You're ok. We're safe now."

Slowly and without saying a word, Mia lifts painful and tormented eyes, studying Shelby closely, responding to Shelby's gentle touch cleaning as best she can the dirt and dried blood from around Mia's eyes, and face. Standing back to give everyone room to breathe, I marvel at what their clothes are telling me. Each of them are wearing ragged, torn and dirty designer clothes with what surely must be a volume of dried blood down one side of Max's long sleeve dress shirt. Both of my friends quiver uncontrollably, sitting on the edge of my sofa, knees to knees, holding hands, Max's eyes darting around in his head, muttering softly, under his breath to Mia. A chunk of hair is missing from the back of Max's head. Mia has that gash and the same bed-hair look that Max is sporting. She has torn most of her fingernails back of the nail bed; many of the tips are sprinkled with bright red slivers of blood. Max has bloodstains and deep bruising around his neck and upper arms. Looks like bite marks everywhere.

As Shelby continues her work with the medical kit, I turn my attention outside in anticipation of securing the mangled front gate, hanging limp by one hook on the gatepost. I am not needed inside and repairing the gate will give me time to think. On the way to the shop to retrieve the tractor I stop by the dog pen. Zoie and Little spring free when I let them out in the yard with me. With every step, I can't stop asking, "Why hasn't power restored? Why can't I get an emergency signal? What has Max and Mia survived? What's going on out there? Is it coming our way?" On my way to and from the gate, for good measure, I drive the tractor over Papé Cap lying in his grave, out of sight, but not nearly out of mind.

"Told you to leave my dogs alone. Look who's paying attention now."

While working the tractor back and forth over the mangled gate, trying to get it bent back into workable shape, I worry about my battered and traumatized friends, disheveled and looking as mangled as their car. They have been married twenty years, true-life high school sweethearts. Mia was on the rally squad and Rose Festival Queen, and Max worked hard at being a contribution to the basketball team. After high school, they went to separate colleges. Mia comes from a family of means and as expected was enrolled in preparatory school. Her parents had designs of introducing Mia to opportunities surely she would embrace as a result of her enrollment and social status.

Max on the other hand funded his education by two part time jobs; making pizza dough at a parlor on campus, and cleaning a radio station at night, making sure prerecorded programming functioned as it should. Their love found a way. The bond Max and Mia nurtured through high school endured time, distance and convention, and while both were still in college, Max proposed marriage. Mia gleefully accepted over vehement objections from her parents. They had their difficulties as everybody does. However, they stuck together and believed in each other and here they are today, having survived something horrific I hope is not coming our way.

Riding the tractor back and forth over the mangled metal gate I chuckle out loud remembering how, on more than one occasion, Max would recall with a good deal of pride in his voice, 'We made do' like many newlyweds did 'back in those days'. Making-do for them on more than one occasion was going to a local restaurant that had a nice salad bar with all the trimmings. Their budget could not afford the salad bar but they filled a bowl with croutons and poured one of their favorite salad dressings on top. On more than one occasion, their date night consisted of good conversation, glasses of water, and a "crouton salad" for each. 'Thankfully those days are behind us,' they would conclude with a chuckle and a wink exchanged between them. That's how those two are – practical, down to earth and committed to each other. Over the years, their unshakable commitment to one another, dedication to hard work and adherence to tight budgets started paying off. Hard work in entry-level positions eventually led to other doors opening with greater responsibility, influence, and money.

Max and Mia have the depth of character to be kind and caring to others less fortunate, while enjoying the fruits of their labor garnered over a lifetime of fiscal and professional discipline. They enjoy nice things and take care of what they buy; such as their home in the hills overlooking the city and the once immaculately kept all black BMW. "All black and chrome. Reminds me of Big Biker's hog. Now that was a nice ride," I think to myself with a smile that feels good doing it. My smiles fades when I look closely again at Max's car parked sideways on my gravel drive; dented, completely muddy, with multiple troughs of bright bare metal along the top and sides. The entire car looks like a beast bigger than the car itself had attacked it.

With my mangled gate and its "Positively No Trespassing" sign now wired into a closed position and the tractor back in the barn, I shed my muddy boots outside the patio door. Returning barefoot with Zoie and Little, I join Shelby and friends gathered in the back bedroom. It's not long before I am shooing the dogs out the door. They each quickly sniff Max and Mia one more time before I am successful at herding them; including Zeke, out into the hallway. Closing the bedroom door behind me, the room is exceptionally quiet but for intermittent sounds of soft breathing or someone fumbling with their coffee cup. The room has the somber feel of a doctor's waiting room. "Anybody need anything while I'm up?" I haltingly ask the quiet threesome around me.

Shelby softly replies everyone is fine, and with her reassurance I gingerly settle on my blanket next to her while Max and Mia huddle together in a far corner.

The four of us, with our backs against the wall, holding hot cups of coffee or tea in our hands, sit on the floor in silence. Although awake, Mia hasn't uttered a word since they arrived two hours ago. She holds a cup with hands that shake uncontrollably from time to time, never making eye contact with anyone, simply sitting and sipping her tea.

After a while longer, and clearing my throat I ask as gently as possible, "Max. Are you able to tell us what happened?"

My question hangs in the air like a ghost while Max stares into his cup with eyes that look as if he is searching for words that refuse to come to mind. The room remains quiet for a long time until Max tries to speak. What comes out doesn't make sense and he tries again saying with a faltering voice, "We thought we were safe at home." He doesn't speak again for a long time.

"Yes, and" attempting to gently nudge him to open up more fully. I trade concerned glances with Shelby. She too understands we need to get Max talking. We need to know what happened and if it's headed our way.

Max suddenly comes to life, looks up with swollen eyes, clears his throat and apologizes, "We didn't bring anything CW," he says. "We left everything behind. There just wasn't time." His voice cracks and tears well in his eyes, on the verge of bursting uncontrolled. Somehow, Max fights back and maintains composure.

"I understand," I reply, without understanding but encouraging him to go on. "Don't worry about any of that. You're safe now."

"You made it," Shelby adds reassuringly, now sitting alongside Mia - holding her hand.

Max begins reciting how he was in the city, across the river at the courthouse defending a client when all the lights suddenly went dark. With electricity gone, he immediately became afraid for Mia, recalling the last he knew of Mia's whereabouts, she was working from home that day.

"After the lights went out we just sat in the dark courtroom for a minute wondering what to do next." Max continues, "After a short while there wasn't anything to do but leave. So we did."

Getting to his parked car was the easy part. Getting home was not. He recalls talking to himself on his trek home, repeating all the way, "Mia is at home. Home is Point B. Going home to Point B." It took him several hours just to work his way across the nearest bridge, then more hours through clogged downtown city streets, finally making his way up to their house in the small-gated community in the hills above the city center. It was after midnight before he was at faux iron gates shut across the entrance to their neighborhood.

"When I pulled the car to the entrance gate I instinctively went for the electric gate opener. I think I even pushed it once. I remember thinking it funny I automatically did that."

He manually opened and closed the gates and in so doing, looked up and saw for the first time the large smoky orange glow of fires reflecting on low hanging clouds above the city.

"I was nearly in a panic, worried about Mia. I had been in traffic for hours with all the time in the world to think the worst. I had no way to call her and she couldn't reach me so all I could do was sit behind the wheel, my foot on the brake, and worry. What made things worse, through my window glass I watched looting a few feet from my car."

With the gates closed behind him, he returned his car home again safe and sound. As soon as he pulled up, Mia came rushing out from the house to meet him, falling into his arms outside his car door. Holding tight to each other, kissing for a long time, smiling and giggling about being safe together, Mia too saw for the first time the glow on the clouds from fires burning throughout the city. Exchanging concerned looks, they clung to one another, finally making their way into the pitch-black interior of their spacious home. Together at last, they locked themselves behind heavy doors and double pane windows and hoped for the best. When daylight broke on the first morning, a few neighbors still left joined them in their kitchen.

"We felt a sense of security and found it useful to discuss next steps for our community behind the gates. These were good people. We had to stick together."

Gathering together each morning quickly became everyone's daily ritual, finding comfort in the company of their friends around Max and Mia's kitchen table. Everyone was doing the best they could to make the most of a tough situation without power and with dwindling resources. Each morning the skyline showed more columns of smoke from fires in the city below. On the fourth day, everyone could smell the smoke, thick and acrid. It only got worse after that.

Describing the smoke columns Max says, "They multiply at night." Despite everything, "We stayed put. We felt safe behind our gates with our neighbors. Besides, this was our home. If you can't feel safe in your own home, where else can you?"

Max goes on to describe how they made the most of the situation for close to a week, eating what they had in their cupboards and everyone sharing what little they had among new friends. This morning, as they had done each morning since the blackout, they were together with their neighbor's in the kitchen when suddenly loud shouting and profanity broke through windows and walls, coming from the direction of the cul-de-sac.

"We all jumped up and ran to the windows." Peering through living room draperies the small group of neighbors stood motionless, shoulder to shoulder, with growing fear. Hordes of outsiders rampaged through their gated neighborhood, busting windows on cars and kicking in doors on houses. They threw anything and everything they could into the street. Realizing what was descending upon them, everyone scattered.

Max and Mia went running upstairs to pack and get out of town - successful only at making it to the top of the landing when they heard their front door kicked in. Hearing the door crash open, Mia nearly screamed, but Max grabbed her just in time, covering her mouth completely, stifling the scream now only Max and Mia could hear. Sounds of heavy boots rushing in all directions paled in comparison to sounds of cracking, breaking, tearing and shredding in the rooms below them.

"The look in my wife's eyes was terror beyond description."

Max describes backing Mia against an adjacent wall off the upstairs hallway while looking around frantically for some kind of self-protection. He armed himself with his father's five-iron golf club hanging as part of a display nearby, his body shielding Mia against the wall. Waiting from their concealed space at the top of the landing, listening to the sounds of rage downstairs, Max remembered thinking how the weight of the club was heavier than what they make these days. His thought was cut short when two intruders made their way upstairs. Max met home invaders with the blade edge of the five-iron club, slamming with all his might across their foreheads followed swiftly by repeated blows to the back of their heads. Each intruder buckled and fell with muted thumps to plush beige carpet - deep red blood spilling out and mingling together with diminishing pulse beats.

"I think I killed them," Max says in a voice choked with emotion. He pauses and takes a quick sip of tea from a cup noticeably shaking in quivering hands.

The fight was on as Max and Mia battled their way down carpeted stairs, through a gauntlet of close quarter's combat that stretched through the kitchen and family room. They were beaten, kicked, scratched, and clawed from all sides, while fighting back with all they had. Mia, screaming wildly, tore away fingernails while exchanging blows with attacking home invaders while Max swung the heavy club for all it was worth. Kicking, scratching, and head butting female and male attackers alike in a fight for their lives through rooms of their once peaceful home, Max and Mia finally managed to lock themselves in the BMW they had moved to the garage a few days ago. Their attackers kicked heavy boots against the doors and side panels as a shovel was being swung against the back window. Lifting the garage door was not an option. Max yelled to Mia to hold on. Bracing herself, Max revved the car engine into the red and with tires pouring smoke, exploded the trunk of the car through the metal garage door that gouged ribbons of bare metal into black car paint. They drove away from hell unfolding in the house he and Mia had raised their children in, abandoning their house full of memories of birthdays and anniversaries and Christmas celebrations. Speeding away as fast as possible, leaving everything behind, careening nearly out of control, headlong toward the gates beyond, they nearly drove over rampaging criminals intent on stopping the car with their bodies. Max and Mia each caught fleeting glimpses of several neighbors in bathrobes on their knees, being kicked and beaten down to immaculately kept exposed aggregate driveways, devoid of cracks and oil stains of any kind in keeping with Home Owner Association rule 1.7 (c).

Mia collapsed against the passenger door as Max drove through faux iron gates. He pauses for a moment with his head bent down; gazing into a far off space beyond the room we are sitting in. They made their way to "Stanton Mountain", driving at break neck speed for close to an hour, nearly out of control at times on the wet curves down the pass road. Several times, police officers parked off to one side of the road leading into Holbrook flagged them, signaling them to stop. Max and Mia sped past, never slowing down; even though police had guns drawn and other cars and motorcycles had dutifully stopped at the side of the road.

"No one chased us and I kept going. Even if they had chased us, I wouldn't have stopped. To Hell with them." Max's voice trails off as he turns and looks at his battered wife now safe among friends at Stanton Mountain.

"I'm surprised they didn't shoot you." I give the group a quick rundown of my experience at the blockade several days ago when Big Biker, Biker Woman were gunned down on our way up the river highway toward Holbrook. The only response any of us could make was to shake our heads in disbelief, collectively asking the proverbial question, "How could it come to this?"

Looking over at Shelby I notice she is looking at me with a serious, pained expression nearly bringing tears to her eyes. She gives me a quick smile as if saying she had been thinking of seeing her family killed and how close she came to being killed herself in the pitch black shed.

Her smile is assurance to me she is safe now. While smiling back we hear a truck race down our road from the left. Shelby looks out the window and immediately backs away with terror in her wide eyes. "It's the pickup truck from the other night, the night the store was burned," she says in the same fearful and quivering voice I heard when she ran down the railroad tracks away from her two would-be killers.

Peeking over the windowsill, I see the truck race down the road from left to right followed by two other rusty, dented pickup trucks. I have seen those two before but I've not seen the one with the confederate flag. Shelby is trembling and holding tight to Mia's hands. Kneeling in front of her, gently stroking her hair and smiling, I ask if she wouldn't mind staying with Mia while Max and I look around the property. Shelby nods without saying a word and brings her shotgun close to her side.

"Good girl."

"Max, take my shotgun. It's loaded so watch out. I'll show you how to use it when we get outside." Max and I suit up against sheets of heavy rain. I sling my rifle across my shoulders and we exit the house with the dogs following us. While walking the property I tell Max how I met Shelby and why she is terrified seeing the truck speed past the house.

"I'm sorry to hear that. Shelby seems like a nice girl. I can tell she likes you a lot," Max says.

"Yes. She is a nice girl and I like her a lot too, but this isn't the time or place to be making long term plans if you know what I mean," although my heart doesn't want to believe it. Clipped wings and all, way out on the limb, my heart refuses to listen to reason. It continues its lovesick song at the top of its tiny lungs.

Max nods and I direct the focus of our conversation to how the shotgun works. "Cycle the pump like this," and I demonstrate, "to chamber a shell and eject a shell. Click the button at the back of the trigger guard to the left to fire. Click the button right for safe. The shotgun holds five shells with one in the chamber. You know how it kicks. You've shot it before. Only thing is, if you can, let them get close, the closer the better, and then pull the trigger. No need to aim down the barrel with a shotgun, especially at close range. Simply let the buckshot take care of the rest."

"Seems straight forward."

"Oh yeah Max, it's straight forward alright, but you might be thinking differently when you remember firsthand how this sucker kicks." We continue our walk, surveying the property. Scanning the hills with my range finder, after awhile I conclude the property is clear of any sign of danger. The only sounds we hear are big drops of rain falling on vegetation around us, a few birds off in the trees somewhere, and the creek babbling over rocks.

We return to the house and check on Shelby and Mia, finding them sitting quietly together, shoulder to shoulder. Our group huddles near the picture window of the living room to take advantage of the available light as I familiarize everyone with equipment, weapons, and ammunition available to us, in case we are forced to defend ourselves. I explain each one to Max and Shelby, while Mia listens from a distance outside our tight circle, with her head bent down, not saying anything.

"These are the usual shotgun shells; double 00 buckshot meaning nine lead balls coming at you at once, each equivalent to a .33 caliber bullet." I proceed to explain the other shotgun shells I had stored away. "These are rifle slugs, one 60-caliber piece of lead at a time. In addition, here in this pouch are specialty shotgun shells. I have shot only one of each. They are amazing and quite expensive."

"First up, the flechette shell that blasts 12, one inch steel darts into the target. Second, the flame-thrower shell spraying a 3000-degree flame 100 or more feet. It's called 'Dragon's Breath' and consists of zirconium particles that attach themselves to whatever they hit and do not stop burning until their fuel supply is gone. Water doesn't put it out, effectively making the shotgun a flamethrower. Impressive at night that's for sure."

"I'll bet," Max replies in a somber tone while turning a flame-thrower shell end over end in his hand, thoroughly inspecting it.

After our group is refreshed with soup for dinner and a bottle of wine shared among the four of us, darkness has settled in and it's time for bed. Shelby leads Mia, still not saying a word, to the bedroom across the hall from ours and Max follows. They all turn and stand with me in the hallway outside their door. My friction flash light I previously carried in my mouth through the dark metal pipe on my way home, with its small blue light, now washes over our faces before Max shuts the bedroom door.

"It's good to see you, Max. "

"We were lucky," he says.

Nodding my head yes I say, "Mia is going to be ok. You'll see. You'll feel better soon. After all, you made it to Stanton Mountain" smiling a weak smile he probably couldn't see. "Remember," pointing to the shotgun in his hand, "that thing is loaded. Don't start shooting until you know what you're shooting at." He smiles for the first time and assures me he'll be careful.

"Thanks, CW. Thank you and Shelby for everything." The door closes with the unfamiliar sound of my bedroom door being locked. My friends are safe in my house for the night - that's all that matters.

Shelby and I cuddle for a while in our bed but I am too restless and cannot sleep for very long, yet again. Trying as gently as possible, I successfully roll myself out and tuck the covers around her as she sleeps.

Having pulled my clothes on as I moved to the living room, I sit on a seat cushion, with a blanket covering me, to one side of the picture window with my night vision unit in my lap. My loaded AR15 is at the ready propped against the windowsill. The landscape outside is quiet and dark. I am on security detail and I feel good doing it. Zoie, her toenails clicking lightly on the laminate flooring, comes out of her room and lies down next to me with her head resting in my lap. The other two dogs are snoring in their bedroom, comfortable on their king size mattress. Zoie takes a deep breath and lets it out slowly. I smile when I feel her body relax as she contents herself to sleep for the night at my side. "Good Girl. You're my best little Zoie Girl."

CHAPTER FOURTEEN
FLASHPOINT

Thursday, October 25

Low rumblings deep in Zoie's chest nudge me awake. Hearing her low rumble again, I open my eyes fully. Zoie hasn't moved from her sleeping position, head laid on my lap, her big body curled up tight against me. My right hand goes instinctively behind her right ear and along her thick neck muscles. My fingers behind her ear tell me where I should look. Her head is resting across my lap but her eyes are open. She thinks she hears something but isn't quite ready to commit. Looking through the window toward the gate, in the direction her attention is pointing, I see what my gut tells me are two people in a low crouch on my side of the fence. Whoever these people are, they are out by the road, near the gate and making their way toward the bridge in the middle of the night. My family and friends, sleeping comfortably in their beds are at most 80-yards away from unknown men that may have guns. Aside from Zoie, I am the only one that knows they are there.

Grouped in the shadows at the corner of the bridge, those two are on my property and sneaking up to my house. They don't know for sure if anyone is home but they're sure acting like someone is. Zoie sits up next to me, ears perked up and eyes laser focused on the road. She senses evil intent and loves to protect me - I have always encouraged her to be herself. Rumblings deep within her chest come more fully now. Looking through the infrared night vision monocular I am able to confirm, two figures - one on the right of the bridge near the low evergreen shrubs, and one on the left. I am unable to identify exactly what weapons they have but pretty sure those are semi-automatic something's they are carrying. The unidentified figure on the left motions to the other to go across but the man on the right hesitates. Seems he doesn't want to. I mutter softly aloud, "You've got two choices, Prick. The bridge or cross the cold creek and get your socks wet." Zoie darts a serious look at me and then immediately toward the intruders. Without making a sound I slide the window open an inch or two along its vinyl track, steadying the barrel of my rifle on the windowsill in the open space.

Zoie is now standing next to me about to really bark, but I calm her before she gives away our position. If I can, I would like to see what's going on a little while longer. Zeke and Little sleeping in the next room aren't yet stirring and that's a good thing. "Good girl Zoie" I say quietly as I position the red dot holographic sight center mass on the dark shape at the left of the bridge giving hand signals. At this distance, I am aiming center mass at a dark blob.

"What's the protocol in situations like this?" I ask myself absently. "Does the homeowner initiate the introduction? Or, is it the other way around?" Assuming the person doing the waving is in charge of their two-man foray, I keep my aim in his direction. Not knowing the hand waving leader was beginning to stand up to cross the bridge, I shout into the darkness, as deep and authoritative as possible, "Stop! Or I'll shoot!" Zoie immediately erupts with urgent barking, each one echoing into the night. In an instant, both figures go prone on the wet ground. Their body shapes are now barely discernable within shadows that envelop them nearly completely. I am confident neither of them have a fix on my position. Because of the darkness and echo off the hillsides, my voice and the direction of Zoie's barking are hard to pinpoint. I could be in the house or out on the property. For all they know I am somewhere in the dark behind them. They do know for sure I have commanded them to stop or, "I'll shoot". That means either I'm bluffing or I am armed. They will have to find out which.

In an instant Zeke and Little join Zoie and me, and if all their whining and jostling is any indication, I am evidently not opening the window fast enough. Finally, with the window fully open, all three Great Danes repeatedly bark their commands into the darkness of the small valley Shelby and I call home, their authority reverberating off hillsides cloaked in early morning darkness. Zeke, Zoie, and Little have had their say and I shoo them away. Shelby, followed immediately by Max and Mia rush in and kneel next to me with weapons at the ready.

Looking out the window and back at me, Mia is visibly frightened and clings to Max, not saying a word. After a quick rundown of what I have seen, I ask Mia and Shelby to please move the dogs to the garage and lock them in. "Be sure the garage door to their pen is locked; and when you come back; lock the interior house door as well. Ok?"

"You got it," Shelby says and she and Mia funnel the dogs into the garage and lock them in.

Shelby and Mia are back at my side in less than a minute. Turning my full attention again to the front yard I cannot tell if anyone has moved. I scan the area with the night vision unit but can't determine for sure if anyone is out there or not.

"Max. I think it is best if he you take Mia to your bedroom. Your shotgun will be the perfect thing we need to cover the windows at the back of the house."

"You got it Cdub."

"Position yourself on the floor with the heavy footboard of the bed as protection. If anyone tries to come in, let them. Even if they break the glass, let them. Rest your shotgun on top of the footboard of the bed and put the butt firmly in your shoulder. Remember, the gun is gonna kick like a mule but don't let go. Point it at the window and fire only when they are silhouetted. That's when they'll be most vulnerable." Max doesn't seem able to concentrate.

"This is a lot of information coming at you. Are you tracking?" I ask Max with an urgent whisper.

"Yes... yes I am. Copy," Max says halting and unsure.

Talking rapidly I continue, "Keep your bedroom door open so you don't shoot me or Shelby coming down the hall. Ok?"

"Yes," he says.

"Remember Max, you have a pump-action shotgun that hold five shots. Put more shells next to you and load when you have fired four. Always keep one in the chamber ready to fire. Click the button left to fire and right for safe."

Max looks me in the eyes and repeats with more confidence in his voice, "Copy".

"Go" and Max takes his weapon down the hall with Mia closely following.

Shelby comes up close. "I don't know who they are," I whisper. "I do know they have guns. Of what type I can't be sure."

"Are we going to be ok?" Shelby asks in an urgent voice.

"Yes" encouraging her with a smile and a squeeze of her shoulder. "It would be best if you would watch my back with that hand cannon you've got. Take a position behind the sofa in the TV room with your back to the wall. You will be well concealed and can cover the patio doors and dining window from there."

"Sounds good," she says confidently, giving me a quick kiss on the cheek, and then takes a position to cover my back.

We have our bases covered and I turn my attention toward the bridge. "Perhaps they'll go away, knowing now someone is home," I find myself saying aloud. Unfortunately, they don't.

The two shapes reposition themselves. Aided by the night vision monocular, I watch quietly from my armed position at the windowsill in the living room. Neither of the two want to cross the cold creek, if I understand their hand gestures correctly. Nor do they evidently want to expose themselves on the open bridge deck. I told them I have a gun and I have ordered them to stop. I cut my thinking short and burst out shouting toward the two men about ready to assault the house, "Stop! Back up. Go Away. Now!"

Again, they stop and this time bunch together at the left of the bridge. Placing the night vision monocular to one side, I settle myself at my windowsill firing position with the rifle in my shoulder. Softening the red glow of the sight reticle, I focus my aim center of the bridge deck. Almost immediately, muzzle flashes erupt from the two figures.

Their bullets hit hard, high and low along Louisiana Pacific siding of the house. Several rifle bullets make their way in places into the interior drywall. My aim is steady and my breathing controlled as I watch the first shadowy figure peel away in a low crouching run, attempting to cross the bridge. Covering fire provided by his buddy is coming in hot and heavy. I recognize the sound of his 7.62 caliber AK-47. I would recognize that sound anywhere, let alone the one shooting into my house right now. I squeeze the trigger of my rifle four times. With bullet impact, Running Man on the bridge stumbles, and falls dead face  first to the bridge deck. Keeping my right eye closed, with the night vision to my left, the thump of my heartbeat makes steadying the monocular that much harder. Nonetheless, I am able to make out the remaining dark shape hiding in the bushes. He has stopped firing, and has gone prone again in the wet grass. I suppose he is lying there trying to decide what to do next now that his friend is dead. I know that's what I would be thinking if I were him. The command at that moment I am sincerely willing into his mind is, "Retreat, you son of a bitch." My thoughts evidently bounce off his thick skull. When I am about to yell for him to back off, he inexplicably jumps up screaming wildly as if charging a bunker in World War Two. I guess he is incensed at seeing his friend shot dead in front of him. While the second assailant runs, he fires his semi-automatic rifle, spraying bullets wildly - some striking randomly along the house front and others into the eaves. One even nicks the weather vane on the roof, spinning it with a sharp, metallic ping sound.

The guy out front quits shooting, falling hard on top of his friend, when I easily cut him down with two bullets shot into him center mass. D-Day Boy's last breath is forced out his lungs as he falls on top of his dead friend. The sound of his rifle falls into the tall grass and comes to rest. Morning sounds return. If there are other intruders outside, they know where my firing position is based on my muzzle flash. Quickly taking my weapon I whisper softly to Shelby to stay in place, "I'm moving to the back bedroom."

"Ok" she replies softly from the dark corner of the TV room.

Whispering loudly for Max to hold his fire I say, "I'm coming your way."

"Copy," he whispers and then, "Did you get 'em?"

"I think so. We'll talk later. I'm going to the bedroom across from you. I'll let you know when the coast is clear."

"Ok," Max replies.

"How's Mia?" I ask as I pass by their door into the back bedroom that will be my next firing position.

"Shaking, but ok."

"Glad to hear she is no worse. Be ready to fire."

Max adjusts his position on the floor, protected by the bed footboard, Mia tucked in behind him. The house is dark and becomes quiet. Ten minutes or more go by resting my weapon on the sill of the back bedroom window keeping watch until suddenly I catch a glimpse of movement at the far right corner of the night vision lens. I was scanning in the opposite direction and caught only a glimpse. The best I can do is trust my gut instinct. Instantly dropping into a prone position on the carpet I turn and face Max's direction, "Max" I whisper loudly. "Max... they're coming your way."

"Copy," Max replies with a resolute and deadly tone of voice.

A minute later their bedroom window is being jimmied open from outside by person or persons unknown. Gunfire out front starts up from assailants I didn't see get into position; directed toward the picture window in the living room I previously occupied - incorrectly thinking I am still there. Good thing I moved. Max and Mia hear the window latch break apart and the bedroom window slide free. Bullets hitting the front of the house punch holes through the double pane picture window glass with multiple hard, sharp spitting sounds, bullet lead embedding along interior walls, splintering parts of door and window trim. Holding my fire, I sit tight in my new position at the back bedroom window in our living quarters. In the bedroom occupied by Max and Mia, a dark shape laboriously muscles himself onto the window ledge. Max said later, as he watched; he could tell the man pointed a weapon through the window first to see if anyone would fire. When no one did, the man laid it down against the interior wall.

The dark figure outside jumps up and supports his outstretched body with both hands on the sill, arms fully extended - half of his body up and leaning in. Several days later, around the campfire, Mia said she remembered the intruder wasn't able to keep the toes of his boots from making a thumping sound against the outside of the house as the lower half of his body tried to find footing to leverage himself fully into the interior before the boys out front stopped shooting. Max's timing with the double 00 buckshot was impeccable. At a distance of eight feet, the blast from his shotgun tore a massive bloody hole in the man's chest, starting his shirt on fire. Nine lead balls explosively ejected the intruder out the window, launching his body into a sitting position on the muddy grass, his back against the ivy, his left leg dangling down into the open latrine pit nearby. From my position across the hall, I hear Max convincingly rack another shotgun shell in the chamber. He's ready to fire again.

Hearing his shotgun blast, I immediately open up with my rifle aimed where I had seen muzzle flashes coming from the other gunmen out front. I shoot all remaining twenty-four rounds of armor piercing bullets I have in the magazine, shouting through it all at the top of my lungs, "Go away! Go Away!" When I stop shouting and quit shooting, I let the empty 30 round magazine fall to the soft carpet at my feet and immediately slap in another magazine, sharply closing the bolt with firm authority - locked and loaded again. My ears are ringing and I can't see clearly because of repeated muzzle flashes in a dark bedroom. From the same window I was at this morning when I woke up suddenly and needed to suck fresh air, I marvel at our living quarters now.

When I woke up this morning and knelt at this window, life was basic, comfortable, and reassuring. It is now full of empty rifle casings and the pungent aroma of cordite and burnt gun oil. I don't know what those people want and I actually don't care. All I want is for them to go away.

Keeping my aim down my sight, I sweep the area looking for movement - seeing nothing out of place. The early morning darkness is dead quiet outside. Seems either the assailants are dead on the far side of the bridge, or they escaped. I cannot see anyone out there but into the darkness I yell, "Stop! Stop NOW!" My voice dies away but not before darkness seems pleased to echo my words back to me more times than usual off black wooded hillsides that surround us.

Waiting a while more I'm satisfied it's safe to move and I make my way to Max and tell him I think our attackers have left. I remind him to reload, and he does, shoving the shell into the shotgun tube with a convincing click. "I'm going to check on Shelby but I'll be back shortly."

"Copy."

Shelby, armed and dangerous, hears me coming down the hall and whispers from the dark corner she is sitting in, "Hey Fella. Over here." Sitting down next to her, we slide ourselves as close as we can and sit in the dark with our backs against the wall, listening to the sounds of our breathing. She is doing fine in her concealed spot.

How's Mia?" Shelby asks in a soft voice filled with concern.

"She's on the floor of their bedroom not saying a word - laying on the floor with her eyes open. I don't think she's made even one sound since she's been here."

"Give her time. I think she will be ok. There was strength in the eyes I looked into today."

"You're right. Time will tell."

Talking about not making a sound reminds me, the dogs have been awful quiet. They hate the sound of gunfire, and I imagine they are cowering together, shaking uncontrollably from all the loud noises, but unharmed in the garage. To think anything else is too painful and I avoid those thoughts altogether.

"Shelby, I think the coast is clear. I'll make sure and be back soon."

Crouching low at each window, I peer out and each time the night vision unit assures me the property is clear of movement. The four of us nevertheless stay in place for another hour, sitting quietly in the dark, intently listening for any sound while I continually scan the darkness outside the house. "Better safe than sorry" Max said. Only when daylight thankfully begins to lighten the morning sky do we feel comfortable enough to move out of our firing positions. We don't know what the attackers were after, or who they are.

My wristwatch glows 5:56 AM. Time to view the damage. With my rifle slung in a ready position across my chest, I lead Max outside, while Shelby intently follows our progress, window to window, room to room. At the corner of the house, I scan the hills beyond to try and detect movement that may indicate a sniper position.

"Max, the area looks safe to me. Let's go outside and see what those Pricks left us." Around front we find bullet-holes dot the exterior walls and a few have creased roof shingles. Nothing I can do about any of that now and we turn our attention to the two bodies on the bridge. We ponder leaving D-Day Boy and his friend out front instead of burying them.

"It would be a warning sign until the lights come back on. You know, for anyone thinking they can come up here and start trouble."

Max replies, "It could be a provocation too. Two bodies lying exposed. We don't know who they are or where they came from."

"You might be right. I'm just wondering if I need anything more than a Positively No Trespassing sign."

We mull the options and each possible implication, ultimately deciding to leave the bodies where they lay. Their deaths are a done deal. We are not exploiting them or desecrating them. "Whoever wants them can come get'm. They had just better leave as soon as they do. My 'Positively No Trespassing' sign at the front gate is still in full force and effect as far as I'm concerned."

Max nods his head in agreement. Our decision feels good to both of us and we make our way to the back of the house to Latrine Boy. Shelby continues her vigil from the bedroom window as Max and I stand over the corpse. Seeing her, I smile and give thumbs up. She smiles weakly. Latrine Boy is a blond haired kid with sad unblinking blue eyes and a dark red hole where his heart used to be. Lying there with his tongue drying out, limp at one corner of his partly open mouth, he is oblivious to hundreds of blow flies buzzing in and out of his gaping chest wound.

"We're going to have to move this guy."

"Yep," I reply, surveying the damage.

"I can't take a piss with someone watching."

We laugh at the expense of Latrine Boy - his foot in the shit. Max helps me bury the guy in a trench we dig next to Papé Cap. "They can keep each other company."

"Nice," Max says with a smile as he fires up the tractor and then makes his way to the barn after our work is done.

Somehow, Shelby sees a group coming at us from the direction of the neighbor's field. She bangs on the window and calls us to get in the house. I guess at the time we were too busy burying Max's kill to notice movement coming in where Papé Cap and friends made their first appearance a week ago. Glancing quickly over our shoulders, a heavily armed group of six to eight men is heading our way, out about 200-yards.

They have to slog through that cow pasture full of mud and thick field grass. Some of the men carrying guns hug the tree line along the hill on one side of the pasture. Others are among trees along the creek. Many in the group avoid the open ground. In the house, Max and I take up the same positions we had the night before; however, I realize we are blind on the side the attack is coming from. I don't like it and tell Shelby what I'm thinking while we sit next to each other in her concealed spot guarding the patio door. I run and grab Max's shotgun and extra shells and give the weapon and ammo to Shelby. "Use the sawed off first," I tell her quickly. "If you need more, go for the pump after that."

Hurrying back, I find Mia awake and talking, kneeling next to Max at the foot of the bed. "What can I do?" Mia asks in a weak but urgent voice.

Max and I look at each other, smile, and then turn back to Mia. Those are the first words she has spoken since they got here. "Glad to have you back Mia," I respond. "We'll give you a job. You can help Max," and she nods in agreement. Tearing into a hiding space, I bring out my other AR15, load it up, and hand it to Max. Extra magazines loaded with full metal jacket rounds are laid out next to Mia, and after a quick instruction, I leave them and run to Shelby. Along the way, I place the loaded M1 Garand battle rifle with a bandolier of 30.06 rounds in en bloc clips in the living room where I can run and reach it if I need to.

Kneeling in front of Shelby, she tells me she has everything she needs. I let her know I will be back but, "I have to get outside because we're blind in the direction those men are coming from. Watch the door and don't let anyone get in." She sends me on my way with a kiss to my cheek. Helped by Max I exit the house through their shotgun blasted bedroom window and head in the opposite direction of the assaulting force coming from the neighbor's field. Twenty yards further on I hook right and charge up the hill. I am carrying my AR15 rifle in one hand and in the other, the 30.06 bolt-action rifle with scope I picked up along the wall near the picture window.

Halfway up the sloping hill along the back of the house, I find a concealed position with a clear view of assaulting forces coming in from the neighbor's field. I haven't been spotted and jump into a depression behind a tree uprooted when it fell years ago. I have the high ground, concealment, and the element of surprise. Immediately deploying the rifle's bipod along the rim of my natural foxhole, I easily rest crosshairs of the scope on the chest of the closest approaching figure 120 yards down range. I take a breath, exhale slightly, hold and squeeze the trigger. The man drops dead. The impact of the heavy 30.06 full metal jacket bullet flips him backward into the tall grass where he disappears: "One down."

Hearing the shot, everyone in the field pauses in place; some crouching, while others hit the ground. In short order, I find a guy crouching down, probably on one knee, but not fully concealed. He's turning his head left and right trying to figure out where the shot came from.

My riflescope has excellent lens clarity, allowing me to see bullet impact to his left temple. The Greek 30.06 battle ammo I am firing jerks the man's head violently around with the impact as if he were kicked in the jaw by a mule. My punch to his skull spews blood and brain fluid through craggy fissures of skin and bone. Crags rimmed with blood-drenched hair crack apart like chunks of watermelon rind and fly away, spraying multicolored fluids in all direction. Everyone in the neighbor's field not already on their belly goes flat to the ground after my second kill. I don't have another target of opportunity and quickly start running down hill, trying desperately not to trip and fall as I gain speed. Somehow I manage to reload two 30.06 bullets in the internal magazine of the rifle without tripping and falling – a miracle in and of itself. After charging downhill from the backyard, I swing wide right to make my way along the creek bank out front in the direction of the neighbor's field.

At the underside of the metal bridge, I pause, gasping for air, slowly lifting my head up over the deck. The men are up and moving again. Peeking over the two dead bodies lying nearly one on top of the other I count five men at or very near the fence line. "Climbing the fence will slow them down a bit" I say to myself, hoping I can pick them off one at a time. The back of the dead man lying closest to me makes a good rifle rest. Quickly, I put a bullet through the neck of the man in a position to make it over the fence first. He falls backward surprised and grimacing. While swinging my aim to the next target I previously identified, suddenly a rapid succession of bullets thud into the mud, saplings, and rock inches around my position.

Bullet shrapnel hits me with driveway rock and bits of metal from the bridge deck - peppering the right side of my neck and upper arm. A sniper is firing a semi-automatic rifle from the high ground to the rear and has me nearly in his crosshairs. Propelling myself off the embankment, I land with a loud splash, feet first in the creek, half running, half wading through knee-deep water as quickly as I can - staying low along the side of the creek bank that conceals me from gunfire coming from the hill across the road. A minute later, I hear a blast from Shelby's shotgun, a pause and then another shotgun blast. Echoes of shattering plate glass reverberate back to me from the hill behind the house. A pause and two more blasts report from Shelby's position indicating she has dropped the sawed off and is working the 870 pump. Good girl. "Give'm hell Shelby."

At a protected spot down the creek, I make my way out and onto the grassy bank. Running as fast as I can, I cross open ground to the corner of the house near Max and Mia's bedroom window. Crouching low and peeking around the corner of the house I see a man at the far end, dead at the foot of the concrete steps on the back patio – a mountain of razor sharp plate glass surrounds him. Another man with a rifle, very much alive, is on the hill in the backyard fifty yards away making his way toward my original firing position. If he is successful getting into position, he'll have excellent cover to shoot into us. I hear myself say aloud, "He will be extremely difficult to root out if he gets in the there."

Dropping my 30.06 rifle to the muddy, wet ground, I steady my AR15 against the corner of the house and begin firing a volley of fire that instantaneously matches that coming from Max's AR I just now notice poking out from the open bedroom window. Through the recoil and smoke of our weapons, I see the man hit an invisible wall of lead, dancing in place among the spray of leaves and twigs that remind me of Kia gunman dancing at the crossroad. He ceases his herky-jerky dance when our rifle bullets stop hitting him. Only then does he fall to the ground dead, rolling ten feet down the sharp slope of the hill until his body comes to rest out of sight in the tall field grass.

With assistance from Max, I make my way back through the window into the house with both riles in hand. "Everybody ok?" I ask.

"Yes," they both reply.

"Excellent. Good job. Thanks for the help back there Max."

"I didn't think I could hit anything with this," he says with a smile.

"See. You never cease to amaze," smiling and then quickly making my way to Shelby, finding her shaking but otherwise composed. No one has made it into the house and no one has been able to get a shot off toward her. "You feel ok where you are?"

"Yes," she says and I tell her we have company coming in from the front.

They will likely also try around back again. I open pouches along the Army-surplus web belt containing both the flechette and flamethrower rounds, and load the 870 full of those. Shelby already loaded the sawed off with two double 00 shells. "When you raise hell with this," I say, giving her the freshly reloaded 870, "try to make sure they're outside the door; if you can. We don't want to burn the house down if we can help it." I try a goofy smile. Shelby looks nervous and doesn't smile back. I am nervous too. I leave her with a kiss on the forehead, making my way quickly to the picture window in the living room. A short time later Shelby's shotgun goes off and lights a man with 3000 degrees of burning zirconium pyrotechnic, instantly igniting his easily combustible clothing, and hair. The blast propels his flaming body backward several feet in mid air out the patio door, barbequing his eyes shut. His screams continue until flames melt his vocal chords. Falling out of sight to one side onto the wet ground, his body burns, lying face down along the back fence of the dog pen.

Max's AR begins firing methodically from the confines of the back bedroom: nothing from the front. My senses tell me I'm going to be next. Sure enough, a late model off white Toyota LUV pickup truck swerves off the road and heads toward the gate. My 10-pound M1 Garand battle rifle is in my hand, loaded with eight rounds of 30.06 caliber ammunition. I do not remember picking it up. I level the muzzle toward the lightweight pickup truck crashing through the metal gate, heading full speed toward the bridge, not slowing down for the two dead bodies clearly visible in its path. There are two people in the bed and one in the cab.

The truck is ten feet from the bridge when I lay in four well-placed rifle bullets aimed at the radiator. I shoot all remaining bullets through the windshield and driver sitting behind the wheel. Rifle recoil is hard to control, slamming into my shoulder with each squeeze of the trigger. Regardless, I keep the rifle leveled and continue firing in a methodical rhythm, bullets smashing into their intended target with devastating effect. Impacts from bullets cause the pickup to veer left over the side of the bridge, doing a header into the creek, smashing its grill into the opposite bank. The sudden, crashing stop catapults the two gunmen out of the pickup bed, into the air, each one falling out of sight to the rocky creek bank. My empty en bloc clip ejects from the M1 rifle chamber with its classic ping sound and falls to the laminate flooring. Effortlessly, I reload the Garand with another eight rounds of ammunition, and sight in on a newer model navy blue pickup coming down the road toward the house at a high rate of speed. This one has an oversized black front bumper that looks something you would ram things with in a demolition derby more so than anything I've seen on the road. The truck looks familiar but I don't know why it does. My immediate attention is drawn to a man from the Toyota having crawled out of the collision, on his belly, onto the creek bank. I fragment his head with a full metal jacket bullet. When the bullet hits him, his body immediately goes limp, his dead ass dragging his body back where it came from, out of sight to the creek below.

With a tremendous crash, an intruder kicks in the door leading into the TV room from the garage. Two blasts from Shelby's shotgun go off in response.

Thankfully, for us those were flechette shells and not the flamethrower. Twenty-four steel darts impale deep in the face, neck, and chest of a huge Lumberjack of a man carrying a sawed off shotgun in one hand and a drywall hammer in the other. Blinded by steel darts in his eyes, he stumbles and falls to the floor inside the TV room screaming and clawing at his wounds. I jump back from the picture window toward the immediate threat and shoot two 30.06 bullets at point blank range into his chest. He dies instantly.

Wheeling back around to the window, I take up my firing position again, watching as the huge steel bumper on the front of the blue pickup knocks a man over that had been running along the bridge toward the house. The body crumbles under the truck, cracking and crunching as bones fold onto themselves, stuck in the undercarriage. When the truck hits the two bodies lying on the bridge, the force tears away large chunks of red meat from D-Day Boy, nearly causing the driver to lose control of the pickup. Gut instinct had told me to hold my fire. Good thing I did. From the short distance now between my firing position and the truck with its front tires off the ground, I get a good look at the driver. My friend, Airisa Severn has arrived and in time to take out one of the bad guys all by herself. She pulls the pickup to a sliding stop parallel to the sidewalk leading to the front deck, turns off the engine and exits the cab in a smooth, fluid motion, spinning, crouching low, scanning the area for any threat - her Chinese model AK47 locked and loaded, ready for action. There are no bullets coming in and Airisa makes her move through the front door I have standing open for her.

"Good to see you Airisa," and she and I take up opposite positions at the picture window facing the bridge and road beyond.

"Good to see you. Just in time too it seems," she says.

"You got that right. Thanks," and in a loud voice toward the interior I ask if everyone is ok. Max, Mia, and Shelby all reply they are. I yell again over my shoulder, "Everyone, meet Airisa. Airisa, this is everyone." Voices from various locations within the house greet Airisa and she says hello back, still scanning her line of sight toward the road left to right, right to left. Crouching low, I individually check each firing position and find everyone in good spirits, all things considered. After an hour goes by, we all agree the immediate danger seems to have passed and regroup in the middle of the house.

With formal introductions made I find the time to be 2:20 in the afternoon. In less than four hours, it will be dark, and before that happens, we need to determine a security watch schedule, cover the windows that have been blasted, get ourselves something to eat and fortify our positions in case there is a repeat attack. Airisa asks if we know what these people want. No one does. I speculate it's because they think I have food to spare, but who really knows. "That's all speculation. I haven't asked and they've never said. If they come again I'll ask, until then," I pause for a deep breath. "Good job today. All of this is way more than I would have ever expected to happen regardless of anything I've seen before."

Shelby adds, "Let's get these guys out of here," shrugging one shoulder toward Lumberjack bleeding on the carpet in the doorway from the garage.

"You're right," and we all take off in different directions with our guns at our sides. The dogs haven't barked and they hadn't charged into the house when Lumberjack did his thing. I fear they caught a stray bullet or were killed outright before Lumberjack forced his way into the house. Thankfully I find them in a far corner of the garage, huddled together shaking wildly, tails between their legs, worried eyes fixed on me, ears drooped as low as they can go. They look how my heart feels, and the best I can do in the moment is huddle with them as close as we can possibly get and stroke their heads, rub their droopy ears, and repeat softly how proud I am of them. Shelby comes in, stands next to me, and pets their backs as well. After a few minutes, I ask if Shelby wouldn't mind filling up the dog's food and water bowls in the laundry room down the hall to the right, which she does immediately. As she takes care of filling those, I gather their blankets and pile them all on the floor of the bathroom as fluffy as I can. With all three dogs inside, I shut the door, enclosing the dogs with Shelby and me in the dark tight space. She and I sit shoulder to shoulder on the edge of the tub, bury our faces in the midst of their large heads, and let their hot, panting breath course over our faces as we rub their droopy ears - assuring them repeatedly what good dogs they are. Zoie's tail starts wagging a little and bangs against the drywall in our closed space for the few remaining moments we spend together. There's work left to do and we have to go. Shelby follows me out the door, closing it behind us.

Mia meets us on the other side of the door. Putting Shelby's hand in hers she assures me she will take care of Zeke, Zoie, and Little. Does my heart good knowing they will be in her good hands. "Thank you, that means a lot." As she passes on her way to sit with the dogs I think to myself it's good to see Mia has her color back. Shelby was right - Mia is a strong woman. Shelby and I clean away shards of broken patio glass, enough to allow us to tack a bed sheet in place over the opening and, for good measure, stack furniture inside across the opening to help act as a barrier. That's the best we can do and it's really not much. She and Max help me move Lumberjack out the door and onto the cold concrete of the garage. Pulling him by his boots and pant legs, his head thumps down hard on each concrete step until we have him cleared away from the entry. Without nails, we are unable to secure the exterior garage door he busted through to get into the house. We improvise and prop the door closed with the generator wedged against the door from inside. After Max and I stack nightstands against the opening of their window, we have done all we can in the house. Congregating around Airisa at the picture window, still keeping watch toward the front of the property, I ask, "What do you think about you and me taking our trucks and parking them end to end on the bridge as a barrier against anyone coming in with a vehicle."

"I like it." Airisa replies.

Max and Shelby stand watch out front as Airisa and I drag the two bodies to opposite sides out of the way and position her pickup truck with its steel front bumper halfway down the length of the bridge. We set the truck in gear, engage its parking brake and start bringing over rock to put under the wheels. In the process I notice, wedged in places in the undercarriage of her truck, body parts and clothing belonging to Origami Boy. She bends down and does a quick inspection. "That's all yours Airisa. You're gonna have a heck of a time cleaning that up."

She chuckles and smiles, "Shut up."

With my truck grill pressed as tight as I can get it against the back bumper of Airisa's pickup, my truck in gear and the parking brake set as well, Airisa grabs gear from her pickup bed and we head to the house. It isn't until then I noticed what looks to be a penis with its pair of shriveled balls skewered to her radio antenna. A thought to ask her what that's about comes and quickly goes, having more pressing matters demanding my attention - mainly arranging security detail, general clean up, and dinner, all before nightfall. We are all emotionally if not physically drained. We need food and rest in a bad way. Shelby puts her hand in mine as we walk together to the house and I squeeze her hand lightly, noticing again how our hands seem to be made for the other. Walking hand in hand I walk taller somehow, more confident, and strong with feelings that electrify me, feelings I have not felt for a very long time.

CHAPTER FIFTEEN
OFFICER JOHNSON

We have done all we can to secure the house and defeat any run across the bridge. Back in the house, our group reconvenes to confirm our security watch schedule: two-hour shifts starting at sundown. I'll take the first watch. I set out energy drinks if anyone wants it for their shift. Our group settles in, inspecting and cleaning weapons as Mia puts water on to boil for top ramen soup cups and instant oatmeal. As Shelby cleans and dresses my shrapnel wounds, I decide Airisa is right, and if the opportunity presents itself, I am going to ask what these people want. For now, we settle back and have a good meal. While we eat dinner, huddled together in our makeshift living space, Airisa describes how she barely escaped the city to "Stanton Mountain".

Airisa has been a server at the City Grill for five years and makes good money doing it: due in large part to the fact she is a hard worker and energetic. Being attractive doesn't hurt which also lends itself well to her hot pursuit of a modeling career. In order to help make ends meet and have a little money left over for fun, she holds down a second part time job, the one she finished before clocking in for her shift at the Grill. To say she is extremely busy is an understatement.

On the afternoon of the blackout, she had clocked in moments before the lights went out. When station management told everyone to evacuate the building, she dutifully obeyed but couldn't help stop thinking of how much money she was losing because of the forced night off and the very real impact it may have on her ability to pay house rent due at the end of the month. Along with everyone else in the building, she dutifully made her way down thirty flights of stairs lit by emergency lights, to the parking structure in the basement garage. She jumped in her truck, presuming a normal 15-minute drive home – a drive that ultimately took three hours through traffic snarls and the first signs of looting.

Finally home, she parked and locked her truck in the alleyway garage, and made her way to the house hoping to find her roommates. Unfortunately, the place was uncharacteristically empty and quite dark. After a considerable amount of waiting and twiddling her thumbs, she decided it would be a good idea to pack her things to get out of town in case, "for some reason", she needed to leave in a hurry.

Listening to her instincts, she grabbed a flashlight and stuffed a gym bag with extra clothing and a toothbrush, and headed to her pickup truck, along the way retrieving her AK47 from a hall closet and the Army tote bag containing ammo and magazines. During the process of packing her truck, she saw fires lighting up the sky from the city center. Within two hours, fires had spread North and West of her house only six to eight blocks away. The main road down the block was clogged with cars and droves of people walking away from the fires; everyone seemingly in a panic. Airisa isn't prone to panic. She tossed the bags in the truck and headed back to the house with the loaded AK47, taking refuge in the darkness of her bedroom, watching light of the burning city reflect on her ceiling through her locked windows. Bringing the AK47 rifle closer into her lap, she sat on the bed with her back settled against one corner of the wall, knees to her chest and her favorite beat up pair of ladies Danner boots laced up snug. Feeling the weight of the rifle in her lap made her feel glad to have the self protection, never imagining her rifle might come in handy for something more than taking down a deer. She learned about the AK from a favorite Uncle of hers. He had served several combat tours in Vietnam and raved about how tough it was; basic, compact, fool proof and hit with a punch that made it ideal for deer hunting. On her eighteenth birthday, he gave her the AK he had been carrying. It became her prized, workable, possession ever since. With nothing left to do in the dark house, she let her head fall between her knees, fitfully in and out of sleep.

When daylight finally arrived, she had aches and pains up and down her back and neck from sleeping in such an awkward position. Stretching, trying to work out the cramps, she assessed her options. Although her roommates hadn't returned and there was nothing to do and little to eat, she nevertheless decided to stay put and wait a while longer. Airisa was confident they would arrive soon; and when they do they'll buy a bottle of wine and all have a good laugh about the madness, close but not too close to home. Airisa is a self-sufficient, independent thinker, and true to form, she believed she would be ok. "The lights will come back on any time now." With not much food in the house, she nevertheless made do: eating dry cereal out of the box, peanut butter from the jar with a spoon, and raw tuna from a can accompanied by half stale Wheat Thin crackers until those were also gone. Drinking water came from the water heater tank and she sucked on ice from a warming freezer compartment, several times opening the darkened refrigerator in hopes of finding the last warm beer she drank the first day had miraculously reappeared. More days of boring misery passed, dozing much of the time, always cradling her loaded rifle. Finally, she had enough of a cold, dark, lonely house and decided to head out to "Cdub's" place. "Staying put is stupid."

In preparation for leaving, she wrote a note for her roommates and taped it to the refrigerator door telling them she's ok and has gone to "Cdub's for a while. I'll be back soon. Don't wait up." She raided cupboards of what paltry edible food was left and put it in a plastic shopping bag along with her lavender scented hand lotion.

Before putting the travel size perfume spray into the bag, she sprayed her neck and wrists, and then threw eyeliner in the bag for good measure. Everything else she thought she might need was already in the truck in the other two tote bags from the night she first arrived home. In no time, she was done packing and stood for a moment contemplating contents of a nearly empty bag. It was better than nothing. "It wouldn't be right to show up empty handed," she said. Airisa left through the back door, saying in a loud voice over her shoulder as she went, "Ta Ta, I'm leaving," and while chuckling to herself, she shut and locked the door behind her.

The alleyway garage that housed Airisa's full size GMC pickup truck is especially tight given the custom-made steel bumper she had installed on the front. She often said she is, "going to get a killer winch for that thing someday." Squeezing herself through the tight space she slid herself into the driver seat, positioned the loaded AK in the front passenger seat and set down the small bag of miscellaneous items. She then backed the truck out halfway into the alley to give her access to the dusty kitchen cupboards along the front wall of the garage. Running down the mental list of camping gear she wanted to bring, she thinks she hadn't unpacked the camp stove and sleeping bag from her last camping trip. Those should still be in the truck bed, but she'll double check the cupboards anyway. While she is at it, she'll grab the rolled up ground pad she knows is in one of the lower cupboards.

Her truck headlights illuminated the interior of the garage and shone deep into every corner of the cupboard where she is wedged when a short blast from a police siren announced she had company. Exiting the cupboard with a sleeping bag in one hand and the camp stove in the other, she squeezed her compact 5'5" frame between the truck and the garage door and set both items down in the pickup bed on her way toward the police car blocked by her truck. With a fake smile taped to her face, usually reserved for boorish customers, she approached the driver side of the police car while mumbling under her breath, "Not you again." In a singsong fashion, not convincing enough to be sincere but not enough to be offensive, she said aloud "Hello Officer. Is there something wrong?"

"Ma-am, I'm going to have to ask you to remove your vehicle from the alley. We're in a state of emergency, and emergency vehicles like mine have the right of way." He is trying to be funny, but they both knew he wasn't. The immaculately clean and pressed police officer smiled and ran his eyes up and down Airisa's taut athletic body, studying her olive skin, finally returning his gaze to her piercing black eyes. "Yummy. What's that sexy perfume you're wearing?"

Airisa described Officer Johnson as a 32-year-old 6 foot 1 inch muscular police officer with thinning brown hair and pale eyes that remind her of light blue marbles. Her rented house is in his patrol district, affording him frequent opportunity to flirt suggestively with Airisa from the first day she began renting the place two years ago.

She has played nice each time, never flirty, always courteous but with a strong undertone, "Look Officer, I respect cops but there is no way in hell you and I will ever hook up." It is a message he didn't take to heart, although it was delivered consistently at every encounter. Perhaps he had completely ignored her message, or he's stupid, or perhaps he believed Airisa was playing hard to get. Regardless, there he was, impeding her progress from getting out of dodge. "Damn it," she thinks to herself, "If I had been ten minutes sooner I would have been out of here by now."

Rolling her eyes, and without answering his question about the perfume she was wearing, she remarked, "I need to get one more thing from the garage if that's ok with you?" and made her move into the garage and toward the front of her vehicle without waiting for his response. She bent down, reached in a far corner of the lower set of cupboards, and came out with the inflatable ground pad she uses when deer hunting. She stood up, turned around and ran smack into Officer Johnson's immaculately pressed light blue uniform shirt. She was immediately startled and concerned. He had never invaded her personal space before and she never heard him come in. In a split second, he grabbed both her shoulders and menacingly bent his towering muscular body slightly toward her face, "Young Lady you've been a smart ass way too long. Who do you think you are? I'm a nice guy! I've let slide all your smart-ass remarks, thinking you'll come around one day. Oh no, not you. You just keep being a God damn Bitch."

With a menacing stare radiating a fierce passion in his eyes, Officer Johnson was no longer friendly. Airisa dropped the rolled up ground pad she had been holding. She started to answer the Officer's question but choked it off in her throat, thinking it was best to shut up. A momentary silence passed as they stared into each other's eyes. That's when Officer Johnson tried forcibly kissing Airisa Severn - wrong thing to do. Revolted, she turned her head, squirming, trying to break free. There was no breaking free from him. His grip was so tight; her shoulders would remain bruised and hurting for a week and a half. Her involuntary reaction sent Officer Johnson over the edge. He spun her around, grabbed a hand full of her black hair, and threw her headlong into the counter top of the old kitchen cupboards, using a physical force technique he had perfected over the years manhandling countless criminals as a trained lawman. Airisa stumbled and hit the counter top hard with her hips and arms, doing her very best not to be injured by the assault. Officer Johnson stood his ground, nervously laughing.

"I'm darn lucky I didn't crack my head wide open on the overhead cabinets," she says to our little group huddled together not saying a word and hardly breathing.

She continues by telling us how he picked her up around her waist and threw her down to the garage floor to the pile of newspapers and magazines loosely tied in bundles waiting for recycle day next Tuesday. In her position on the floor, Airisa turned and tried to kick him hard in the groin with her right boot.

Trained in hand-to-hand combat, Officer Johnson anticipated her move in plenty of time for the kick to hit high on his left thigh without much force. Her move simply angered him and he responded by reaching down and grabbing a handful of sweatshirt, lifting her up and slapping her hard across her face; hard enough to make Airisa see stars. At the time, she wondered if she would ever get her wits back.

He let her fall limp to the newspapers and magazines and took a moment to savor the feeling of power his domination was having on him. Unbuckling his black leather utility belt, it fell to the garage floor at his feet. Its jangle of keys, chrome Peerless brand handcuffs, black plastic canister of pepper spray, and Glock 9mm handgun he affectionately called 'Suzie' hit the garage floor behind him. Edging the belt away behind him with a sweep of a black boot, he picked her up and slapped Airisa even harder than before, letting her fall to her knees, dazed and disoriented. He laughed powerfully as he stood over her, while unzipping his uniform pants, opening them from around his waist to fall free over his boot tops. He is in the mood to take what has always been denied him and no one is there to stop him. Not then. Not ever again. Airisa felt her body lifted from the floor and aggressively forced face down, bent over at the waist on the dusty counter top of those old kitchen cupboards in her garage at the back alley of her rented house. Her dazed and disoriented mind registered Officer Johnson's strong, nervous, grabbing hands forcing her tight jeans down from around her hips. Her naked thighs exposed to the chill morning air awakened inside her a sense of survival rage she never knew slumbered there.

Officer Johnson pushed one hand down on her strong back, keeping her bent down on the counter top, forcing her sweatshirt up her back with his other hand, becoming even more aroused by the full length tattoo on her back he never suspected was there.

"You're a God damn slut all right. I always knew you were."

While his right hand worked a flaccid penis pressed against her butt, trying to work up the erection he was fearful he would not accomplish when he wanted it most, her rage caused her to do something quite surprising in that moment. In a calm husky voice, that at the time sounded to her as if coming from someone else, she moaned alluringly and asked him if she could help.

"All you ever had to do was ask, Big Guy," she said, in a cooing tone of voice, while ever so slightly rotating her body to face an Officer Johnson possessed by an all-consuming lust for athletic, olive skin, raven haired, Airisa Severn.

As she slid down to her knees between his legs, he furiously stroked his limp organ, feeling himself on the verge of a monster erection, altogether elusive and frustrating. His wild, staring eyes followed the steady progress of her mouth down between his legs, nearly fainting when Airisa looked up at him with dark, sultry eyes, running the tip of her tongue slowly along her full lips. Releasing the death grip around his penis, he leaned over her, spreading his legs wide apart - resting his upper body weight with both hands along the dirty counter top he had thrown her against moments before.

He is a controlling, all-powerful badass cop, about to cum harder than any fantasy he had ever had while masturbating in his patrol car in the alley outside Airisa's rented house.

Driven nearly insane with lust, his body shuddered repeatedly seeing her on her knees in submission in front of him, feeling her hot breath millimeters away from his limp organ hanging free between his legs in the morning air, her lips full and seductive, excruciatingly close. She cradled his balls lightly in her finger tips and then pulled down sharply, a move that took his breath away, transporting him to sexual heights he was sure he would never return. Her touch rocked his head back and he clinched his eyes shut: Officer Johnson's wet dream was about to come true at last. "Oh Yes. Give it to me Slut," he moaned on the precipice of a sexual release he has no imagination sufficient to create.

Officer Johnson inhaled fully with the pinprick, eyes clinched tight, mouth open, head rocked back, bracing for his ecstasy the moment Airisa's sexy mouth takes his monster cock down her throat - massaging his balls with her finger tips the way his slut always liked to do it just for him. In that moment, his man-hood pulled away easily in the grip of Airisa's left hand as the surgical steel knife blade she had taken from her bra strap sliced through his buttery tissue without resistance. In the split second before pain beyond description set in and life ending blood loss took hold, he straightened from his bent position and looked down at Airisa - beads of sweat forming above the quizzical look on his face, as if saying, "Is it over? I haven't cum yet."

Airisa describes how she rose up from her position between his legs, and while doing so, for good measure, flicked the surgical steel blade deep along the inner fold at the back of Officer Johnson's naked right knee - a move that gleefully opened his popliteal artery - releasing volumes of hot blood. Horny Officer Johnson dropped immediately to his knees, eye level to his severed genitalia held in Airisa's quite bloody left hand. With hardened, piercing eyes she watched Officer Johnson become painfully aware of what just happened to him.

Pain for would-be rapist Officer Johnson arrived as a tsunami of fire from thousands of nerve endings exposed to trauma and cold air; overwhelming, all consuming, engulfing flame coursed through his body, causing him to vomit his breakfast down the front of his neatly pressed light blue uniform shirt. He collapsed sideways in a fetal position clutching with all his might his castrated stub, his body writhing in unending, unspeakable pain amongst strewn piles of newspapers and magazines on the garage floor. As Officer Johnson lay on the floor screaming incoherently, crying like a little boy, blowing snot bubbles out his nose, the only sound Airisa heard was adrenaline pounding in her ears from her wildly beating heart. She pulled her jeans back up around her hips, stepped over Officer Johnson, picked up her ground pad and, at the passenger side of her truck, skewered his genitals to the radio antenna. Sliding easily into the driver seat of her warm and waiting pickup truck, she shifted gears hard into reverse and repeatedly struck the police car until her truck was free to turn and make her way out of town.

Numb to it all, she drove out of the city, hardly noticing entire neighborhoods in flames and people looting whatever they were inclined to loot. At one point, she caught a good look in her driver side mirror of the building where the City Grill is, flames ringing the top. The entire thing was on fire. If Airisa could have thought of it, she would have sent a prayer heavenward for her friends wherever they might be. However, the best she could do was drive out of the city with a mind on autopilot, not waking from the trauma induced fog until her truck turned onto my road and she heard volumes of gunfire surrounding my place. Coming to her senses, she increased her speed and made the careening turn through the gate and over the bridge, mowing down Origami Boy in the process.

When Airisa is finished describing her ordeal, no one moves. Everyone sits in silence on the floor not wanting to look at the tears streaming down Airisa's face - tears she has been shedding for most of the telling of her story of survival and escape. Mia and Shelby have been crying too.

We sit in silence for a while longer until Airisa blows her nose, wipes tears from her eyes, looks at each of us and says, "But it's all good now, right?"

"Yes. Yes it is," we all meekly mumble in response with more hope in our voices than perhaps real conviction. I lean over and hug her and she hugs me back. "You are one special girl," I whisper as I look into her tearful eyes.

"Shut up. You're gonna make me cry," she replies with a short chuckle, a soft smile and more tears welling up in her eyes. She does her best to quickly wipe them away.

"By the way, what's that perfume you're wearing? I noticed it when you rolled in."

"Covet by Sarah Jessica Parker. $69.99 but I got it at the clearance price," she says, smiling with a look of pride having been smart with her money.

"Smells nice," I say and looking to the group I continue, "I have first watch. Are you guys ok cleaning up and finding a comfortable spot for the night?"

"Sure thing, no problem," and we break loose from our tight conversation and begin settling in for the night. I set the timer on my watch for two hours, position myself at the picture window, and begin my security watch, looking out the window in the living room toward the bridge and road. My loaded AR15 rifle is close by. Everyone settles in for the night and the house is quieting down. The dogs have been curled up in their sanctuary and have not come out although the shooting stopped hours ago. I don't blame them. I would hide too if I could. Just at that moment, I hear Shelby and Airisa in the back bedroom. I imagine Shelby is holding tight to Airisa and Airisa to Shelby, sobbing into each other's shoulders. If anyone can relate to the horror they have each survived, those two can.

In a few minutes, Shelby makes her way softly down the hallway to me while wiping remaining tears from her eyes. She lies down and settles herself close to my side with her head on my lap and my arm across her shoulder.

"Cdub," she says with a soft whisper in the dark before falling asleep.

"Yes Shelby."

"I love you."

My heart leaps and I can do nothing but let it prance. It has become a young colt on a beautiful summer day. My heart is unrestrainable, joyously celebrating all that life offers. Shelby presses against me even closer than before and falls asleep in my lap as I hold her close. Two hours come and go, and I take her security watch as well. I am wide-awake and she needs rest more than I do. While everyone sleeps, I scan the blackness outside with my night vision device. Everywhere I look the property is all clear. Keeping my eyes focused on the darkness outside, I stroke her sandy blond hair and allow my heart a response that only I can hear, "Shelby, I love you too."

CHAPTER SIXTEEN
KX79L Mobile

"Power Station A5 KX79L mobile transmitting on 62.3 kHz to KX53L mobile at Power Station L25. Are you there Bill? Over."

"KX53L mobile to KX79L mobile. I hear you Tom. Good to hear your voice. Over"

"Bill, Everything on your end ready to roll? Over."

"Ready and waiting. We have the team assembled. What do you need? Over."

"KX53L mobile, Power Station A5 needs one fully operational EMS server and one SIEMENS generator and all the spare parts you can send. Can you handle that? Over."

"Shouldn't be a problem. We'll load them up and head your way. ETA your location 8 hours. Tom, we are factoring in time it may take us to reroute ourselves if we run into trouble out there. Likely, that will be the case all things considered. Over."

"Bill, I understand. You guys be safe. Hearing help is on the way is wonderful news. We've been waiting a long time to hear a friendly voice. I'll let our guys know the good news. They will be ecstatic. In the mean time, we'll keep working the debugging protocols. Maybe we'll get lucky. Nothing has worked so far though. We are dead in the water here. Over."

"KX79L mobile, do you know what's been going on out there since the cascade took everyone off line? Over."

"We know some and what we've heard is pretty ugly, terrible stuff. Bits of information we have received indicate this is a much bigger event than '03. Nothing we can do about that. Right now, our job is to stay focused and get power stabilized. I've been tracking radio transmissions from unaffected geographies reporting power has begun stabilizing within the blackout sector with limited success thus far. Reports estimate 20 to 30% grid complete across all affected areas. Everyone has a long way to go. We haven't been anything close to successful here so we have to stay on the job until our area is stabilized, reconnected and powered up.

With equipment you're bringing and our coordinated efforts, I am confident we can bring our two stations and then our sector on line within the next twenty-four hours after the equipment is installed, tested, and operational. I should say I am hopeful, as long as nothing else catastrophic happens. Over."

"KX79L mobile, You say, 'Ugly!' I'd say that's an understatement Tom. You've been out there. You know what's going on. They are killing each other, ransacking power stations, even burning some to the ground. We're sitting ducks with no way to defend ourselves. Cops aren't even responding. I've heard reports that cops and National Guard troops are shooting first and asking question later! Damn it, Tom. The world is coming to an end!"

"KX53L, hang in there Buddy! We have work to do. The only way out of this mess is to stay focused. We need this grid back on line and some God damn power flowing! You with me Bill? Over."

"KX79L mobile, sorry. I'm with you Tom. It's just… Just… Never mind. We're on it. Looks like our region is the last holdout. Have you heard entire power station teams being killed? There's no making sense of that Tom. Who in their right mind would want to keep everyone in the dark ages? Over."

"KX53L mobile, yes I've heard that too and on my way through town I've seen some horrible things. I'm damn lucky to be back at A5. It's unbelievable but I've even seen people partying in the streets while the city burned, and it looked to me as if everybody in the whole city was looting, burning something, or killing somebody. I don't understand any of it either. You're right; it doesn't make any sense, but with you guys at your station and us here, we are safe and sound. Snug as a bug. Thank God. We need that server, the generator, and the spare parts you have. Get'm here as quick as you can. Ok Bill? When your crew arrives, I will ring you and we'll coordinate the restart protocol and get us out of the dark ages. Over."

"KX79L mobile. You got it Tom. Who would have thought having a job like this I would be wishing for some way of defending myself. Regardless of anything else, we're going out there into the mess and we will get to you. You are not alone. We'll do the best we can and we'll see you when we see you."

"Bill?"

"Yes, Tom?"

"We'll keep good thoughts going your way and we'll see you soon. Just hang in there with me. Everything is going to be ok."

"Roger that. Thank you. KX53L mobile signing off."

"KX79L mobile signing off."

CHAPTER SEVENTEEN
MY BROTHER'S KEEPER

Wednesday, November 7

It's been thirteen days since the first full scale attack on the house. Skies since then have been drizzling cold rain for several days in a row helping wash blood away and I'm praying for snow this winter that will blanket all the ugliness and start purifying things. After we were attacked, we kept the security detail to make sure we weren't letting our guard down before it's truly safe to do so. There were times, when the weather wasn't too terribly nasty, I suited up and spent hours in the dark outside, hunkered down along a likely route of attack if someone was going to sneak up on us in the night - securing a spot at the far meadow and other times along the ridgeline behind the house. Relying on my Army training, I surprised myself that I was able to endure long hours in the wet and cold. Each time Shelby would stay with the others in the house, but she was always the one on the walkie-talkie set answering me when I would check in, every hour on the hour.

Before the set could be put into operation, it had to be powered up. I couldn't figure out how to make that happen without firing up the generator, and with our gasoline ration running low, it would be overkill for such a small thing. We all agreed having two-way communication is critical for any of us venturing outside, especially at night. Mia surprised us all, including Max, with a tid-bit of knowledge from high school electronics class. Her rudimentary knowledge on the subject was exactly what we needed to rig up a connection from the emergency crank radio to the walkie-talkie power source. It isn't too bad with everyone pitching in to get the set recharged except the constant whirring sound of the crank gets irritating after awhile. Everyone is grateful for the technology though, especially Shelby and me.

Seems everything has calmed down; however, the mystery remains why we were attacked in the first place. As days pass, we have settled into a comfortable routine once again. Most hours of the day and into the early evening hours our small party of five plus Zeke, Zoie, and Little, huddles in the makeshift living space Shelby and I first set up when we arrived home. We have rationed our food stores, and our efforts are working ok for now, although there's hardly any gasoline left to fire up the generator. It has been wonderful being able to use it several times, even though each time only long enough to get hot water for each of us to take a quick lukewarm shower. Lukewarm or not, the infrequent shower lifted our spirits and sure beat using wet wipes.

For a short while, sharp edges of our routine have been softened by pulling a cork from a small supply of what was at the time a cheap $2.99 Australian Shiraz purchased a year ago from the discount grocery store. Those bottles are now our delicious luxury. On rare occasions between fronts of rain rolling through, we've all bundled up, braved the elements, and taken a couple bottles down to the fire pit in the meadow that borders the creek; that same meadow where in the summer before the blackout the dogs and I lay in the sun for a nap after playing all day. After gathering dry wood from the  woodshed, I am able to light the pile easily using a 15-minute road flare. Standing around the glorious bonfire this time, even as the sky misted on us, with our weapons locked and loaded at our sides, we thoroughly enjoyed our family and our bottles of Shiraz. Because of the circumstances that have thrown us together, we have come to know one another more deeply than we otherwise would.

During one session around the bonfire, we decided to reveal one quirky thing about our personalities that none of us knows, an exercise that is sure to be most difficult for Max and Mia. However, they even surprise each other with a morsel of information buried deep, but nothing earth shattering either. After all, it's all in fun in the strictest sense of the word and so, I start.

"I put black electrical tape over every logo in my house after I've bought the item, such as the TV, the stereo, and even the microwave oven and espresso machine." I explain it's because I don't want the thing marketing itself to me on a subliminal level each time I look at it. "I know what I have and why I bought it. It did its job the first time." One by one, with the roaring fire in the middle, we pass the bottles and peel back the curtain to reveal little bits of ourselves.

Shelby is next and says, "I never eat anything red like jelly-belly candy or licorice. I even pick out red colored fruit loops." We all laugh with her and ask why. "It's because when I was a kid, maybe eight years old, I got sick one time when I ate a red jelly bean when I wasn't supposed to." She has the group intrigued and we listen intently. "The Sunday school teacher gave each kid one jelly bean as a treat when we left the class one Sunday morning, but we were told not to eat it until we got home. Well, I didn't wait. During church, I popped it in my mouth and ate it, knowing full well I shouldn't, and by the time church was over, I was very sick. I mean, bad. I missed a week of school because I ate that red jellybean. Maybe God was punishing me for disobeying a direct order. Whatever it was, 'red' colored stuff never tasted any good after that."

We are all chuckling and I reply, "God works in mysterious ways."

It is Airisa's turn and she laughingly tries to dodge and pass the bottle to Max instead. Of course, we are having too much fun to let her pass. She couldn't do that and had to play along.

Airisa laughed her husky laugh and told us how she believes she doesn't think she will ever find Mr. Right. Now that's a kind of opening line that got all our attention and she knew it and stood there letting the pregnant pause linger a moment longer as she smiled and drank slow, big gulps from the wine bottle. "Well," she said starting again, "Guys like girls that are prim and proper, who cook, and clean house and keep everything in order and I'm not that way. I am much more practical and nothing like a little Miss Susie Homemaker. For example, I see no need to participate in the endless chore of folding and putting away each and every item of clothing."

Everyone is laughing and having a good time, and Max asks Airisa, "So, you don't believe in washing clothes? That's pretty gross if you ask me."

She quickly retorts, "Butthead! I didn't say that. I wash everything; I just don't fold socks, bras, and undies. Everything else, yeah, sure. I get that. What I don't get is the obsession with folding all those damn little pieces and therefore, I don't do it." Airisa takes a few more swallows from the bottle before passing it left to Max.

Shelby is grinning with a big smile that lights up her face and asks, "So, what do you do with them?"

"After I wash them," Airisa says, pausing, turning and smiling while staring at Max, causing Max to laugh, "I dump them all in a cardboard box on top of the dryer. I pick through the box as I need something.

After all, don't you all pick through the stuff you have folded and put away? So, why bother going through all the hassle in the first place?"

Everyone around the bonfire ponders Airisa's pragmatism and turns our attention to Max. "Ok Max. Tell us something Mia doesn't even know," I ask prodding him to dig deep.

Mia turns to Max with a big grin on her face and says, "Yeah. Tell me something I don't even know."

Our tight group is enjoying our outing at the bonfire and the camaraderie contained in our collective laughter as we watch the comfortable exchange between Max and Mia.

He thinks for a minute or two while sipping Shiraz and says, "Ok. I've got something. When I was in college, I believe it was my third-year; we had a class assignment from one of the professors who wanted to familiarize us with the process of doctoral thesis writing, for any of us with designs for a PhD.

Mia pipes up, "Oh this is good. I haven't heard this before."

Looking at Mia, Max continues, "See. I am still a man of mystery after all these years. Well, I was thinking long and hard about the class assignment the professor gave us, and for the life of me couldn't come up with anything intriguing enough to write about. Until that is, one night Mia and I were drying our clothes at the laundromat and I found myself staring at the clothes in the dryer tumbling round and round.

Watching those clothes, I remembered when I was a kid my brother and I would stand and watch clothes tumble in the dryer at the laundromat my Mom took us to. My parents didn't have a washer and dryer of their own for quite some time, so we used to go with Mom every Thursday evening. Thursday was washday. Friday was payday and grocery night. Saturday was bath night for my brother and me.

"And…," injects Mia, politely prodding Max.

"And, as I watched our clothes tumbling in the dryer, I recalled even as a kid I wondered if there ever was a time in the history of tumble drying that clothes had ever come out folded, even once simply from the tumbling process. Think about it, surely there could be at least one time it happened, or could happen given the number of times people dry their clothes."

Everyone in the group is laughing heartily. I think I have tears in my eyes because of it but can't really tell because of the mist in the air. Mia laughs more so than anyone, especially at the rather serious look on Max's face, indicating to us all it was a theory worth investigating further and one he still believes could actually happen.

Brushing off our good-natured skepticism, "And so, I did my research and wrote my paper, concluding it was a mathematical possibility but not anything I personally experienced or heard of occurring. I don't remember what reaction the professor had when I turned my paper in."

Mia turns and lightly punches his left shoulder and says light heartedly, "So that's why you suddenly started doing all the laundry! I never said anything at the time because I didn't want to jinx it. I thought your Mom had a talk with you."

Max and Mia hug and he turns to the group and replies, with a proud smile, "I got an A on that paper," and Mia replies, "And I loved the free time too." They turn and exchange a peck on the lips.

It's time for Mia to tell us a little quirky thing about her that Max doesn't know. She turns her face slightly to him and looks up with a mysterious and mischievous, albeit playful look in her eyes.

"In the early days, before we had kids, we had a dog named Harley. He was our first, a yellow lab puppy and a very good dog. While Max would be at his job as a new Deputy DA, I would stay home with Harley. For being a puppy, he sure was a fussy eater. So, to help him get the idea of eating I used to taste his food before feeding it to him."

"Yuck," Shelby and Airisa say - standing amongst the group in the misty, drizzle of the early evening; warmed by our companionship and the bonfire, and the bottles of wine shared between us. I practically spit my wine out laughing so hard and that makes everyone else laugh even harder, this time at me.

Mia continues, "I never took whole bites," lightheartedly defending herself. "Some of it actually did taste as advertised. Well, not half bad that is. Harley seemed to appreciate what I was doing for him, and took to eating his food, as a healthy little puppy should. Just wish he had been a bit more restrained as he got older. He got to be a fatty with a vacuum mouth."

Max replied, "You were practicing for when we had kids," showing solidarity with Mia.

"Yes. Exactly."

With laughter all around, and full hearts and light heads, we finish the wine and return to the comfort of a dark house, and let the fire die down on its own in the fire pit in the rain outside.

Those were good times around the bonfire, and the last time we did that was three days ago. Since then, we've spent our time indoors out of the elements, napping, playing cards, and talking. Thankfully, our spirits are ok, our health is good, and our little family gets along well with one another. Mia's head wound is healing nicely and she is back to her old self. The shrapnel wounds on my neck and shoulder are nearly gone as are the scratches and bite marks Max suffered.

Airisa's bruised shoulders remain intensely black and blue, and when she raises her arms over her head, she is reminded of how painful they are. We jokingly tell her not to do that and she responds each time with an affectionate, "Butthead" retort, and we all have a good laugh. Shelby is my constant companion, at my side wherever I go, even sleeping next to me on the floor each time it's my turn for security watch.

Eventually, despite the rain and weather turning colder each day, we have to bury the bodies we had left in place where they fell. Not only are they a constant reminder of the assault on the house but they simply smell too bad for us to ignore any longer. By leaving dead bodies in place were they fell, we thought they would be a deterrent to other intruders. Perhaps they were. We haven't been attacked again. Regardless, waiting as long as we did also makes the clean up that much more disgusting. In spite of the stench and gore, we all pitch in and get them scooped up and buried next to Papé Cap and Latrine Boy. Several of us, including me, vomited repeatedly during the process.

After the putrid task of burying the bodies is complete, including Officer Johnson's man-hood, I survey the long rows of naked earth left behind because of the extensive trenching in the expanse of grass. I am thoroughly perplexed how the blackout could result in all this death. Standing over the graves, I count the number of bodies buried there. In addition to Papé Cap killed the first morning, and Latrine Boy Max killed, I count two bodies from the bridge from the first night attack.

And then, there's the one Airisa dug out from the under carriage of her truck after she folded him into something a human body would look like if it could be folded into an origami. One I killed with a 30.06 bullet through his forehead down at the creek and two of his pals in the crashed and beat up Toyota pickup, still on its side in the creek leaking oil and gasoline. Then there is Burning Man Shelby lit up with the flame thrower shotgun shell as he tried coming in through the patio door, and another she took out with her sawed off shotgun. To my growing mental body count I add Lumberjack who came through the garage door into the TV room Shelby first blinded with two flechette shells and I finished off with two 30.06 bullets from my M1 Garand. Lastly, there is Rolling Man on the hill behind the house Max and I executed with dual AR15's. I don't count the bodies we left in the neighbor's field. They have likely become coyote food by now so we decided not to spend our energy cleaning up for the neighbors. At this point, I have lost count and repeating the mental exercise is too gruesome to repeat, so I turn away and leave them in their graves in peace.

It's amazing how the human spirit needs familiar routine to rely on. Even with all we have been through, including the unpleasant task of burial detail, and not knowing what the future holds, after a time we let our security detail lapse. It is as if the human spirit must ease into a comfortable routine, albeit without desserts and lattes, text messaging, email, or Facebook updates. As our individual needs and wants shrank to core values of food, water, and shelter, our caring for one another's wellbeing within our small family exponentially increased.

We have successfully created for ourselves a tight knit family right here in our darkened corner of a large and unyielding world, all the while doing what we can to benefit one another. The lights will come back on at some point in our future, when that will be we have no clue. In my ordinary life before the blackout, I had been used to near instant gratification: I took for granted electricity for the house and the various pieces of equipment, tools, and entertainment devices that were integral to my world. If I had a question about something and wanted to know more, all I had to do was connect to the internet through any number of ways. If I wanted to talk to someone, all I had to do was use a cellular phone or talk via the internet. If I were bored, I would download or rent a movie and sit back comfortably, losing myself in the story enhanced by Digital Theater Sound. In my life before the blackout, I never thought patient endurance would be the most difficult opponent to master.

Over the years, as I was gathering what we share now among our small family, I speculated the worst I would have to endure would be the lack of running water, or a porcelain toilet to sit on, or even a hot shower. Now that I've been living this blackout, I understand how wrong I was. Sure, I wish for those amenities that I had taken for granted as part of a comfortable life. However, a recurring question haunts me: Could I have better prepared myself mentally to patiently endure what seems to be an endless unknown? Sitting on the floor with the others in the back bedroom while they play cards, it's easy to second guess myself and get pretty rough in my thoughts about what I should have done or should have done better.

The Angel on my shoulder whispers I shouldn't be too hard on myself, that I should relax and enjoy what food, cooking fuel, and clean water we have, the roof over our heads, effective guns nearby, and ammunition to go in those guns.

Without calling them, my thoughts somehow find their way home and come back into the room from far off places they have been wandering. Looking up from my lap, I find Shelby's caring gaze has quietly watched me as I rode my thoughts to places beyond our four walls. She has been holding my hand, all the while not saying a word. I love the gentle spirit of this young woman with strength beyond her years, with an ocean of calm inside her that trusts she will get all her answers soon and with patience enough to wait. I want to be more like her in that regard. With my thoughts fully back, present, and accounted for, I pat her hand with mine and smile into the loving eyes of Shelby Gales.

"Cdub, need anything?" she gently asks.

"Just thinking. I'm ok. Thank you."

She plays her next few hands of cards and comes up with "Fish". I look up and stare outside; it's raining steady, hard and grey. My thoughts wander to the bodies buried in the yard near the chip pile. I think to the dead group of would-be killers how they are gonna get wet before this season is done, that's for sure, "Yer, gonna get chilled to the bone Boys!" Without saying a word, I rest my head against the wall and close my eyes, smiling. Shelby's soft, warm hand alternates in and out of mine as she handles her cards.

CHAPTER EIGHTEEN
HAIL MARY

Miraculously, through heroic efforts of technicians, there are sectors of the power grid that have been restored across several of 11 affected states. Within pockets where electricity is operational and stabilized, violence and civil unrest, as if by magic, slinks back into the darkness - civil order begins to restore. Power grid operators in CW's sector have been unsuccessful in their attempts to repair and reconnect to the grid. Fate has decided the worst of the destruction within any affected region be concentrated within power grid sectors A5 and L25.

Power Station A5 has been waiting for the arrival of personnel from their sister station L25 across town, and they are now overdue by forty-eight hours. For a long while, KX79L mobile maintained a consistent communication link with KX53L mobile after the estimated time of arrival came and went. There is no way of knowing what happened to the men and women transporting EMS server equipment, a generator and spare parts or if they are still en route. It's as if they drove away and disappeared off the face of the earth.

While waiting for equipment and parts from L25, Power Station A5 personnel two and three at a time ventured away from relative safety and brought back food and sanitation supplies from nearby stores for the rest of the group holed up in their cinder block box. They could only conduct foraging efforts a few times because each time they went out, they had to go further and further away from the station to find what they needed. On the fourth and last time, the group of engineers barely made it back alive, having been ambushed by looters who beat and kicked them senseless with bicycle chains and lead pipes. A few of the attackers severely slashed a couple of operators with knives across their backs as they fled. The operators dropped most of what they had scrounged as they ran for their lives. Without help arriving soon from the outside, Power Station A5 will be unable to survive much longer. The station has been attacked by marauding bands of criminals who got inside a couple of times. They smashed some of the equipment and burned transmitters and generators before A5 personnel, fighting with their bare fists and even wielding metal folding chairs, finally succeeded driving the invaders from the building. A5 personnel quickly locked the doors from inside, "entombing ourselves" according to I-Don't-Give-A-Shit grid operator about to retire.

At one point, the handset from KX53L mobile at Power Station L25 activates and ham radio receivers monitoring the frequency listen to an open microphone, transmitting static and nothing more. Power Station A5 KX79L mobile attempts to raise KX53L but is unable to because the microphone is keyed in the open position.

Several times sporadic voices, shouting in unison and sounds of furniture being thrown around are heard, followed by silence and then the open microphone again transmits what sounds like gunshots echoing in a closed space. Transmission from KX53L mobile at Power Station L25 is suddenly cut and the connection cannot be reestablished.

Ham radio operators in bordering states outside the affected area scale insurmountable odds and miraculously establish communication links with several National Guard forward bases stationed within the blackout. Dire need of armed protection for power station personnel and equipment is repeatedly relayed. After a time, the absolute critical need to protect the last remaining infrastructure is fully understood by military commanders. Stretching even further their capacity protecting other high value priorities, National Guard troops have been mobilized into patrol size convoys of two Humvee's each and dispatched to protect larger power stations from being thoroughly destroyed. A military convoy usually consists of six to eight well-armed military Humvee's with five soldiers in each vehicle; however, there are simply not enough resources to go around for the incredible amount of need. Therefore, only smaller size convoys can be deployed. The reduction in force puts military personnel at increased risk of attack, thereby increasing the soldiers outward facing threat response. Simply put, under severe conditions such as this, smaller sized convoys are more likely to shoot first and ask questions later.

Armed troops deployed into the city realize early gains. Several National Guard convoys have successfully woven their way through riot torn, burned out sections of the city and have already surrounded their designated power stations allowing grid operators to rest, eat, sleep, and work. Some units have begun ferrying personnel, equipment and supplies to other stations, while some Guard units protect linemen as they attempt to repair or otherwise replace critical elements of the power grid. Civilian attacks on military personnel are generally one sided in favor of the well-armed and well-trained military. With mobs indiscriminately attacking anything moving, the shoot-to-kill order is exercised frequently with devastating effect. Other power stations remain unprotected with personnel like sitting ducks at the mercy of fate. Some stations have been abandoned altogether and burned to the ground by person or persons unknown. If the trend isn't halted soon, there simply will not be enough grid infrastructure left for anyone to connect with, resulting in an extended blackout for an indefinite period.

"Charlie Six Niner Five to Base. 10-11. 10-14 N/NW Lombard proceeding Papa Sierra Lima Two Five. ETA Three Zero Mikes. Over."

"Base to Charlie Six Niner Five. Acknowledged. Threat-level Four gentlemen."

"Charlie Six Niner Five to Base. Threat-level Four acknowledged. We are locked and loaded."

As the two-vehicle convoy rumbles its way down Lombard devoid of civil control of any kind, it discovers its route of travel to Power Station L25 blocked by massive barricades of burning tires, furniture, cars, and anything else that can burn and be thrown in the street.

There seems to be no straightforward approach to make it through the city; therefore, they are forced to turn down alleyways and narrow side streets in their efforts to flank barricades to reach their objective. As they pick their way through the city, Molotov cocktails splash flaming gasoline across the body of Humvee's, thrown from unseen rioters from above. More than a few bullets strike their vehicles at random angles from snipers no one can locate. All other two-vehicle convoys on the same channel dispersed elsewhere throughout the city monitor urgent radio calls to Base from another six man, two Humvee convoy within the bowels of the city. The two Humvee convoy has become hopelessly trapped after detouring around a barricade, turning into an alley the crew did not realize was blocked until it was too late. The unit could not back out in time before a couple of burning vehicles were pushed into place behind them, blocking any route of escape. No one was available to come to their rescue. After a valiant three-hour effort, all six soldiers were burned out of their vehicles and then massacred after they ran out of ammunition. Their weapons and grenades were never recovered, and both vehicles were torched in place.

Not one of the dead soldiers was awarded the Purple Heart, let alone a combat citation for bravery under fire. They died conducting military operations in a civil action, not during combat against a foreign nation. Not receiving full military honors didn't make sense to their families. Their sons and daughters were doing what they were trained to do, and they all died together doing their duty. For some unknown reason, hardly anyone saw the military burial ceremonies captured by independent film crews.

National Guard convoy Charlie Six Niner Five arrived at Power Station L25 in time to fire their turret mounted .50 caliber machine gun into a large group of people actively engaged in tearing down transmission lines and in the process of setting the building on fire with power station personnel locked inside. Heavy bullets at close range tore bodies in half, severing arms from shoulders, heads from bodies, and in some places, piercing the Power Station walls into interior spaces, barely missing several grid operators trying to debug a defunct server. After the crowd fled beyond the fire they had set, one Humvee covered the North side of the building and one covered the South while the remaining four soldiers took up security detail inside the building with automatic weapons locked and loaded. After securing their objective, one Humvee was sent into the city with a shopping list, returning several hours later with much needed medical supplies, food, and water. After having something to eat, tightly wound nerves began relaxing, and a large majority of station personnel collapsed into comatose sleep as a result.

More than fourteen hours pass before Power Station L25 is able to return to the job at hand, repairing their own damaged equipment and gearing up to transport to Power Station A5 one SIEMENS generator, one EMS server and spare parts. The original plan between the two stations is still a viable one and made even that much more urgent because of lost time, equipment, and personnel throughout the region. Power station personnel go about their missions with renewed vigor, feeling more secure in the presence of their personal armed bodyguards. In less than eight hours, their power station is repaired and ready to transport equipment to A5 and ultimately assist in a sequenced connection to the power grid. No one has heard from Power Station A5, and there is no possibility of determining what the cause is, whether it's a failure of L25's ham radio equipment or of Power Station A5's radio equipment or, God forbid, A5 personnel are dead or the station abandoned all together. No one will know until someone arrives.

Finally, L25 personnel have a flatbed semi-truck loaded up for transport across town with a SIEMENS generator and all the spare parts they can manage to do without for their own needs. Station personnel were surprised to find two operational EMS servers in the back of their storage room, one server still in the box, wrapped in cellophane. They kept one for themselves and packed the other on the flatbed.

"Charlie Six Niner Five Alpha to Base, 10-10 Papa Sierra Lima Two Five with four civilians and one semi with grid equipment. 10-14 Papa Sierra Alpha Five ETA Six Zero Mikes. Over"

"Base to Charlie Six Niner Five Alpha, acknowledged. Be safe out there boys. Let us know what you see."

"Charlie Six Niner Five Alpha, 10-4. Proceeding to objective Papa Sierra Alpha Five to assist grid connectivity mission. Charlie Six Niner Five Bravo holding fast at Papa Sierra Lima Two Five as security detail. Over"

Humvee "Bravo" consisting of three soldiers stand fast at station L25 as security against further attacks while Humvee "Alpha" escorts grid operators and replacement equipment to station A5 across town miles away. The sheer size and weight of the semi-truck, its precious cargo, and the terrain they have to pass through, result in slow progress for the two-vehicle convoy in their trek across town. The convoy is forced to thread slowly and cautiously along city streets strewn with debris and flaming wreckage, a dark city landscape looking more like the streets of a war torn third world country than a moderate sized American city in the new millennium. Success of their mission is far from assured, with death and destruction all around them, repeatedly forced to back track, blindly feeling their way through the holocaust. The slim odds of success, let alone making it out alive, are not lost on L25 personnel driving the semi-truck loaded with spare parts, or the three soldiers in the lead Humvee.

Arriving at their objective at all, let alone with undamaged cargo, is to say the least, an incredible long shot, but a long shot worth taking. L25 personnel will know what to do if they find Power Station A5 abandoned, burned to the ground or worse - everyone dead.

CHAPTER NINETEEN

12:00

Friday afternoon, November 16

Grey skies and steady rain. We are all huddled together as usual in the back bedroom playing cards and drinking coffee or tea when suddenly all three dogs jump up and stand with feet spread wide apart, intently watching the bedroom door, hair on their necks and backs raised high. Deep rumbling sounds come from each of their chests. Cards and coffee cups go flying in all directions when 425 pounds of dog spring to attention in the middle of our cramped space. As the dogs continue their deep low rumble, everyone in the room grabs for guns. Shelby backs in a corner with her sawed off and takes Mia with her. Airisa peeks low over the windowsill looking right, and I do the same scanning left. Max moves to the closet wall opposite the door and covers the entrance to the bedroom with his rifle. I see him pull the charging handle back slightly to ensure a round is in the chamber. He sees me and nods, indicating he is good to go.

Listening intently, we hear the floor creak somewhere down the hall. Someone is in the house and trying to walk softly. When the dogs hear it, they erupt in boisterous barking with a deafening volume that makes it impossible to detect anything happening outside our closed door - that's not a good thing. Airisa and I exchange concerned glances. We instantly realize the danger of our vulnerability. Neither one of us sees anyone coming down the road toward the bridge. Our two trucks are still in place blocking access from that direction and we quickly conclude we are being invaded from one or both of our blind spots. The dogs keep barking in the direction of the closed door but don't attempt to go near it. Putting my finger to my lips I signal for everyone to keep quiet and to stay put, followed by a motion pointing at my weapon to make sure we are all able to respond immediately to any threat. While weapons are being checked and ammunition secured for a quick reload, I release the revolver from the shoulder holster under my left arm, dig out several speed loaders of ammunition from my pants pocket, and whisper to Mia as I give her the revolver and ammunition, "Take this. Shelby will tell you how to use it." Mia's hand dips as I place the weight of the gun in her shaking hands, her eyes expressing unbridled concern as she looks down at the heavy revolver and then back to me for reassurance.

In a calm, reassuring voice Shelby whispers to Mia, "Don't worry. It's easy."

"Are you ready to look after Zeke, Zoie, and Little?" I ask Mia.

"Don't worry Cdub. We won't let anything bad happen to them," Shelby responds as Mia nods her head in agreement.

"Thank you, Ladies." Shelby and Mia will be good to their word and knowing that allows me to concentrate my attention on other priorities. Everyone has weapons at the ready, including Mia with the heavy revolver held in a tight grip with both hands after having organized shotgun shells for easy feeding to Shelby. All three dogs barking loudly put us at severe disadvantage. We are unable to hear what is going on outside the bedroom door. However, their barking does afford Airisa and me the cover we need to open the bedroom window and slide ourselves out to the front lawn undetected by any intruder in the house. What we don't know yet is who is outside, or how many there are. Being outside the house is the only way we can find out. After we crawl through with our weapons locked and loaded, Shelby closes and locks the window. We maneuver our way right, around the corner and up the wet wooded hill behind the house, as rain covers our footsteps and thankfully blends our movement with grey sheets of rain. From our vantage point on the hillside, Airisa and I see the bed sheet Shelby and I had tacked to the patio doorframe still in place but pushed to one side. Someone coming in the house would cause that, but Airisa and I don't see anyone as we scan the area to our front and to our right and left flanks.

Suddenly a figure appears from inside the house at the opening of the patio bed sheet. I nudge Airisa and we both direct our attention to the man who has his attention focused toward the dark wooded area up the hill along the far side of my rifle range in an opposite direction from where we are. The spot he is focused on is to our left front approximately 150 yards from the position we have taken to scan the area. The man pumps his arm as if signaling a trucker to blow an air horn and in response, four men in various colored clothing appear, rising up from the soggy under brush and make their way over the low rusty fence. On my property, they fan out, making their way cautiously in the direction of the patio entrance to my house. Several of the men have AR15's and the others have other rifles I can't identify from this distance because rain smears my glasses and makes it difficult to see clearly.

Whispering urgently to Airisa I tell her, "We can't let them get in," but if we make a move right now, we will be exposed to their fire and that means we can't make it back inside the house. "We're going to have to pin them down and try to get inside the house through the patio door." I outline my thoughts and although she doesn't like the idea of running into their line of fire, we have no other choice if we are going to have any chance of helping the others inside defend themselves. "This is going to be incredibly tight and will require a huge amount of luck. Are you ready?" I ask.

"Yes," Airisa responds as confidently as possible.

The attackers are now approximately one hundred yards from the house and the man at the patio has his head out looking left and right and urging the slow moving group to hurry up. "Can you take out the man at the patio?" I whisper into her left ear.

"Yes," she says with much greater confidence as she levels her aim at the man's chest and follows up by saying slowly and with convincing assurance, "Oh Hell yeah."

"When you take him out, I'll fire at the group and get them to pin down. As soon as I start, you haul ass down this hill and make your way to the patio door. I will follow and keep firing in their direction. When you hear me yell to you, you start firing at them on the run. We want to have at least one weapon firing at all times. Ok?"

"Got it," she says never taking her aim off the man who is leaning half way out the opening at the patio door.

My red dot reticle shines bright, showing me the way to the nearest threat coming down the hill. While aiming down my sight I say, "Anytime you're ready." I hear Airisa take a shallow breath, hold it, and then let loose with three rapid well-controlled shots from her AK47. The first of three 7.62 bullets from her AK slam through the chest of Patio Man 2. Rifle recoil walks her second bullet two inches high into his esophagus and out the other side, burying itself deep into the soft wood of the doorframe. Her third bullet obliterates his head, painting the bed sheet, and doorframe in a spray of tissue, brain matter, and volumes of blood that fountain out the hole onto the concrete patio step.

With her first shot, I open up with my rifle and the man in my sight display window tumbles backward and doesn't reappear. I swing my aim left to the next nearest threat, but the remaining group on the hill has already hit the ground.

Airisa jumps up from her position on my right and leaps over and through the slosh and muck of the hillside. She makes her way toward the edge of the hill at the back of the house above were Latrine Boy died three weeks ago. As she runs, I put five more rounds down range, spraying the general area where the men have hit the ground out of sight, and then I start downhill as well. Without aiming, I nonetheless try as best I can to keep bullets striking near their area. My only hope is to keep them pinned  down and for me not to fall while I make my way off this hill following Airisa. Before I stop firing, I see her on flat ground and about ready to jump over the split rail cedar fence into the backyard near the house. While continuing to fire, I yell and she immediately and fluidly swings her AK toward the threat area while going to one knee - unleashing her own version of hell from the muzzle of her semi-automatic battle rifle. As she fires, I run past and jump higher than I thought I could in one motion over the rail fence, landing harder than expected onto the muddy grass at the back of the house. I tumble forward onto my knees nearly losing my balance altogether, and skid to a stop in the wet grass.

Breathing heavily, I brace myself against the wall of the house under the window of the bedroom Max and Mia stay in. Airisa is continuing her controlled methodical firing right and left into the tall grass where the men are pinned down, approximately sixty yards from her position. I reload quickly and when she hears my rifle shots join hers, she stops firing and jumps down next to me, reloads and begins firing again as I reload. We make our way along the back of the house, toward the patio, both methodically spraying the tall grass in the direction of the assaulting force - successfully pinning them down as we make our way into the house over the quite dead and mangled body of Patio Man 2.

"Damn Airisa. And you use that AK for deer hunting?"

"Yep."

"Good job Girl," I say as we each make our way through the patio entry and take up positions in the house: Airisa covers the patio door, while I cover the front of the house through the picture window in the living room. We're in the house and we aren't receiving incoming fire yet from the assaulting force on their bellies in the grass outside, but we do not have long until all that changes. Yelling to everyone in the house that Airisa and I are inside, I call everyone to the open space between the kitchen, living room, and TV room. Max, Mia, and Shelby come down the hallway, crouching low with weapons locked, loaded, and ready to respond to the eminent threat yards away. Zeke, Zoie and Little are behind the closed door in the back bedroom, barking loudly and pawing at the door.

"Shelby, please take Mia and secure the dogs in the guest bath. Lock yourselves in. Lie down in the tub with shotguns loaded and pointed at the door. Ok?"

"I don't want to leave you, CW," Shelby replies in a shaky voice.

"I know but it'll be best this way. I'll feel better knowing you are out of the line of fire. We'll be ok out here. Do you trust me Shelby?" I gently ask as I put one hand on her smooth cheek. She looks deep in my eyes with a worried look, and presses my hand into her cheek more fully.

"Yes Cdub. Yes I do," She says, swallowing hard, trying to bury growing emotion she is nearly unable to contain.

I kiss her soft lips and study deep for a moment her lovely, worried, brown eyes, "I love you Shelby." Her entire composure changes with a flash of a smile that lights her eyes and face. In the instant before having to rush off to help defend her home and friends, she visibly becomes a new woman. Shelby makes her way down the hall carrying her double barrel shotgun, looking back over her shoulder with a smile for me. I swear I see a small skip in her step as she goes. She leads Mia to the guest bath and then retrieves the dogs. I hear a jostle of noises as they all fit themselves in the tight space in the guest bathroom. "Max," I say, "Airisa and I saw four guys out back in the field coming at us from about 60 to 80 yards out. One I know I took out. The others hit the deck in the tall grass as soon as we opened up. Airisa obviously got the one at the patio door. Do you have enough ammunition?"

"Yes," Max replies flatly and adds, "I'm good to go."

"Airisa, how are you doing? You all set?"

"Yep, Ready to roll," is her forceful response right at the time bullets splinter wood and drywall at the back of the house, coming from various angles right and left from the hill outside.

Airisa yells loud from the living room, "Cdub, you better come here and see this. We've got trouble."

Max covers the back of the house from his crouched position in the kitchen, and I low crawl over the laminate flooring to see what Airisa is seeing.

"What is it?" Max yells in a loud and urgent voice, keeping low from bullets flying in overhead.

I peek above the sill and see a rusty orange pickup truck with a large confederate flag flying from the back right quarter panel and a two-tone grey and blue striped pickup with two guys each in the bed holding onto light bars across their cabs. Both trucks are coming onto the property at a high rate of speed and the men in the back are getting ready to throw what I soon know are pipe bombs, one from each pickup. At the exact moment each truck brakes to a sliding stop along the gravel drive before they plunge over the side into the creek, the men in back use the momentum to hurl their homemade grenades high into the air toward the house.

Covering the back of the house, Max begins firing his rifle from a kneeling position along one corner of the kitchen and yells, "They're coming!" as Airisa and I helplessly watch two metallic grey cylinders arc end over end, tumbling toward the house spewing sparks from their fuses. We duck down as they fall several feet apart on the gravel driveway and explode almost at once. One pipe grenade blasts a jagged man sized hole in the soft metal of the garage door, allowing easy access through it and then into the house from the interior door through which Lumberjack, days before, entered and then died. The other bomb detonates with enough force to disintegrate into splinters the corner of the wood deck where Papé Cap and his two buddies had riffled through the emergency food container the first day I was home. The blast causes the front door to slowly open inward and rest in position along the wall and simultaneously shatters the picture window - razor sharp broken glass fly inward slicing into the right side of Max's face and shoulder. I hear him cry out in shock and pain from the explosion and shrapnel hitting his body. "You ok?" I yell out.

"Yeah, I think so!" and his rifle shots quickly pick up where they left off seconds before; firing into the backyard and along the hill at targets as they become available.

One of the killers on the front lawn runs toward the house with another lit pipe bomb - Airisa and I kill him as if we were a two-person firing squad. He falls and explodes into red, wet meaty chunks spraying mud, grass, clothing, and flesh into the air that rain down onto the lawn. Simultaneously Max is attempting to kill a couple of bad guys that have actually made it into the house. Our efforts are not nearly enough.

Rifle fire is coming in earnest from various positions along the creek bank to our front giving the assaulting force excellent protection, pinning us down while other attackers come at us from our blind spots. Good for them. Bad for us.

"They're going to try and out flank us," Airisa says calmly, continually firing her AK repeatedly toward muzzle flashes coming at us from the creek bank.

"I know," is all I can say in response as I also rhythmically fire my AR - reloading magazine after magazine. Brass shell casings litter the living room floor around us, thick gun smoke undulates in the interior air, as bullets streak through the smoke and hit hard into wood, drywall, glass, and upholstered furniture; filling the room with particles of dust and bits of cloth that mix together and float like snowflakes. Our worst fear is coming true. We have been outflanked. We are pinned in with no escape and with no alternative but to battle close range, hand-to-hand. Any thought of asking them why they are doing what they are doing has long vanished. It is kill or be killed. Answers may come later. Perhaps not.

Airisa is firing her well-aimed AK47 and is yelling something to me but I don't understand what she's saying. Backing away, she fires from her hip out the broken front window, making a move toward the TV room. As she makes her move, a bullet hits hard in her right thigh, taking a chunk of flesh with it. She screams in pain as the velocity of the impact spins her on all fours in a 360-degree turn in mid air, inches about the floor, as if she's levitating. Damndest thing I ever saw.

When she stops spinning, she retrieves her rifle and low crawls into the TV room to assist Max who has been covering the back of the house, but is down on the floor and bleeding, hit by bullets from two more men coming in on him through the patio door barricade. He's been shot through his left arm and right side, but successfully takes out one of the attackers with rapid firing from a point-and-shoot position on his knees in the dining room. Airisa arrives next to him in time to kill the other.

From my firing position at the living room window defending my home and my family, a surreal cocoon of slow moving clarity and all-consuming physical exhaustion envelops my reality. Exerting monumental will to survive against an equal or greater force intent on killing life causes my mind to float out of body in the midst of the fury of battle. I am aiming and shooting my rifle but no longer hear the shot or feel the recoil. I hear distant sounds of shotguns joining the fight from down the hall. Zeke, Zoie, and Little are barking, crying, and screaming in tones I never knew dogs could make.

"God bless Shelby. God bless us all," as I continue aiming and firing and reloading magazine after magazine of armor piercing ammunition from my red-hot AR15 rifle.

Moments before Airisa made her move to help Max; Shelby and Mia hunkered down in the confined space of the guest bathroom with Zeke, Zoie and Little, listen with growing apprehension to sounds of raging battle drawing closer and closer outside their door.

As instructed, they are lying as low as they can get inside the tub, with their shotguns resting on the tub rim, leveled toward the locked door. All three dogs on the floor in front of them whimper and shake uncontrollably in an animal version of a nervous breakdown.

Suddenly the guest bathroom doorknob rattles, followed quickly by a shotgun blast that explodes through the hollow core door, spraying wood into the dogs. A large sliver impales Zoie's chest near her left leg, and she howls in fear and pain. Mia and Shelby are lucky; lead pellets fly over their heads and embed into the fiberglass tub surround while at the same time the 870 shotgun Mia was holding instantly goes off, her trigger finger startled by the attacker's blast. Mia's load of buckshot hit the intruder full in the neck and face with nine lead pellets, and he falls backward, spilling dry dog food and the water bowl, and dies on the laundry room floor in front of the washer and dryer. After Mia kills the attacker, Shelby climbs out of the tub and stands on the sink counter top, pressing herself against the wall with her sawed off shotgun pointed at the door below her. At that moment a second intruder steps over the dead body of his friend and kicks the guest bath door hard expecting it to fly open - certainly not expecting it to be stopped as it did when it hit the dogs lying on the floor nearby. As dogs jump up, Shelby's shotgun goes off, wounding the man but not stopping him. He is able to reach through the door and throw her off the counter onto the tub rim as Mia tries to break her fall. Shelby's back hits the tub rim hard, and she cries out in pain.

Mia's shotgun and revolver lay helpless beneath them at the bottom of the tub, while Shelby's shotgun is out of reach, flung between the sink cabinet and toilet when she fell.

The attacker forces his way in and is immediately pinned to the floor by enraged dogs frenzied beyond their breaking point. He is mauled to death, unable to defend against clawing paws, and biting, ripping, and tearing canine teeth. Zeke, Zoie, and Little rip and tear unrestrained long after the attacker stops kicking. Blood oozes to the bathroom floor through jagged gashes on his throat, arms, and face. Perhaps dental records, if any exist, will be able to identify him. His face is unrecognizable. One eye is completely gone as is his nose, a side of one cheek and portions of his mouth. Remaining bits of lip and cheek flesh hang ragged free and puffy red, showing too much gum and white teeth. His body, especially his throat, is entirely tattooed with deep black and blue puncture holes. With the guest bath door open, Little Zeke bolts out and down the hall toward the front door followed closely by Shelby, stumbling and falling on bodies as her boots lose traction in slippery pools of blood, water, and dry dog food pellets on the laundry room floor.

Upon hearing the sound of shotgun blasts from the guest bathroom, Max, although badly wounded, picks himself up and runs headlong through a hail of incoming bullets to assist Mia and Shelby. In so doing, he inadvertently tackles an intruder who had come down the hallway through one of the bedroom windows, a killer with me in his sights. If it weren't for Max tackling the man by accident on his way to save Mia, I would have been dead from a hatchet-wielding madman.

Max and the would-be killer fall to the floor of the hallway, their weapons out of reach. Locked in mortal combat with entwined bodies part way in and part way out the dog's bedroom door, both men are screaming, kicking and gouging the other in a fight to the death. Through the struggle, somehow Max is able to sit on top of the man's chest. He pummels the man's face and throat as hard and as fast as he can even after his fists are broken assaulting the attacker pinned beneath him. Max doesn't feel the pain of his broken hands; he keeps fighting with every ounce of fury he has. At one point during their combat, Hatchet Man rakes fingernails down Max's face and blood streams from the wounds into his eyes nearly blinding him. This allows the attacker to grab at a knife from a back pocket but he is successful only at giving Max a good look at what is in store if he doesn't kill this man. With all his might, broken hands and all, Max squeezes the man's throat, desperate to choke every ounce of life from the violently wriggling and clawing killer beneath him. Pressing down on the crushed neck between his knees, Max stares at his would-be killer's bulging eyes and purple face. The man's expression becomes frozen in death. Regaining his senses, Max has an emotional breakdown. He cries hot tears that drop onto the dead man's face without notice by either the living or the dead. Close quarter's combat rages throughout the house but for Max it is far away, muted in the distance. With no strength left but to straddle his barehanded kill, Max doubles over and weeps uncontrollably.

As Max sobs uncontrollably nearby, Zeke and Zoie in the guest bathroom shake spasmodically, whimpering and whining, their heavy bodies lying on the dead man pinned beneath them. They periodically sniff their kill, lips and whiskers foaming white with their fury and stained red with the man's blood. Stunned by the explosive noise and carnage, especially within confines of such a small space, Mia laid back in the tub to regain her composure. Quickly regaining her wits, she stumbles over the dogs and bodies and into the laundry room at the entry of the guest bath in the hopes of following Little and Shelby. As she does, she comes up behind a figure raising the butt end of his rifle, ready to bring it down hard on the back of her husband's head. Max is sitting and weeping tears onto the purple face of the dead man beneath him. The blow from the rifle butt cracks into Max's skull. He cries out, slumping forward, knocked semi-conscious, unable to defend himself, at the mercy of the killer standing over him ready to deliver the coup de grâce. Although Mia had forgotten the 870 shotgun in the tub as she left the guest bathroom, somehow she had taken the revolver with her, now firmly gripped in both hands.

Seeing her husband being attacked, she yells a guttural scream of rage and fury and takes a few steps from the laundry room to a position directly behind the man with the rifle held high for one last lethal blow. She pulls the trigger of the revolver repeatedly until the only sound left echoing in the hallway are metallic clicks of the hammer falling repeatedly on empty chambers. Five semi-jacketed hollow point .38 caliber +P bullets hit the man hard, mushroom outward, and fragment as each pass through muscle, lungs, heart and bone.

Mia is so close that when she fires, parts of the man's jacket ignite in blue and orange flames around bullet holes that breathe smoke. The man falls forward and dies, lying on the king size pillow top mattress my ex-wife loved so much. Mia drops the revolver and rushes to Max's side, pulling him from under the dead man, cradling her husband in her lap while stroking his brown and graying hair. He is alive but severely wounded and moaning incoherently in the lap of the love of his life. Cradled in Mia's arms, Max succumbs to unconsciousness. Mia sobs and rocks back and forth, brushing her tears from Max's placid, bruised, and bloodied face. They both fought hard, and they both fought well, and for those two there is nothing left to give.

As all three dogs tore their attacker to pieces in the guest bathroom, I am hit hard on the side of my head by someone I never saw coming. I instantly see stars and nearly vomit from the blow. My AR falls to one side out of reach, and I am immediately thrust into a hand-to-hand, life and death struggle with a burly muscular man with a flattop hair cut more stylish in the South in the 1950's than in this day and age. He is wearing grease-stained jeans, a dirty white tee-shirt, and a faded brown Carhartt jacket opened down to a John Deer belt buckle around his waist. He clearly outweighs me in pounds, sheer muscle, and the advantage of the surprise blow to the back of my head. His hammer strike has peeled back a large flap of skin - the gash on my head bleeding freely as I roll along the dirty laminate floor.

My attacker is sitting on my hips with my back pinned to the floor, but I have somehow locked my hands tight around both his wrists. In his right, he is clutching a brand new 24-ounce Ace Hardware ball peen hammer he would very much like to bury in my skull and very nearly did with the first blow. His fierce brown eyes bore a hole in me, bloodshot red, radiating a maniacal passion for my death that pierces me like the point of a knife deep into my soul. We exert every ounce of strength we have in the struggle for and against my life. Straining with all his might to overpower me, his neck veins become engorged ropes on the verge of bursting bloody contents. I am fighting with all my strength to keep my wrists locked around his while simultaneously trying to deflect his repeated attempts at head butting me.

Out of my peripheral vision, I glimpse a black and white shape and then feel one of Little's back paws scrape the right side of my face as he loses traction on the laminate flooring, sliding into me in his desperate escape from the house. Little recovers his balance and bolts through the open front door and out into the wide-open spaces beyond with his tail firmly tucked between his legs. Through tears in my eyes from being scraped in the face by his back paw, I recognize Shelby's boot dart past me in Little's direction but then change quickly and run to the TV room. Airisa has a guy twice her size by the shirt front, kneeing him repeatedly in the groin without much effect; damn the bullet wound to her thigh.

Mingling with the chaotic sights and sounds of the melee, I hear five loud shots from Mia's revolver go off close by, but I am unable to know why as I fight the man intent on killing me with a hammer and the horrific realization my strength has ever so slightly begun to fade. Trying, even in this moment, to be my own best friend, I think if I can just hold on a little while longer I'll be all right, but I don't know how I can.

Shelby arrived to help Airisa in time to knock the legs out from under Airisa's attacker. All three fall to the floor, scratching, kicking, and clawing. At one point Airisa tries to get at the knife in her bra but can't find it in time and is instead hit horribly hard across the face by a backhand from the attacker who recovered from the fall and had also pushed Shelby away. As Airisa falls back, he turns his attention to Shelby and punches her full in the face with a closed fist. Her body shudders and she immediately collapses to a sitting position on the carpet near the entrance to the garage. All she can make out at the time is a spinning room as blood flows freely from her nose and around loosened front teeth. Her left eye swells intensely black and blue. Dazed and disoriented, Shelby can do nothing in the moment but sit and watch.

The attacker turns his full attention to Airisa in time to catch a painful blow to his nose, the forceful strike from a fist delivered with all her might turns his head hard left, spraying Airisa with snot and gushing blood. Unfortunately, the attacker does not go down but bends in a wrestling stance and picks Airisa up by the waist, and slams her into a nearby wall, her back shattering the glass of a framed picture hanging there.

As she slides down the wall, broken glass slices deep ribbons along her elbows and through the exquisite tattoo on her back. The impact also causes my M1915 bayonet to fall to the floor from the World War One Springfield rifle it had been attached to as part of a wall display. The intensity of the pain and mortal fear ignite an internal firestorm of rage inside her. She explodes with an incredibly forceful backhand hard across his bleeding nose with the flat metal of the bayonet blade. She didn't know it was a bayonet she held and did not know it was the flat side. The only thing she knew for sure was she was holding something when reacting with everything she had to fight with, and fight back she did with good effect. The guy shrieks in pain from the hideous trauma delivered to his broken nose and can do nothing but stumble backward and pause, putting both hands to his nose and face. Instantly Airisa kicks him over with one Danner boot hooked behind his left ankle and one Danner boot hit hard to his left knee.

In that moment, fog lifted from Shelby's mind, in time for her to focus on Airisa starting to kick the man onto his back. Scrambling up, Shelby grabs a handful of hair and assists him to the Persian rug in the TV room while Airisa jumps and lands hard with all her weight, knees first, onto the guy's chest, taking all the air out of him. Her crushing blow breaks several of his ribs, each one with a loud snap. Unable to catch his breath, he lies bleeding from his nose, gasping for air - the razor sharp edge of the bayonet Airisa hit him in the nose with, now pressed across his throat. Shelby and Airisa, shoulder to shoulder, press down with all their combined strength.

As the attacker fights for his life, his struggling, flailing, and squirming beneath their combined weight, assists the sawing action of the blade through his neck. Misty blood mixed with foamy white phlegm spurt outward from his esophagus as his windpipe cuts in two, allowing him finally to catch a much need breath, albeit his last. When the blade severs his carotid artery, volumes of deep, dark red blood fountain out with each diminishing heartbeat; until the blade can continue no further, stopped in place by grayish white cervical vertebrae of his spinal column. Airisa and Shelby have nearly decapitated the man and the look in his eyes testifies he is very much surprised by that fact. Airisa and Shelby turn their heads attempting to avoid his fluids, nevertheless, saliva and sticky blood completely cover their hands and arms. He stops moving, and they turn and stare at the carnage of his gaping fatal neck wound. The dead guy looks like he can hold his breath forever, with a thick purple tongue sticking out between blue lips and white teeth - as if in death, he mocks his killers. Airisa averts her eyes and releases her hands from the blade. Opening her eyes a moment later, the sight of the clock on the old VCR I have been meaning to give away but found useful from time to time puzzles her. That old thing is blinking "12:00" again, and again, and again the same way it does every time it powers up after an outage. For an instant, sitting there on the chest of the dead guy, she stares at the phenomenon of the blinking clock display, its meaning not yet registering.

Shelby looks over to see what has captured Airisa's stare and instantly recognizes what it means and says weakly at first and then with an ever increasing shout, louder and louder, and more insistent, "God! Oh my God! Oh my God!" Airisa slides off the dead body, sits on the floor shaking uncontrollably, with tears gushing from her eyes, and shouts at the top of her lungs, "THE POWER IS ON! THE POWER IS BACK ON!" Disregarding bullets coming in from all directions, Shelby jumps up and flips light switches wherever she can find them, instantly illuminating our close quarter's battlefield.

When Shelby flipped those light switches, my killer instantly froze, his ball peen hammer held high and free over his head. A fraction of a second later I would have been bludgeoned to death on my living room floor. I hadn't enough strength to hold his wrists any longer and he was able to break free. A fraction of a second before the lights came back on, and with nothing for me to do but prepare myself for the unthinkable, I prayed to God not to make it hurt. I don't care what anyone says, my life didn't flash before my eyes. All I saw was the instrument of my inevitable death clutched in my killers determined and exceedingly capable right fist held high over his head. Mercifully illuminated, bathed in incandescent light from every bulb Shelby could find a switch for, the man slowly lowers his instrument of my death, edges himself off me, and sits without saying a word with his back against the wall adjacent to the broken front door.

I scoot away and rest my back against a far wall battered with several hundred-bullet holes of all sizes. Panting heavily I am fearful I will not find enough air to breathe, convinced I will surely die at any moment.

When the lights come back on all gunfire from outside quickly ceases and silence, thick and luscious, blankets the battlefield and every combatant. With my back against the wall, panting for air, unable to move, I watch as my would be killer stares blankly at a spot on the floor in the middle space between us, his neck veins, once rope like and ready to burst blood, are back to normal. A full minute later, he shakes his head violently side to side as if trying to wake up. When the head of the ball peen hammer clutched in his right fist absently strikes my laminate floor with a loud jolting click, he rolls to one knee, stands slowly, and then walks with steps unsteady at first through the front door and down the drive - all the while rubbing his head with his opposite hand. Without looking back or saying a word, he walks away, his boot steps fading into the distance as he walks down the gravel driveway, past our two trucks blocking the bridge and toward his armed men gathering at their pickup trucks near the front gate.

Shelby helps me up and I lean on her for support as I gingerly touch one of her swollen cheeks. She stands at my side and snuggles into my chest holding tight to my arm. Airisa is crying as she hobbles over, and Max and Mia stumble into the living room. We gather our battered wounded selves at the shattered picture window in the living room and watch the man carrying the 24-ounce Ace Hardware ball peen hammer gather his men with him, weapons in their hands.

Only when they are sliding into their pickup trucks do I remember the question I wanted to ask - but my voice cracks and "Why?" is stuck in my throat. I do not get a second chance to ask because they speed away, out of range, beyond my front gate with its thoroughly mangled "Positively No Trespassing" sign still firmly attached. Their confederate flag flutters hard in the wind, snapping loudly at first and then diminishing, along with the rumble of their loud engines as each pickup truck drives down the road and then turns hard left at a high rate of speed toward the river highway further on.

At last, everything is quiet again, another peaceful, rainy late autumn afternoon in the country. For a very long time, with every bulb shining bright in the house, we stand together and gaze out at the fall day, not concerned at all about evening's gathering shadows closing in fast. Finally, we put our guns down and huddle tight together, not saying a word. With our heads bowed and our eyes closed, someone begins softly sobbing. All the while, our battered and bruised bodies are bathed by an incandescent waterfall spilling over us. I open my eyes. Electric light is gathering itself in pools around our feet.

CHAPTER TWENTY
AFTERMATH

Our family stayed together for another three weeks, tending to our wounds, cleaning ourselves and burying bodies in the soft ground between the chip pile and the rifle range. Everyone believed Papé Cap and Latrine Boy appreciated having new faces in the ground with them. Lastly, we searched the neighbor's field for other bodies we knew were there at one time; but couldn't find much to bury once we started looking. We cleaned the house the best we could, patching bullet holes, ripping up putrid carpet, bloodied and gouged flooring and we burned the revolting mass in a funeral pyre on top of the graves where the large barren patch of earth displayed tire tread patterns from my tractor.

Eventually, Max, Mia and Airisa made their way home to begin their lives again, carrying with them memories of solidarity and pain, friendship, survival, and triumph beyond anything they could have ever imagined. We remain friends to this day.

A junk-man whose number I got from the local paper hauled the beat up white Toyota LUV pickup truck out of the creek. He took the heap some place down the road and sold it for scrap - never once asking how it got there or about the many bullet holes in its grill.

God answered prayer and winter blanketed all the ugly scars with fresh, clean snow that was thicker and lasted longer than usual. In early spring, after Shelby and I put a fresh coat of paint on the house, we listed it with a property management company owned by a young couple new to the area and hungry for our business. We did not say what had happened there or of the buried bodies. Shelby and I moved far away and never returned. We made a new life together in a place without bad memories at every turn.

Zoie recovered from her chest wound but was never again able to run as full and free as before. She never left our side and died at an exceptionally old age for a Great Dane. She remains my best little girl, and there is not a day that passes that I don't miss her.

Zeke never recovered from the nervous breakdown he suffered because of the home invasions. When it was all over, he no longer found joy taking walks with us to the creek or the meadow, where in sunnier days we would play, and then nap together in the grass warmed by the sun. In the end, Zeke was content to stay in his room with his food and water nearby and lie in front of the wall heater we kept on for him. He passed away peacefully in his sleep not long after.

Little was two-years old when the blackout hit. He never returned home after he ran from the house that day. Before we moved away, Shelby and I drove country roads calling him home. Several times, we caught a glimpse of what looked to be a black and white shape in deep meadow grasses and thick woody places along hillsides that are so beautiful in the autumn season with their leaves painted orange, yellow and rusty red.

CHAPTER TWENTY-ONE
POSTSCRIPT

In Congress, Joint Interagency Energy Task Force Hearing –

[2.] *"Over the past decade or more, electricity demand has increased and the North American interconnections have become more densely woven and heavily loaded, over more hours of the day and year. In many geographic areas, the number of single or multiple contingencies that could create serious problems has increased. Operating the grids at higher loadings means greater stress on equipment and a smaller range of options and a shorter period for dealing with unexpected problems. The system operator's job has become more challenging, leading to the need for more sophisticated grid management tools and more demanding operator training programs and certification requirements."*

~ YEARS LATER ~

My friends, Louis and Marge, sit reverently across from me at their kitchen table in their quiet, comfortable home on a beautiful autumn morning. I am nearing my 75th birthday.

"Cdub" Lou says, softly nudging himself into my thoughts.

"Hmm. Oh, sorry. I guess I was daydreaming." Turning my gaze away from the cup of coffee Marge set on the table in front of me, I look up into my friend's sad and caring eyes.

"It was a nice funeral." His hand quivers as he raises his cup to take a sip.

"Thank you. Yes it was." I swallow hard. "I'm sure Shelby thought so too. Gerber Daisies are her favorites. I never saw so many in one place before."

"Those were sure pretty," Marge replies. "I've always enjoyed Gerber Daises too."

"Pastor Ron did a good job. He kept his part short. I'm sure Shelby appreciated that. She and I prefer less than more when it comes to preach'n." I'm biting my lower lip and trying my best to hold back tears that threaten to spill from my old eyes.

No one says anything for a couple of minutes as we sit at the table enjoying each other's company, drinking our coffee and listening to the sound their clock makes ticking on a wall in the living room - reminds me of love at first sight at Big Meadow. Seems like yesterday.

Marge breaks the silence, "She was a beautiful woman, Cdub. We were blessed to know her."

"Thank you Marge. She was a gift to me and to a lot of people. I don't know how I got to be so blessed."

"It's good she's not in pain anymore," Lou replies somberly with Marge agreeing softly.

"It was hard letting her go, but we knew it was time. Fight'n the cancer didn't give her any quality of life; and at the end, she was in such awful pain, even drugs couldn't touch it. When we knew it was getting close, I slept in the hospital bed with her. In the middle of the night when she couldn't sleep, we would lie there in the dark holding each other, listening to the quiet night sounds, loving the feel of each other pressed in close. During all our years together, I tried my best to give her the Moon, but all she ever cared about was my love. Shelby made love enough. I had plenty of that and never held back; neither did she." I can't help gulp air, trying my best to breathe.

Wiping tears away quickly and sighing deeply I add, "Tonight will be the first night in 32 years we've been separated from one another. Did you know that?"

Marge replies, "I don't believe we did. We were curious how you two found each other 'cuz you were perfect together".

"You were the most in love two people could be; well, besides Marge and me," Lou says with a smile while wiping away a tear and leaning slightly, giving Marge a light kiss on her cheek. Turning back to me he adds, "I always told you real love would happen for you."

"Well I tell ya, you believed it for me when I couldn't. Thank you for that and for being a good friend to Shelby and me all these years." After blowing my nose and wiping my eyes, I continue, "We met in the middle of the night in a broken down ol' shed when she was 24 years old, during the early days of the devastating blackout way back when. After the night we met, we never left each other's side. Never wanted to, figuring there was nothing out in the world important enough to experience alone." I pause and feel the weight of my words pressing on me. With a voice full of emotion I say, "Before Shelby, I was dead but didn't know it. Out of the darkness she became my gift of life and I became hers."

Staff Sergeant Charles William Stanton

First Armored Division, U.S. Army

Balkans Campaign

APPENDIX A
CHARACTER BIOGRAPHY

Charles William (*Cdub*) Stanton
    5'11"
    200 pounds
    Brown hair
    Brown eyes
    43 years old
    Divorced
    Occupation
        Insurance Risk Manager
    Work history
        Police Officer
        Staff Sergeant, US Army

Shelby Gales
    5'2"
    125 pounds
    Blond/Brown hair
    Brown eyes
    24 years old
    Single
    Occupation
        Gales Market Country Store

Airisa Severn
    5'5"
    119 pounds
    Black hair
    Brown eyes
    25 years old
    Single
    Occupation
        Restaurant server
        Aspiring model

Max West
    6'0"
    155 pounds
    Brown hair
    Hazel eyes
    45 years old
    Married to Mia for 20 years
    Occupation
        Attorney at Law

Mia West
    5'6"
    110
    Blond hair
    Blue eyes
    45 years old
    Occupation
        Wedding Coordinator
        Etiquette coach

APPENDIX B
WEAPONS

Colt AR15 Sporter
  PMI 55 gr. FMJ 5.56
  30 round magazine
  18" barrel
  1:7 twist
  Velocity 3080 ft/s (2,100 mph)
  Max effective range 500 meters
  Blackhawk three-point sling
  A2 adjustable rear sight
  Fixed front sight post
  Six position collapsible stock
  Ergo no-slip pistol grip
  YHM free float quad rail hand guard

Springfield Armory M1 Garand
  152 gr. 30.06 M2 Ball FMJ
  Eight round En bloc clip
  Adjustable peep sight
  Velocity 2,805 ft/s (1,912 mph)
  Max effective range 800 meters

Ruger M77 bolt action
  152 gr. 30.06 M2 Ball FMJ
  Five round capacity
  Velocity 2,805 ft/s (1,912 mph)
  Max effective range 800 meters
  Nikon Prostaff 3x9-40 scope
  Harris fold away bi-pod

Remington 870
  12 gauge
  Five shot capacity
  Pump action
  18" barrel
  Velocity 1600 ft/s (1,090 mph)
  Max effective range 100 meters
  Double 00 buckshot 2 ¾ inch
  Rifle slug 2 ¾ inch
  Flechette shell (12 x 1" darts)
  Zirconium-based pyrotechnic shell

Rock River AR15 Operator
  5.56 Lake City Arsenal M855 65 gr.
  steel penetrating core
  30 round magazine
  18" barrel
  1:9 twist
  Velocity 3025 ft/s (2,062 mph)
  Max effective range 500 meters
  Blackhawk three-point sling
  A2 adjustable rear iron sight
  Collapsible front sight post
  EOTech L3 holographic sight
  Six position collapsible stock
  Ergo no-slip pistol grip
  Half Quad free float hand guard
  Grip Pod Systems fore-grip
  FA556AR SureFire suppressor

AK 47
  7.62 NATO 147 gr.
  30 round magazine
  16.25" barrel
  1:10 twist
  Velocity 2785 ft/s (1,898 mph)
  Max effective range 500 meters

Mossberg
  12 gauge
  Two shot capacity
  Double barrel sawed off
  Velocity 1600 ft/s (1,090 mph)
  Max effective range 50 meters
  Double 00 buckshot 2 ¾ inch

Ruger SP101 stainless steel revolver
  Caliber .357
  158 gr. 38+P SJHP
  Five round capacity
  Velocity 906 ft/s (617 mph)
  Max effective range 50 meters

APPENDIX B - CONTINUED

B. Svoboda Bowie knife, Solingen Germany

Kershaw 4" spring assist lock blade knife

Springfield Armory M1915 bayonet

APPENDIX C

BACKPACK CONTENTS

PACK
1. Metal frame Dana Design K2 Short bed
2. Extra set of clothing:
   a. Black T-shirt
   b. Boot socks
   c. Dry-fit lined running shorts
   d. Woodland camouflage bush Hat
   e. Black leather gloves
   f. Dry-fit long pants
3. (2) US Army military waterproof bags
4. (3) ORION red 15 minute road flares
5. (2) Butane lighters
6. 250' Jute twisted cord
7. (2) rolls toilet Paper
8. Terry cloth towel
9. (3) Water bottles
10. Bota Outback water purification unit
11. Portable Aqua water purification tablets
12. Foot powder
13. Smith's brand knife sharpener
14. Pocket watch
15. Needle nose pliers
16. Cleaning rod and 5.56 brush
17. Remington oil wipes
18. Forest green 8' x10' tarp
19. (2) 2.5 hour Sterno gel fuel cans
20. Duct tape
21. Waterproof coveralls
22. Rubber boots
23. Utility shovel
24. Utility spoon
25. Metal quart cooking pot
26. Metal flask: Maker's Mark whiskey
27. Food:
   a. Plastic jar, Peanut butter
   b. Packets:
      i. Tea
      ii. Coffee
      iii. Wet wipes
   c. (5) Top Ramen soup packages
   d. Cliff bars, Oatmeal Raisin
   e. Butterscotch hard candy
28. Medical kit:
   a. Alcohol prep
   b. First-aid cream
   c. Burn cream
   d. Five hour energy
   e. Ear swabs
   f. First Aid waterproof tape
   g. Peroxide
   h. Disposable shaving razor
   i. Antacid
   j. Lip balm
   k. Adhesive bandages
   l. Elastic knee brace
   m. Elastic elbow brace
   n. Off insect spray
   o. Sinus tablets
29. YUKON night vision monocular with infra-red illuminator
30. NIKON 550 6x21 60 degree waterproof range finder
31. NIKON Travelite III binocular
32. ETON FR-300 AM/FM/Weather receiver
33. Batteries for all devices

CLOTHING
1. Poncho
2. US Army woodland camouflage pants and shirt
3. Woodland camouflage wide brimmed hat
4. Glacier Glove black neoprene waterproof gloves
5. Caterpillar steel toe, lug sole lace up ankle protective boots
6. Brown US Army T-shirt
7. Boot socks
8. Dry-fit lined running shorts

CARRY items
1. Chewing gum
2. Lip balm
3. Compass
4. Wet wipes
5. (3) HKS.357 caliber 5 round speed loaders
6. Bandoleer of three (30 round) magazines

APPENDIX D

BODY COUNT

In order of appearance

Papé Cap
Female driver
Kia gunman
Bryan
Mr. Middleclass
Big Biker
Biker Woman
Bully cop 1
Bully cop 2
Killer 1
Killer 2
Momma Gales
Skipper the dog
Sheri Gales
Shelly Gales
Running Man
D-Day Boy
Latrine Boy
Neighbor's field:
    Unknown assailant 1
    Unknown assailant 2
    Unknown assailant 3

Patio man 1
Rolling Man
Burning Man
Lumberjack
Toyota pickup:
    Driver
    Assailant 1
    Assailant 2
Origami Boy
Officer Johnson
Neighbor's field:
    Unknown assailant 1
    Unknown assailant 2
Airisa's patio man 2 kill
Home invaders at the house
Man with pipe bomb
Hatchet Man
Mia's kill in the laundry room
Dog's kill in the guest bathroom
Mia's kill in the front bedroom
Airisa and Shelby's kill in the TV room

ADDITIONAL READING

[1.] HOW DID THE (2003) BLACKOUT HAPPEN?
BRET PETTICHORD APRIL 13, 2004
www.io.com/~wazmo/blog/archives/2004_04.html

[2.] (Page 139) U.S.-CANADA POWER SYSTEM OUTAGE TASK FORCE
FINAL REPORT: CAUSES AND RECOMMENDATIONS
https://reports.energy.gov/

A HURRICANE KATRINA SURVIVAL STORY
http://recessionreadyamerica.com/2009/12/what-you-can-learn-from-my-hurricane-katrina-survival-experience/

UNITED STATES GOVERNMENT
www.ready.gov/
www.foodsafety.gov/keep/emergency/index.html

THE READY PROJECT
www.thereadyproject.com/

RECESSION READY AMERICA
http://recessionreadyamerica.com/

FOOD SHORTAGE SOLUTIONS
www.foodshortagesolutions.com/

FOOD STORAGE MADE EASY
http://foodstoragemadeeasy.net/

THE HUMANE SOCIETY OF THE UNITED STATES
www.humanesociety.org/issues/animal_rescue/tips/disaster_preparedness_pets.html

L. Charles Holt

lives in a quiet corner of Oregon
with Zeke, Zoie and Little.

Contact the author at:
ZOIEPRESS@hotmail.com

Made in the USA
San Bernardino, CA
23 March 2013